BETTER THAN GOLD

MONTE CRISTO MEMORIES - BOOK 2

JOAN RAWLINS HUSBY

RainSong Press

Better Than Gold
Monte Cristo Memories Book Two

Published by RainSong Press
Copyright © 2024 by Joan Rawlins Husby. All rights reserved.

Cover design by Lynnette Bonner of Indie Cover Design, images ©
   www.istockphoto.com, File: # 1314056883 - woman
   www.depositphotos.com, File: # 395257852_XL - mountain
   www.depositphotos.com, File: # 226884098_XL - sunburst
Book interior design by Jon Stewart of Stewart Design
Maps adapted by Thomas Kauffman

ISBN: 978-0-9821681-6-5

For every Melinda or Quin out there, who in faithfully meeting their challenges leave legacies for the rest of us.

Acknowledgments

Grateful thanks to all who read Monte Cristo Memories' first volume, Heart's Gold, and patiently (or impatiently) waited for more of the story. Your encouragement carried me through!

To Irene Sandburg Philips, Inez Kollmar, and Ruth Youngsman, for reading the manuscript, catching errors, and for encouraging words.

To Dixie Nash who took time from her own project to offer prayer, new perspectives and suggestions for plotting and characterizations.

To my wide-reading daughter, Lenora Anderson, for her valuable content editing.

To the men and women of the Warm Beach Writers in Residence, for inspiration and enthusiasm.

To the Highway 20 Writers' Group for their friendship, support, expertise, and their encouragement in my battles with technology.

To Tom Kauffman, for adapting the maps to show the scope of the story.

To Hank, who while battling his own challenges, continues to support my efforts.

My thanks as well, to the real men and women who lived parts of this story and helped to inspire my fictional characters and their adventures. I've used some names and histories, but of necessity their personalities are mostly imagined.

Captain William Ralph Abercrombie and his expedition were stationed at Valdez. They crossed the glacier with the gold stampeders, explored the country and laid out the road now called the Richardson Highway.

A young adventuress, Lillian Moore, joined Abercrombie's expedition to help wrangle the packhorses. She left a fascinating letter telling of her experiences crossing the glacier and prospecting for gold.

An African-Native American man named Melvin Dempsey founded and ran the Valdez Christian Endeavor Society, as well as many other enterprises.

The real Dan Sutherland ran a tongue-in-cheek push-car railroad to carry the mail between Silverton and Robe. As children, my siblings and I played on the derelict cable car he probably used to cross the river.

BETTER THAN GOLD

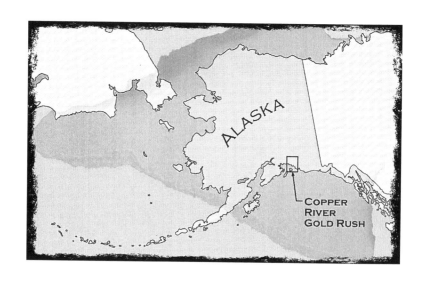

COPPER
RIVER
GOLD RUSH

ALASKA

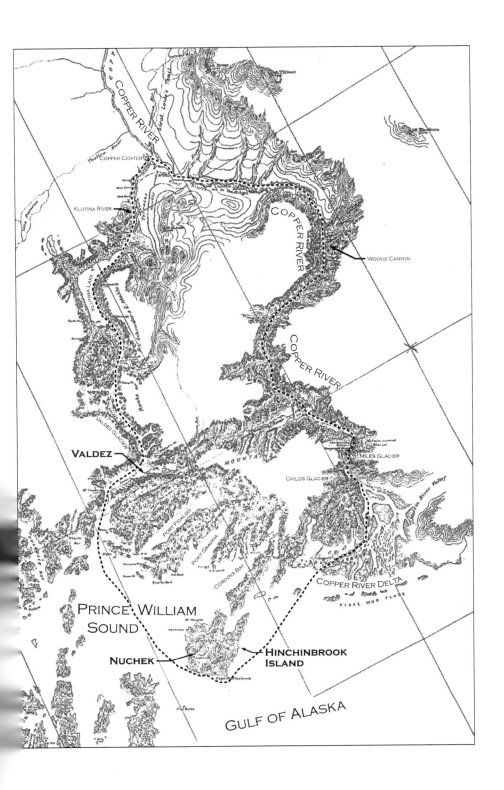

Contents

CHAPTER ONE

THIEF

June, 1898

Melinda McCrae, after a long day of classes at the San Francisco Normal School, felt tired but also jubilant. She'd just finished her first semester. She'd done well, she knew. Now she was on her way to withdraw money from her bank account to pay for the final semester. Dear Grandma Lena had passed away last winter, leaving Melinda funds to realize her dream of teaching. The young woman hoped her grandmother could know how grateful she was.

A strand of auburn hair escaped the small black hat tilting forward atop her upswept hairdo and tickled her nose. She tucked the strand back in place. The absurd little hat did nothing to protect her creamy skin from the early June sunshine. She'd forgotten her parasol. Carrying it would have been awkward, anyway, because her hands were already occupied with her purse, a shopping basket and a parcel of mail from the postoffice.

As she hurried beneath the bank's portico, she glimpsed the handwriting on the top letter. She pulled it free. Yes! A letter from Quin. It was all she could do to keep from skipping with joy. How she wished he was here to help celebrate with her. She wondered if he'd remembered her birthday. Planning to read the letter as soon as she got home, she dropped the envelope into her handbag.

As she passed through the door, the nondescript man lounging against the bank's outside wall barely registered on her consciousness.

He'd noticed her though. As she entered, he moved closer to the door. Under the shadowing brim of a ragged cap, expressionless eyes followed her trim figure to the teller's window. Shifting the basket so she could rummage through her purse, she handed a withdrawal slip to the teller. He counted out what looked like a fortune to the watching vagabond. Stuffing the money into an envelope, the teller handed it to her, along with a receipt.

"That's a lot of cash to carry," the teller advised in a fatherly manner. "Don't let anyone see it." Dropping receipt and money into her handbag, Melinda thanked him. Her mind on the next errand, she hurried outside, past the man lurking in the shade of some tall bushes. She didn't notice as he flattened himself against them.

On to the fish market, then home to the cottage she shared with her mother and Evan, her eight-year-old ward and future son. Her mother had promised to cook a special dinner to celebrate both her 21st birthday and her educational milestone. Melinda was to bring home a nice fresh fish for the meal.

In the morning, she would pay for her final semester at the Normal School. Evan was already enjoying his summer vacation, but she planned to go right on with her studies. When finished, she'd be a full-fledged teacher. Then she and Evan would return to Washington State's North Cascade Mountains, to their little gold mining town, Monte Cristo. And to Quin Chenoweth, Evan's uncle and the man she loved.

As she'd done hundreds of times over the past six months, she touched the heart-shaped locket at her throat Quin had given her last Christmas. Quin's picture inside the locket was all she had of him, here in this bustling seaport town in California. That and the memories of their times together, and his letters. Until today, she'd not heard from him for two weeks. She almost skipped again in anticipation of reading the latest letter.

She turned down a street that led to the fisherman's market. Here, close to the wharves, the streets thronged with men bearing heavy burdens, some leading dogs of all kinds, as well as a few horses. The men were seeking passage to Alaska's newest gold rush.

According to the newspaper stories, nuggets as big as hen's eggs lay scattered on the banks of a river called the Copper, waiting to be gathered by whomever found them.

Only yesterday she'd talked to a barely-out-of-his-teens future prospector. He showed her several burlap bags in which he planned to carry his nuggets home.

Most of the hopefuls crowding the waterfront were much older than that young man. Life had been difficult during the depression of 1893. The West Coast was beginning to come out of it now in 1898, with the help of the Klondike gold rush, but there were always some whom prosperity left behind. The good claims were mostly taken in the Klondike, but new rumors of gold along the Copper beckoned. Many of these men swarming the street had the hangdog look of people grasping for their last chance.

Melinda worked her way through the crowd to an open-air fish market on the wharf at the end of the street. A boat moored near the market was unloading its catch. She looked over the glistening offerings and chose a fish of medium size. She paid for it and tucked the change into her bag.

Just as she snapped it shut and reached for her newspaper-wrapped purchase, a tremendous weight smashed into her back. Fish, purse, basket and mail went flying as Melinda slammed to the ground. An outcry went up from the people around her. Hands reached to lift her from the splintery planks of the wharf.

She replaced the hat someone handed her and felt blood trickling down her cheek. She reached for the handkerchief in her bag. Her bag! Where was it?

"Stop him. Stop that thief!"

Shouts marked the path of a man who bowled people out of his way as he sprinted through the crowd. He ducked into an alley. She'd seen that lanky form and battered cap minutes before. At the bank.

"Are you all right, Ma'am?" The fishmonger held out her basket and newspaper-wrapped parcel.

"I'm all right, I think, but that man took my purse!" Melinda's hands trembled with the shock of what had just happened. She dropped the fish into the basket. Someone else picked up the scattered mail and handed it to her.

Several men had raced after the fugitive into the alley. Now one of them pushed through the group of people hovering around Melinda. "He got away," he announced, "but he dropped this!" He held up the missing bag.

"Oh, bless you!" Melinda took the bag and checked its contents. She pressed the handkerchief to her bleeding cheek. Here were her bankbook, her comb. Her heart sank. Where was the envelope of money she'd just withdrawn from the bank? The money to pay for next semester's studies?

Chapter Two

Best-Laid Plans

Someone must have directed a policeman to the scene, because suddenly a man wearing a badge and a uniform stood at her side, asking questions. She shook her head to clear it, pressing the handkerchief against her stinging cheek.

"Did you see who knocked you down?"

All Melinda could think of was her dream, broken; Grandma Lena's gift, gone. Her eyes blurred with tears. "I only saw him running away," she gulped. "I probably couldn't identify him."

"Well, I could," the fishmonger said. "I looked right at him as he grabbed her purse."

"She has her purse, right here," the officer pointed out.

"He threw it away. After he'd taken the money I just got from the bank." And Quin's letter. She felt like wailing. She told the officer the amount of cash, and that the thief must have been watching her.

"Yes, probably. Well, give me your name and address. We'll try to find him, but don't expect to get the money back. There are a lot of dark holes where vermin like that can hide in this town."

She thanked the policeman for his time. Feeling weak and stumbly, she started home. She noticed a tear in the front of her navy serge skirt. Her knee stung, too. She must have scraped it when she fell.

Rose Skinner obviously felt shaken by Melinda's story, but she tried to project reassurance as she clucked over the bruise purpling on Melinda's cheekbone and the bleeding knee. She sat her down after Melinda had washed, and dabbed some salve on the cuts. She taped a small piece of gauze over each. "They're not much more than scratches," she said, and patted the cheek as if Melinda was still her little girl. "You'll be good as new in no time."

The screen door opened to admit Evan with an armload of firewood. "You're home, Mindy! Did Grandma Rose tell you we're baking a cake?" He lowered his armload carefully into the wood box, knowing that jarring the stove might make the cake fall. "Doesn't it smell good?" He turned to look at Melinda.

"Oh, what happened!" He touched her face, his gray-green eyes wide.

"Just a scratch, Grandma Rose says." She smiled at the sturdy, yellow-haired child who'd chosen her to be his mother almost from their first meeting at Monte Cristo. Her first priority when she and Quin married would be to officially adopt this boy.

She explained what had happened, trying to keep it light so he wouldn't worry. Evan took things to heart more than most little boys.

"You should have seen all the people who came to help," she told him. "Even a policeman. He said they'll try to find the thief."

She gulped back tears as she remembered he'd also said the money was probably gone for good. Now what would she do? That money had meant her future, at least the one she had planned.

"If I had been with you, I'd have stuck out my foot and tripped that thief. I'd have grabbed your purse back."

She smiled at the little boy's bravado.

"I'm sure you would have. You're a quick thinker, Evan." Then she mourned out loud, "The thief took my letter from Quin, too. I never even got to read it!"

"Why would he take Uncle Quin's letter?"

"He probably grabbed it up with the envelope of money, not realizing he had it. Maybe he'll throw it away and someone will find it and see that I get it."

Rose curled her arm around her daughter's shoulders and drew her into a hug. "It could happen," she said. "Meanwhile, we'll try to think of another way for you to pay the tuition. The school might let you pay in installments. I can take in a few more dress-making clients. Perhaps you could help me a little in the evenings."

Melinda gazed fondly at the older woman. Her hair, once dark auburn like Melinda's own glossy locks, had acquired more streaks of silver since she left Monte Cristo. And when had those lines around her eyes deepened? "No, Mama. You already work too hard. I'll ask if the school can make other arrangements, but you have too many clients already. I know sewing bothers your eyes. You mustn't sacrifice any more for me."

The college had a break of several days before the second semester began. Each morning, Melinda walked to the police station and asked the chief if her money had been recovered.

"I'm sorry if I'm being a nuisance," she said. "But thugs like that are not good for the town's reputation." She added, "Or for that of the police."

The third time she stopped by, she saw the police chief look up from his desk as she walked in. His expression as he glanced toward the other exit looked harried, but it was too late for him to escape.

"Hello, Miss McCrea. I suppose you want to know what progress has been made on your case."

"Yes."

"I already told you that I sent two detectives to investigate. They got a good description from the fishmonger and other witnesses. But it's like he disappeared into thin air. All we can do is keep watching for him. I'm afraid by now we won't recover your money, even if we do find him."

"But .... "

"I'm sorry, Miss McCrea. These things aren't easy. There's nothing more we can do."

She felt tears gathering. It took all the willpower she possessed to keep her back straight and her head erect as she marched out of the station.

She had one more option, her appointment that afternoon to talk to the college administrator. As she waited for the streetcar that would take her to the school, she touched the gold locket at her throat. She saw in her mind's eye Quin's strong face. She would write to him tonight to tell him what had happened.

The streetcar clanged as it slowed for her stop. First, she would ask if the school could grant her credit to finish her studies.

Miss Olive Graydon, the reserved, no-nonsense Head Mistress of the San Francisco Normal School, actually looked sympathetic when Melinda told her what had happened.

"The thief took almost all the money I had, Miss Graydon. I came to ask you if it's possible to make other arrangements for next semester's tuition. I could find a part time job and pay in installments, or I could finish the semester and repay with interest when I get a teaching job."

"I'm truly sorry, Miss McCrea. You are one of our outstanding students. Losing you will be our loss indeed, but the college insists that the entire tuition must be paid in advance. Regarding a part time job: as you know, the work required of our students is heavy. Outside employment is discouraged because we want our students to focus on their studies. Have you considered dropping out for the semester and working full time to save up tuition? You could come back to finish after next Christmas."

"Thank you, Miss Graydon. I will think about it."

As she walked to the streetcar stop, she made up her mind. If the choice was between between school and a job, she would choose a job in Washington, near Quin.

An audacious idea began to take shape in her mind.

She'd have to postpone graduation. Disappointing, but she'd not think about that now. What saddened her more than losing the inheritance was that her mother would be alone again if she left and took Evan.

A second idea sparked.

That evening as they washed the supper dishes Melinda broached the thought of returning to Washington earlier than expected.

The dismay in her mother's eyes almost swayed Melinda's resolve. "But daughter, you're settled here now. Don't you think it's wise to do as Miss Graydon suggested? There are jobs here, and you could save everything you make if you're living with me. You'd only be a few months behind your schedule that way."

But she thought again of Quin, and how she missed him. If she returned to Washington, they could be married now. She could still find work and finish school later. This didn't have to be the end of her dream. She wouldn't think about the fact that many school districts frowned on hiring married women teachers.

She brought up her second idea. "Mama, with Grandma gone, what's to hold you here in San Francisco? You could come back to Washington with Evan and me. You could live with us. You'd have no trouble finding customers for your dressmaking if you wanted to keep on with your business."

Rose bowed her head, considering what Melinda said. "I'd like nothing better than being near you dear ones for the rest of my life," she said softly. Then she raised her head and looked into Melinda's eyes. "But I love this little house, and the sunshine. Right now I have many customers who depend upon my work. One day, perhaps, when I retire, I will join you." She wiped away a tear and hugged her daughter.

"You have your own life to live, Melinda. Just be sure to wait upon the Lord. He will direct your paths."

"Trust in the Lord with all your heart, and lean not on your own understanding ... " Melinda supplied the beginning of the verse her mother had referred to, as she sat down to write to Quin. She didn't understand why things sometimes happened as they did. But she *was* waiting on the Lord. Wasn't she?

She picked up her pen.

> *San Francisco, California*
> *June 10, 1898*

> *My dearest Husband-to-be,*
> *It's been six long months since we said goodbye to each other. I wonder if you miss me as much as I miss you?*
> *I hope all is going well with the rebuilding of the Monte Cristo railroad, and that our friends will soon be able to return to the mountains.*
> *Are you still thinking about the newspaper job you were offered? That sounds well suited to your abilities. You could influence so many people.*

She paused, trying to decide how to tell Quin about her problem.

> *I must tell you, my dear. Something happened this week to change my hopes and plans.*

She wrote about the theft of her money and the refusal of the school to relax its rules about tuition.

> *The thief took your last letter, too, before I got to read it.*
> *Since you aren't here to talk with, I've had to make a decision without consulting you. I hope you'll agree it's a good one. Evan and I are coming home!*
> *This semester of education, plus the experience I gained last year at the school in Monte Cristo, should allow me to find a temporary teaching job this fall. Maybe Monte Cristo will even want me back. If I teach this coming school year,*

I can continue my training during the summer at the new normal school in Bellingham.

I hope we can get married right away and have this whole summer to set up a home together before school starts.

Mother is disappointed, but she understands. I have a little money left in the bank, and she agreed to advance me the rest of the fare.

I've purchased tickets for the steamship, Coastal, leaving in a week. It's to arrive in Seattle on June 20. Lord willing, a faster mail ship will get this letter to you in time for you to meet us.

Soon, Quin, we'll be together. Evan misses you almost as much as I do. We'll be watching for your beloved face as the Coastal docks.

All my love,

Melinda

Melinda sat gazing out the window of the swaying passenger car, scarcely aware of the blue waters of Puget Sound sparkling next to the railroad tracks or the green-crowned bluffs of Whidbey and Hat Islands in the distance.

Her fingers absently caressed her locket. She flipped it open to gaze again at Quin's miniature portrait. His dark eyes smiled back at her. But she didn't feel reassured. Today was June 20, the day she'd told him they would arrive.

But this morning, when the Coastal docked, Quin wasn't waiting on the wharf. What could have gone wrong? They stayed until every passenger had disembarked and the wharf was empty. Then she hailed a trolley to take them and their luggage to the train station. Although she scanned the countenance of every dark-haired young man they passed on the streets, she didn't see Quin among them. Could it be that they'd arrived before her letter reached him and he didn't know they were coming? Perhaps he'd taken the newspaper job and couldn't get away. She hoped that was it, but now, as she clicked the locket shut, a pall of worry dulled the beauty outside the train's windows.

Melinda remembered Rose's suggestion to wait for Quin's reply before leaving San Francisco so precipitously. "His situation could have changed," she said.

Why hadn't she listened to her mother? No, it must be that he'd not received her letter. Very likely she'd find him at Mrs. Collin's boarding house, his home whenever he was in Everett.

As the train slowed, nearing the "City of Smokestacks," the eight-year-old dozing against her shoulder stirred, sat up, and looked around. Suddenly wide awake, he bounced in his seat.

"We're coming to Everett, Mindy! Will Uncle Quin be at the depot?"

She made her voice confident. "If he's not, we'll find him."

As the train clacked along the waterfront, Melinda noticed that the bankrupt shingle mill sitting halfway along the 14th Street Dock was operating again. A line of boxcars waited on the dock, ready to carry shingles to eastern markets. She noted other industrial buildings that hadn't been there six months earlier.

In the town itself, fewer idlers wandered the streets. Everett was obviously recovering from the financial depression of the last few years.

She wished that they could travel on through the town, up into the Cascade mountains, and home to Monte Cristo. But Quin's earlier letters had said that much of the Everett and Monte Cristo Railroad still awaited repairs after last November's savage flooding.

She'd never forget how Monte Cristo's inhabitants had to evacuate the town as the rampaging Sauk and Stillaguamish rivers washed out bridges, even sections of the track, along the railroad. She and her friend Nell had walked fourteen miserable miles to Silverton through cold, pelting rain, leading a pack horse carrying Evan, Nell's son Johnny, and a few possessions. Quin had met them at Silverton and took her and Evan to Mrs. Collins' boarding house in Everett. There Melinda had enrolled Evan in school and gone to work at the boarding house.

She smiled, remembering the scene as Quin's train pulled away from Everett, taking him back to the mountains to help repair the railroad. He leaped onto the platform at the end of the train, narrowly avoiding being left behind as it started to roll. "Marry me, Melinda," he pleaded, leaning out over the railing. "Won't you take a chance on me?"

Though she'd vowed never to marry a miner, she'd not been able to stop herself. She ran after the train. As the watchers on the platform grinned, she called, "Yes, Quin. I'll marry you!"

Later, her mother sent word from California about Grandmother's death and the money she'd left her granddaughter. Now Melinda could have her heart's desire, a teaching education. The difficult choice between going to school or getting married was made for her when Quin said he must first have a dependable job. He urged her to travel to San Francisco, where she and Evan could stay with her mother and both attend school.

They had done that.

Now he had that dependable job, she hoped. Lord willing, she would take that chance he'd begged for and marry him.

As the train pulled into the station, she looked in vain for Quin Chenoweth. She'd marry him. But first, she had to find him.

CHAPTER THREE

DISAPPOINTMENT

Collins Board and Room
Reasonable Rates
M. Collins, Proprietor

Melinda glanced at the sign hanging over the familiar door, then down at Evan's excited face. "Go ahead. Use the knocker." she said. "Mrs. Collins won't be expecting us, so we shouldn't walk right in."

Evan clanged the striker against the plate. They heard footsteps hurrying across the lobby. Their former landlady's pleasant face broke into a delighted smile when she saw who stood there.

"Melinda! Evan! What a lovely surprise. I didn't expect to see you for months! Why didn't you let me know you were coming? Are you here for good?" Without waiting for answers, she pulled them into the boarding house lobby, hugging Evan and exclaiming over how he'd grown. She hugged Melinda, too. "Come in, come in! I just took cookies out of the oven and the coffee's hot. I want to know all about San Francisco…"

She looked them up and down, noting that each carried only a small bag. "Nothing's wrong, is it? Is that all of your luggage?"

"We left the rest in the ticket office at the depot," Melinda answered. "We'll get it later."

"Where's my Uncle Quin?" Evan asked.

Their friend looked surprised. "Why, don't you know?" She led them into the kitchen to sit down at the table where they'd often eaten their meals while Melinda worked there. "He took a job with a new Seattle newspaper, *The Daily Dispatch.* The owner gave him a special assignment in Alaska, covering the gold rush to the Copper River. I haven't seen him for over two weeks."

A Seattle newspaper? Alaska? Melinda's heart plummeted. Over two weeks? He could be hundreds of miles away by now!

The joyful reunion she'd imagined vaporized like smoke vanishing on a breeze.

Mrs. Collins poured milk for Evan and coffee for herself and Melinda. She slid some still-warm cookies on to a plate and set them on the table before sitting down herself. Then she noticed the expression on Melinda's face.

"Now, don't you worry," she comforted. "Your old room is empty. We'll have someone fetch your luggage. You two can stay here as long as you need to."

"I can't believe it. Quin went to Alaska?" Melinda's tone betrayed her shock.

"Maybe not yet," Mrs. Collins told her. "He said he'd suggested assessing the situation in Monte Cristo before he left, for a story on when the railroad will be usable again. Could be he's in the mountains, working on that story."

"Oh, I hope so." She sat thinking. "So even if my letter got here, he wouldn't have seen it yet."

"He's had no recent mail. I know he wrote to tell you about the job offer, because he asked me to post the letter. He was thrilled about the opportunity to learn more about the newspaper business."

"I did get a letter saying he'd been offered a job. But I assumed the newspaper was here in Everett."

"Knowing Quin, he probably wrote again to tell you about the Alaska assignment. He was excited about the chance to see Alaska for himself."

"I'm sure he was. But what about me? And Evan?" Even to herself, Melinda sounded self-pitying. "I'm sorry," she apologized. "He didn't expect us back for another six months, at least. Of course, he would take the job."

"You haven't said why you came back early. Did something happen? Is your mother all right?"

"Mother is fine, but something did happen," Melinda said. She told Mrs. Collins about the robbery and being unable to continue her next semester's schooling. "I decided if I could find a teaching job, or any kind of work, in Washington this fall, I could save money for classes at the Normal school in Bellingham next summer."

"It's really none of my business, but couldn't you have done that in San Francisco?"

Just what her mother and the director of the school had both suggested. "Well, I hoped if I came home, Quin and I could get married right away." She hastened to add, "I would still have looked for work."

She sounded so forlorn that Mrs. Collins smiled and patted her hand. "Don't worry," she said. "Once he knows you're here, nothing will keep him away."

Melinda forced a smile in return. She considered another thought. "If Quin did go from Seattle to Monte Cristo," she said, "he wouldn't necessarily stop here, would he?"

"Probably not. He could go straight to Granite Falls, then travel on from there."

Melinda made up her mind. "We'll take you up on your kind offer for tonight, anyway," she said. "If there's still a morning train to Granite Falls, we'll be on it. If we can get to Silverton, we'll stay with Nell and Ole Swenson...you remember my old friends from Monte Cristo. They'll know if Quin is in the area and can help us get to Monte Cristo. Won't it be fun to surprise your uncle, Evan?" Melinda sat back, satisfied with the plan she'd just sketched out.

"Yes, and I'll get to see all my friends!" Evan grinned and downed his last swallow of milk.

"I don't know, Evan. You'll see Johnny, with his mom and Ole at Silverton. But almost everybody else left Monte Cristo when we did."

Mrs. Collins looked concerned. "What will you do if Quin isn't at Monte Cristo?"

A twinge of doubt stabbed through Melinda, but she refused to acknowledge it.

Her answer sounded a little flippant, but she said it anyway. "I'll have to cross that bridge when I come to it."

Quintrell Chenoweth, originally of Cornwall, England, then of Michigan, USA, and more recently of the little gold rush town of Monte Cristo in Washington State, marveled at the twists and turns that had brought him to this point in life. At the moment, he occupied a seat next to a dirty window on an Alaska-bound steamship. If steamships were ranked according to their ridership, this one would be near the bottom of the list. And that, thought Quin, was being kind.

The old tub was packed to the gills with humanity and their beasts of burden. Those who could afford the cost of a tiny stateroom were tending to their seasickness there. The men surrounding Quin, chasers of the latest gold rumors, were mostly middle-aged and older. Most were down on their luck, hoping that this voyage and the tougher journey that lay at its end would finally reward them with prosperity.

A big wave jarred the ship, bringing a collective groan from those who had to fight their seasickness in public. Some rushed outside to the railing.

Quin peered through the rain-smeared glass. Clouds hid the tops of the mountainous islands they were passing, but he could see waves crashing against their rocky foundations. The ship still plowed through the relatively protected waters of the inside passage. His own cast-iron stomach might rebel soon. He'd better write again to Melinda while he had the chance.

He pictured the lovely young woman to whom he would now be married had not fate caused the postponement of their wedding.

First had come the flooding that destroyed the railroad leading to their homes at Monte Cristo. Without the railroad, ore could not be transported to the smelter in Everett. His job as mining captain suddenly became irrelevant. No, nonexistent. The school where Melinda served as temporary schoolteacher closed its doors as the students and their families fled the besieged town. Melinda and his nephew became refugees in Everett, while Quin went to work helping to rebuild the railroad.

Then Melinda received the inheritance that would allow her to get a teaching degree. Quin insisted she join her mother in San Francisco and take the opportunity to fulfill that dream.

It had been a wise decision. As a new feature writer for the Seattle Daily Dispatch, he was now on his way to report on Alaska's Valdez Gold Rush, while Melinda and Evan were safely (and comfortably) residing in San Francisco. He took pen and paper from his writing case, and using the case as a desk, began his letter:

> *On board the Miscreant*
> *June 10, 1898*
>
> *Miss Melinda McCrae*
> *312 Hollyhock Lane*
> *San Francisco, California*
>
> *My Dearest Melinda,*
> *So often over the past six months I've wished to hear your voice and see your beautiful face! By now you've received the letter telling about my new job with the Seattle Daily Dispatch. I'm on my way to Alaska as I write. I am thankful you're busy with your schooling, although waiting another six months to be together seems more like six years! I pray for you and hope your studies and Evan's are going well.*

Here the ship gave a lurch and his pen jerked a scribble through what he'd just written.

Please excuse my untidy scrawl. We're plugging along through a windstorm. This old tub was the only transport available. It's heavily loaded with hopeful miners, their equipment, their animals, and who knows what else. It positively wallows in the swells that crash against the rocks of the innumerable islands we are passing. Most of the passengers and the animals are miserable, although so far I am feeling well. I'm thankful we're in the shelter of the Inside Passage. It would be far worse in the open ocean.

You'll have received the last letter I sent, telling you of my assignment to report on the gold rush to Valdez.

As you may know, the U.S. government has a military expedition searching for a new route to the gold fields, one that avoids the rigors of the Chilkoot and Chilkat Passes and the heavy duties that the Canadian government lays upon the supplies all miners must carry.

The people on this ship aren't waiting for the government to build a trail. For some of the passengers, the prospect of finding gold is their last hope. Though their journey will take them over the dangerous Valdez Glacier, they are determined to find their fortunes on the banks of the Copper River.

I will be traveling with them, documenting their journey. If you can get hold of Seattle's Daily Dispatch there in San Francisco, you can Read all About it! Tell Evan I send my special greetings to him.

With love, Quin of the Mighty Pen

CHAPTER FOUR
SILVERTON, MUD TUNNEL, AND GREAT WESTERN RAILWAY

The train left several of its cars on the siding at Granite Falls. From there on, the train consisted only of the locomotive, a passenger car, plus a boxcar. The boxcar carried supplies for Robe, the village at the eastern entrance to the Stillaguamish canyon, and for settlers living farther up the valley. Once the supplies were offloaded, the boxcar would carry shingles from Robe back to Everett.

Stillaguamish Bridge Number Two, beyond the little mill town, had not yet been replaced, the conductor told Melinda. Robe was nearly the end of the line now. They'd have to make the remainder of the journey by wagon over a dirt and corduroy road. She remembered bumping over logs laid side by side across the muddy stretches when she, Evan, and Quin had journeyed over that same road last November.

Evan had claimed the window seat next to the river. As they chugged across the first bridge and into the canyon of the Stillaguamish, he exclaimed over the broken trees that last November's flood had tossed high above the present water level. Melinda smiled at his excitement. In the six months they'd been away, he'd grown much taller. She'd have to get him more new clothes, soon.

Then, reminding her he was still a small boy, he squealed as the daylight dimmed. The train nosed into Tunnel Number One and moments later emerged into sunshine. Below, the river sparkled, giving no hint of the raging torrent it had been last fall.

The locomotive edged past a close-enough-to-touch wall of crumbling rock that had often buried the rails beneath slides, and crawled through more tunnels. The canyon ended abruptly just west of Robe. They stopped in the settlement long enough to unload passengers and to uncouple the boxcar. Then the train continued another mile or so to a large, two-story building that served as store and hotel.

"This is as far as we go," the conductor announced. "You can wait for the wagon here." He helped Melinda from the train and handed their luggage down. He tossed a mailbag to the platform. Then the locomotive backed down the track toward the switch at Robe.

She and Evan looked around the clearing. Where was the wagon they were supposed to ride? She heard voices through the open door of the store. A muscular man with a curly beard ambled outside and deposited a large box of groceries in a handcart. He touched the brim of his cap when he saw Melinda.

"Afternoon, Ma'am," he said, slinging the mailbag into the cart. "Are you waiting for the wagon?"

"Yes. We're trying to get to Silverton."

"It's loading supplies at Robe for people up the valley. Might be an hour yet."

"'Scuse me, sir," Evan said. "Are you the mailman?"

The man chuckled. "You might say so. I'm Dan Sutherland, proprietor and conductor of the *Silverton, Mud Tunnel, and Great Western Railway*. I meet the train and carry the mail to Silverton."

"You have a railway? To Silverton? We were told this is the end of the line." Melinda's spirits rose at the prospect of avoiding the long wagon ride.

Dan laughed. "It's a very unique railway. Come along and see, if you like. It's just a short walk."

"Please, Mindy! Can we do it?" Evan's face was so eager she couldn't say no.

"Well, I guess we have time." She looked around. "Should we leave our bags here?"

"Put them in the cart. Then if you like the looks of my railway, you won't have to come back for them."

That sounded like a good idea. Melinda introduced herself to Dan Sutherland and told him they were on their way to visit the Swensons in Silverton. Pulling the cart, he led them along a well-used trail across a small bridge, which spanned a creek running alongside the now-unused rail bed, and down the other side of the berm. The music of the river grew louder as they crossed a grassy meadow. Soon they saw what was left of Bridge Number Two, its sturdy abutments standing abandoned on either side of the Stillaguamish. A welter of timbers cast up on the banks were all that remained of the bridge itself.

Near the wreckage, a wooden frame dangled from a cable strung between trees on either bank. Beneath the cable an endless loop of rope ran through pulleys attached to the same trees. The rope, and the rider's own muscle power must provide the means of locomotion for the cable car, she guessed. Melinda caught a glimpse of homestead buildings in a clearing across the river, almost hidden by apple trees.

"There's my train," Dan told Evan. "See it?" He pointed to what looked like a platform on wheels, waiting on the rails beyond the opposite abutment. "Most of the way down from Silverton, gravity's my engine. Going up hill, I have to pump the car myself."

"You make the trip every day?" Melinda asked. "Can't the freight wagons bring the mail?"

"They could. But people are willing to pay me to bring the mail. It's faster and more dependable, you see. If the road gets muddy, wagons can't always get through. They don't run every day, either."

Evan had been eyeing the cable car, swaying gently in the breeze. "Could I ride with you across the river?"

"Sure, if your mom doesn't mind. In fact, I sometimes take passengers to Silverton if I don't have a big load to carry."

"She's not really my mom, yet." Evan turned to her eagerly. "Mindy, is it alright? Maybe we can ride on the push car."

Melinda had a mental picture of them, pumping that odd-looking contraption all the way to Silverton. "Oh, I don't think …"

Dan Sutherland chuckled again. "Why don't you take a look. If you're nervous about it, I'll bring you back in time to catch the freight wagon." He climbed a set of steps to the cable car, tossed the bag of mail and the groceries aboard, then climbed on himself and reached down to swing Evan up. He directed Evan to sit on one of the narrow benches at either end and untied a rope which held the car at the tree.

"Be right back for you, Ma'am," he said as the pulley wheels at each end rolled down the sagging cable and out over the water. When the car slowed at midpoint, he hauled hand over hand on the rope until the car reached the other side.

Evan hopped off. He helped unload, then started toward the handcar with the mailbag. Dan Sutherland launched the cable car back across the river to where Melinda waited. He set their bags under one of the seats and helped her aboard.

As the tram swooped toward the middle of the river, she gripped the frame for dear life. The car swayed and bounced. Beneath them, clear water frothed over and around boulders. It seemed a long way to fall.

"I'd never believe this river could be powerful enough to wash away that bridge if I hadn't seen for myself how fierce it can get," she said.

The man pulled hard on the rope, hauling them up toward the opposite anchorage. "You were here for the flood?"

"Yes, we were with the refugees from Monte Cristo." She took his offered hand and hopped to the ground. She thought his glance lingered a little too long and admiringly. "Perhaps you know my fiancé, Quintrell Chenoweth?"

He glanced away quickly and picked up the groceries. "Your fiancé? I've met him. He's a lucky man, Miss McCrae."

She smiled. "Thank you. I'm hoping we'll find him in Silverton. You see, I don't think he got my letter telling him we were coming."

"I haven't heard that he's around, but then, I don't see everyone that stops at Silverton either."

Melinda followed him with their luggage. Evan waited on the hand-pumped speeder, swinging his legs over the edge, but when he saw Melinda struggling with the bags, he came running to help.

She studied the speeder. Lettering along the front spelled out "Silverton, Mud Tunnel, and Great Western Railway." She'd seen speeders before, used at Monte Cristo by the railroad workers. There were no seats. Two bars on either side of a central assembly allowed the operator to move a crank, which in turn caused the wheels to roll along the tracks. They would have to stand, all the way to Silverton ... stand, or maybe walk behind the car. Evan's gray-green eyes were eager as he said, "If we can go, I'll help pump, Mindy."

She turned to Dan Sutherland. "How much do you charge and how long will it take to get there?"

"I don't charge for passengers if they're willing to lend a hand with pumping. Can't say how long, for sure, but a lot faster than the freight wagon can travel."

"Well, Evan, I guess we'll take a chance. We can't miss out on an adventure, can we?"

They had been push-pulling for ages, it seemed. First Dan pushed down on his bar. They pulled up on theirs, then they pushed down while he pulled up. The wheels of the one-vehicle-train clacked merrily along. A cool breeze blew up from the Stillaguamish, for which she felt thankful. She used her handkerchief to wipe her perspiring face, then slipped off her jacket and dropped it atop her valise.

"Want to rest?" Without waiting for an answer, Dan allowed the car to glide to a stop. He sat down on the platform. Melinda staggered to the edge and sat down too. Her back felt about to break from the stooping and lifting.

Evan's grin hadn't faded. "I wonder if Uncle Quin got to ride a push car when he was helping to repair the railroad."

"I'm sure he did. It's how the work crews go from one place to another," Dan told him.

Melinda recognized the place where they had stopped. "This is Horseshoe Curve, isn't it?"

"Yes." Dan pointed up the steep bank ahead of them. "Brush has grown over the bank so you can't see it from here, but right up there is where the famous Mud Tunnel collapsed. The railroad workers thought this curve in the river was too sharp for trains to follow, so they tried to dig a tunnel through the hill up there. The soil was mostly sand. But they'd got quite a way in when the workers heard a hissing sound. They noticed water bubbling out of the dirt they were digging through. The foreman told them to get out. Then he ran, with an avalanche of mud and sand at his heels. He scrambled up the bank just as the mud exploded out of the tunnel and the top caved in. They gave up and built the railroad where it is now."

"But you said the curve was too sharp for trains to follow," Evan said.

"They have to use special wheels," Dan replied.

Finally, when even Evan had lost his enthusiasm for the push car railroad, Melinda caught a glimpse of cables swooping down a steep mountainside and across the river. They were part of a new tramway completed by the "45" Consolidated Mining Company the very week last November's disastrous flooding had shut down the railroad. Then they passed new bunkers, constructed to receive the ore from the mines high above them. Silverton at last!

Ahead, buildings climbed a steep, logged-over slope at the foot of Long Mountain on the north side of the river. A plank bridge spanned the Stillaguamish, connecting to the rest of the town on the other side of the river. A jostle of kids ran to meet their conveyance. Evan's playmate from Monte Cristo, dark-haired, green-eyed Johnny Fountaine, recognized and hugged him. They wrestled joyfully, then raced across the bridge to his mom's and stepdad's new boarding house.

Melinda noted where they had gone. She turned to thank Dan Sutherland for the ride.

"You're most welcome, Miss McCrae. I'll drop your bags at the Swenson's on my way home. I hope you'll find your Mr. Chenoweth."

"I hope so too," Melinda said. She gazed around at the people heading toward the push car to see what might be in the mailbag. Quin was not among them. She picked up their valises and followed the boys across the bridge.

CHAPTER FIVE

RETURN TO MONTE CRISTO

After a restful night's sleep in one of the Swenson's guest rooms, Melinda woke to a robin's song coming through the open window, and the sound of rushing river. The sun's rays slanted across the top of the peaks above the town and lit the face of Long Mountain.

She heard the stove door clang in the kitchen downstairs. Pots and pans rattled. Quickly Melinda dressed and hurried down to help her friend with breakfast. Flour puffed from the work table as Nell, sleeves rolled to her elbows, patted a mass of biscuit dough flat, then used a tin can to cut out the biscuits.

Flour covered her hands and forearms, smudged her nose and dusted her apron. Her face positively glowed. Melinda laughed with delight. "You're as beautiful as always, even with flour on your nose," she said. "Marriage obviously agrees with you."

Nell's green eyes crinkled. "I heartily agree with marriage! Ole is a wonderful husband."

"I'm so glad. Johnny seems to love his new daddy very much."

"He does. Ole is a natural-born father." Nell lowered her voice. "Can I tell you a secret?"

"I love secrets."

"Johnny is going to be a big brother sometime around next Christmas!"

Melinda grabbed Nell and hugged her, flour and all. "What wonderful news."

"Thank you. I hope you and Quin will be as happy as we are."

Melinda's face fell a little. "Oh, Nell, what if he's changed his mind about marrying me? I came all this way to find him, and he's not even here."

"He's not here in Silverton. But you said he was to write a piece about Monte Cristo. He could have been in a hurry to get there and didn't stop. He might be planning to stop here on his way back. Why don't you stay a few days and see if he does?"

"Well, maybe. Or perhaps I could go to Monte Cristo somehow. I'd like to see how the school fared over the winter. Maybe I can get my old job back."

Nell finished transferring the biscuits to a baking sheet and slid them into the oven. "There. That should be enough to feed our boarders." She added another stick of wood to the firebox, pushed the coffee pot farther back on the stove, and stirred the potatoes that were frying in a big pan. She handed Melinda a basket of eggs. "Here, Melinda. Would you mind scrambling these? We have our own chickens now."

Melinda found another bowl and a whisk. She broke the eggs into the bowl and beat them.

Ole came into the room, followed by the boys. Each carried an armful of firewood for the woodbox by the door.

A wide grin split his bushy blond beard. "Well, yust like old times," he chuckled. "My favorite people, all together again."

His slender wife smiled back. "Caps off, all of you. Breakfast in ten minutes." She watched fondly as the big Swede and the little boys took their turns at the washbasin.

After they'd breakfasted with the boarders and the kitchen had been cleaned up, the boys ran out to play. Ole sat down for a few minutes with Nell and Melinda.

"Quin didn't stop here," Ole said to Melinda. "But if you want to look for him at Monte Cristo, I'm not too busy today. I can hitch up the buckboard and take you."

"Really? You'd do that?"

"A wonderful idea, Ole." Nell jumped up. "Just give me a little time to pack a picnic lunch. I'll get the neighbor lady to come in and fix supper for the boarders. We'll take the boys and make a day of it!"

They made short work of the preparations. Dew still hung on the salmonberry bushes along the railroad tracks when they started out. Ole drove the horse along the wagon road near the tracks. The miles seemed to go by quickly as the friends laughed and visited.

On one especially rough stretch, Melinda looked anxiously at Nell. "Are you sure this jostling won't harm the baby?"

"Oh, no. I'm doing fine. Besides, it's not much farther now."

They were passing the familiar rockslide where avalanches caused so much trouble every winter. Then they recognized the low spots in the woods that had provided the rink for the school skating party during the cold spell that had preceded the flooding last winter.

Finally they came to the lower townsite, where the shack in which Melinda had lived with Rose and her stepfather Jed Skinner stood next to the track. Heavy snow had bent the stovepipe. The remains of a curtain fluttered in a broken window.

"No, I don't want to go in," she told the Swensons. "Let's just see if anyone is still in town." Some of the buildings closest to the Sauk River, just a creek this time of year, had washed away in the flooding. But the Lucky Strike, Nell's former saloon, still clung to the bank.

They continued toward the upper townsite. Snow had caved in roofs on some of the buildings and splintered some outhouses. A "Closed" sign hung on the door of the Regal Hotel, where Melinda had worked before being hired as emergency replacement for the school teacher.

The Mercantile was locked too, but a man came to the door. "I'm living in the rooms behind the store, taking care of it until folks come back. I can open up if you need something."

"No, but we are looking for someone," Ole Swenson said. "Do you know Quin Chenoweth? A mining captain at the Mystery Mine?"

"Heard of him," said the caretaker. "Haven't met him."

"He's a newspaper reporter now," Melinda said eagerly. "He planned to come here to write about reopening the mines."

The man tipped his hat to her. "There's hardly anybody living here, Miss, but a few miners are still working some of the mines on the chance that they will reopen. I suppose Mr. Chenoweth could have gone to talk with them without me hearing about it."

Melinda was pretty sure Quin would have included the caretaker among those he'd want to interview, but they should also check with any one else they could find. She thanked him.

The boys begged to explore, so they left the buckboard in front of the Regal, tethered the horse in the Regal's neglected garden, and walked up the hill to the school house. It looked forlorn and neglected. Would the schoolyard ever again echo with the shouts of children playing?

Unless the railroad got back in operation, there'd be no schoolteacher's job here for her to apply for.

The adults followed the boys up the track into the clearing where Evan and his uncle had lived. The sturdy little cabin was undamaged, but the window boxes were full of leaves and sticks. A broken branch from one of the surrounding trees had snagged on the chimney. Others littered the clearing. Melinda felt like weeping as they turned back toward the village.

Nell linked her arm through Melinda's. "It's a ghost town, isn't it? But once people move back, they'll fix it up, better than it was before the flood."

Melinda forced a smile. "I hope so. Right now we need to see if Quin is here. Should we walk to some of the closer mines and try to talk to the miners?"

Evan and Johnny ran ahead.

As the adults neared the hotel, they saw them talking to a couple of men. Evan ran to Melinda "They said Uncle Quin hasn't been here, Mindy!"

As Ole walked down the street to the miners, she comforted Evan. "Don't worry. We'll find him."

But what if they couldn't find Quin? What would she do then? On the way back to Silverton, Melinda tried to be cheerful for the sake of the others. Nell and Ole seemed so happy together. She joined in the laughter and joking, despite her heavy heart. She felt almost sure that Quin had gone to Alaska.

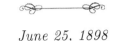

June 25, 1898
Daily Dispatch
Seattle, Washington

Journey to the Copper River Country
by Quintrell Chenoweth

Our vessel, the Miscreant, to the relief of its crowded passengers, steamed safely into Valdez Harbor yesterday. No dock has yet been built there, so at high tide we loaded supplies and passengers into the ship's launches. We made trip after trip to shore. Men, goods, and animals were offloaded in the drizzle onto the mud at water's edge and left there, trying to make sense of our new surroundings.

This reporter is one of the lucky few able to procure a bed in one of the town's few lodging accommodations. It is a small log cabin which the proprietor has stocked with a wood stove and six or eight bunks. Most newcomers set up temporary tent camps while preparing for the trip into Alaska's Interior.

Valdez townsite is located on the outwash from Valdez Glacier, which is visible about four miles from the cabins and tents scattered along the rudimentary roadways. High, snow-streaked mountains surround the townsite and extend along both sides of Prince William Sound. Those mountains are the barrier each of the miners must cross to reach their hoped-for El Dorado.

The U.S. government's military exploring expedition, under the direction of Captain William Ralph Abercrombie, is camped here with orders to search out an all-American route to the Klondike. But most of the gold seekers aren't waiting for a possible trail to the far-away Klondike. They are convinced that closer riches are available in the Copper River country. They simply have to cross the Valdez Glacier, which appears to offer an easy route to a pass through the mountains. Then they will travel down the other side by way of Klutina Lake and the river of the same name to the Copper River. Whether it's an easy route or not, I hope to find out within the next few days.

Quin lifted his pen and thought a moment. Then he wrote, *"More news to follow,"* and signed his name.

CHAPTER SIX

NIGHTMARE

Rain dripped from the brim of Melinda's oiled-canvas hat. Water soaked through her layers of clothing and numbed her hands. She could scarcely feel the oars. It seemed she'd been rowing for hours, but she couldn't get past the cloud-veiled cliff on her right. Why she was here, in a rowboat tossing amongst towering swells, or where she was trying to go, she had no idea.

This must be Alaska. Surely no place else on earth could be as forsaken. Waterfalls poured skeins of white lace down the cliff's face and into the ocean. The falls mingled with the waves slamming against the cliff.

Shouts penetrated the howling wind and crash of the waves. Looking up, she made out the forms of several men, clinging to the nearly vertical rocks. They were trying to traverse the slippery black surface, somehow passing through or behind the waterfalls. The man in the lead reminded her of Quin.

He turned his head toward her. It *was* Quin! His face looked tortured, scarcely recognizable. His eyes met hers. He reached out a hand and as he did, his foot slipped. He scrabbled frantically to regain his balance, but his feet couldn't find purchase. Her own screams echoed inside her head as he fell, disappearing behind the foaming, crashing waves.

Either he lay crumpled on a ledge she couldn't see, or he'd fallen directly into the icy surf. The other men, too, had vanished. She struggled frantically to row toward the cliff, but the waves carried her away.

She became aware of strange noises trying to escape her throat.

Heart pounding, tears wetting her face, she bolted upright. She peered into the darkness. The waves stilled, changing back into rumpled blankets.

No roar of wind or crash of waves disturbed the quiet now. Gradually she remembered where she was. In a guest room at the Swenson's boarding house. Thank the Lord, Evan was sleeping in Johnny's room and she'd not awakened anyone. But what did it all mean? She lay down again and tried to slow her breathing, willing her trembling to lessen. Her heart still raced with the terror of the nightmare. Was it a message of some kind?

God did send messages to people in dreams. She knew that from reading her Bible. When Herod wanted to kill the infant Jesus, the Magi had been warned in a dream not to report back to Herod but to go home another way. Right after that, an angel told Joseph in a dream to take the young child and his mother and flee to safety in Egypt. Was God telling *her* something? Was Quin in danger?

She tossed and turned until the sky lightened, then joined Nell in the kitchen to start breakfast for the boarders.

"Are you all right?" Nell frowned, concerned at the dark circles beneath her friend's eyes. "Didn't you sleep well?"

"Not really," Melinda said. She assured Nell quickly, "The bed was very comfortable. It's just, well, it's just that I had a bad dream. No, more than that. An awful nightmare. It left me convinced that Quin is somehow in danger. Nell, I've been thinking and praying for hours. I've got to find a way to get to Alaska. I've got to warn him."

Nell stared in consternation. "You can't mean that! You told us most of your money was stolen. How could you pay for passage? And how would you find Quin if you do get there? Melinda, Alaska's a huge country, full of grizzly bears and mountains and danger. You can't stake your future on the strength of a dream!"

Melinda related the nightmare in detail, and as she did, the terror struck again in all its gut-clenching reality. Pain pounded through her temples, making clear thought difficult. "I know it doesn't make sense. I can't imagine Quin ever attempting to cross a cliff like the one I saw. But I'm sure the dream means something. If a disaster happens and I hadn't tried to find and warn him, how could I ever forgive myself?"

"But ... "

"Alaska can't be that wild anymore, Nell, with all those hundreds of gold-seekers already there. I have enough money to get there, if I don't insist on the best accommodations." A new idea flashed into her mind. "With all those men eating their own cooking, I know I can make more money once I get there. I can bake pies or cook something else they'll be glad to pay for."

"What about Evan?"

"Could he possibly stay with you until I get back? He's a wonderful little boy, and he could be a big help to you. He can bring in firewood, or sweep floors. He'd love to be with Johnny."

"Of course. He'd be welcome. It's you I'm worried about, Melinda."

Big, gentle Ole poked his head in, just as Nell said this. He looked from one woman's serious face to the other's, but asked with a grin, "Can a guy get a cup of coffee this early in the morning?"

Nell turned to the stove and poured some from the big enameled pot. She handed him the cup. "We need to talk with you after breakfast, Ole." She looked at Melinda. "Is that all right?"

Melinda nodded. She felt sure Nell planned to enlist Ole's help in talking her out of this idea. But discussing the nightmare had only strengthened her resolve. She needed first to know that Quin really had gone to Alaska. If he had, and if it was at all possible, she was going there, too. She would find a way.

"You're my dearest friends. I know you have my best interests at heart." Melinda gazed at Ole and raven-haired Nell sitting together across the table from her. "I'm sure Quin wouldn't have gone away without writing to me about it, but the fact remains, I've not received any message from him at all. He thinks I'm still in San Francisco, so any letters to me would go there.

"He didn't meet me in Seattle. I didn't find him in Everett. He wasn't in Monte Cristo, and he's not been here. All I know is that he took a job with a Seattle newspaper called *The Daily Dispatch*. *The Dispatch* planned to send him to Alaska but we don't know when. I think I need to talk to someone at the newspaper and find out for sure if that's where he is."

"Ya," Ole nodded. "That makes sense."

"Silverton's telegraph is back in order after the flooding," Nell said. "You could send a message to the paper."

"That's a good idea," Melinda said. She thought a bit. "Better yet, is there telephone service between Granite Falls and Seattle? Or Everett and Seattle? I could get more information that way."

Ole looked at his wife, who glanced back as if reading his mind. "No, not yet. If there was, we wouldn't have to go all the way to Seattle to order supplies for the boarding house."

"You're going to Seattle?" Melinda asked eagerly. "When?"

Going directly to Seattle would be the best way to find out about Quin. Ole and Nell could help her find her way around.

"Let Ole and me talk it over," Nell said. "Meanwhile, why don't you take the boys upriver to try out the new fishing poles Ole made? Johnny knows the good fishing spots."

A little while later, Johnny led the way along the river bank. Evan walked close to her, not as excited by the venture as she'd expected him to be.

"What's the matter, Evan? You're very quiet."

He stopped and looked up at her, his eyes more gray than green with worry. "I'm all right." He hesitated, then confessed. "I heard you telling Mrs. Swenson about your dream. I didn't eavesdrop on purpose, really I didn't. You sounded so upset, I tiptoed back upstairs. Do you really think Uncle Quin is in danger, Mindy?"

Her heart jolted. She hadn't meant for Evan to hear that. "It was just a dream, Evan. I was concerned because we haven't found him, and it sounds like he might have gone to Alaska. Sometimes our worries come to life in our dreams. It doesn't usually mean anything."

"But sometimes it does?"

"I don't know. We will pray that God takes care of him. That's the best thing to do."

Johnny called to Evan from the path ahead. "Here's my most favorite fishing place. Hurry up!"

Evan ran to join his friend. Melinda found a spot beneath a tree where she could sit and watch them. Johnny handed Evan a worm from the canful they'd dug. They baited their hooks. Then Johnny swung his pole out over the calmer water on the inside curve of the riverbank and dropped the hook where he thought the fish might be hiding. Evan moved upriver a little way and imitated Johnny.

Melinda remembered her advice to Evan. She prayed for Quin's safety, wherever he might be. As she watched the current flowing around the rocks, tossing sparkles back at the sun, she felt calmer. Nell had known this little jaunt would be good for her troubled spirit.

Evan quickly got the hang of it. When he pulled in a glistening rainbow trout, at least fourteen inches long, both boys whooped with glee.

Johnny showed Evan how to run a piece of fishing line through the gills. Before long they had a string of silvery fish, enough to provide themselves and the boarders with dinner that evening.

In the backyard, Ole helped the boys clean the trout. Melinda found Nell upstairs, changing sheets in the boarder's rooms. She helped make up the beds while she told about the boys' success at the river. "I think Evan is hooked on fishing." She laughed. "Wait 'til you see their catch."

Nell smiled. "By the way, I've got something for you." She led the way to a storeroom down the hall. "We took a trip back to

Monte Cristo when we first moved here to Silverton. I wanted to get the belongings I'd left at the hotel. While we were at it, we brought this back." She gestured to a leather-covered container against the wall.

"Oh, Nell! My mother's trunk! I never even thought of looking for it while we were in Monte Cristo." She knelt on the floor and unlatched the lid. She pulled back the sheet that wrapped an item on top. "The beautiful blue dress Mother sewed for you. You gave it to me to wear at the Chatauqua. Remember?"

"I remember. You looked lovely in it. No wonder Quin lost his heart to you."

Melinda pulled out a pair of boy's knickers. She'd used them for hiking at Monte Cristo. They were still much too big for Evan, but she'd take them with her. Perhaps she could cut them down for his everyday use.

She rummaged deeper. "Here's the little Bible Grammy gave me when we first left San Francisco. I'll take that with me, too. Do you mind if I leave the rest of the things with you? I'm so glad you've kept them where they'll be safe."

"They'll be fine here until you and Quin set up your own home."

A home of their own. She wondered if Quin was as eager as she was for that to happen.

Nell sat back on her heels. "Melinda, Ole and I have talked it over. With the baby coming, he thinks it's wise to make our trip to Seattle a little early. We'll get a friend to stay here and run the business for a couple of days. If you can help me do some baking this afternoon, she'll be able to handle meals. We'll take the buckboard to meet the train at Robe. We'll stop in Everett to see if Mrs. Collins has heard anything from Quin. If not, our first stop in Seattle will be at the office of the Daily Dispatch."

As Melinda rolled out pie crusts that afternoon, she thought about what she'd do if Quin had already gone to Alaska. Would there be some way to contact him? What if she had to follow him? Could she catch up in time to warn him about ... whatever danger might be waiting? Would he think her foolish to let a dream influence her so strongly?

She didn't share her thoughts with Nell, fearful that her friend would also consider her foolish. But she felt it prudent to decide what she might need to buy if she did go to Alaska. It was summer now, but Alaska was colder than here. She'd need woolen clothing. If she had to follow the gold seekers to find him, she'd need sturdy boots for hiking. Maybe a rubberized poncho for rainy weather, warm gloves and hat. Food for herself. Cooking utensils, flour, baking powder, lard, dried fruit for pies for hungry prospectors. What kind of stove could she carry with her? Would she need a pack animal?

The thoughts buzzed in her head. If she were to be gone for a while, she should get Evan some clothes. He was growing so fast. Would the money she had left cover all those expenses, as well as passage on a boat?

She had a hard time sleeping that night. Following Quin to Alaska was a foolhardy idea, she knew, but then the memory of the nightmare came back. Every frightening detail. She must warn Quin of possible danger, even if it did mean appearing foolish.

CHAPTER SEVEN
POSSIBILITIES

Mrs. Collins, at the boarding house in Everett, hadn't yet heard from Quin. She handed Melinda a fat packet from her mother. Inside were letters for both Melinda and Evan, plus money that Melinda knew came from Rose's hard-earned dollars as a seamstress. There was also a weather-beaten letter addressed to her in Quin's handwriting. She opened and scanned it rapidly. He'd written it in early June. Today was June 20. Oh, if only this had arrived before her decision to leave San Francisco!

Skipping over the more personal passages, she read parts of it aloud to the listeners in Mrs. Collin's parlor:

> *We're plugging along through a windstorm. This old tub was the only transport available. It's heavily loaded with hopeful miners, their equipment, their animals, and who knows what else. It positively wallows in the swells that crash against the rocks of the innumerable islands we are passing. Most of the passengers and the animals are miserable, although so far I am feeling well. I'm thankful we're in the shelter of the Inside Passage. It would be far worse in the open ocean.*

Melinda thought of the black cliffs in her nightmare. Had Quin seen places like that?

> *You'll have received the previous letter I sent, telling you of my assignment to report on the gold rush to Valdez.*

No, she hadn't received that letter. Perhaps it was the one stolen along with her money.

For some of the passengers on this sorry craft, the prospect of finding gold is their last hope. Though their journey will take them over the dangerous Valdez Glacier. They are determined to find their fortunes on the banks of the Copper River.

I will be traveling with them, documenting their journey. If you can get hold of Seattle's Daily Dispatch there in San Francisco, you may Read all About it! Tell Evan I send my special greetings to him.

With love, Quin of the Mighty Pen

She smiled as she read the signature. It was tongue in cheek, she knew, but who would have expected a mining captain from Cornwall to turn from pick and shovel to the pen?

"Well, now we know for sure he went to Alaska," said Nell.

"Yes." Melinda folded the letter and tucked it with those from her mother into her valise.

They still had an hour before the afternoon train left for Seattle. Ole took Evan and Johnny outside to play while Nell rested. Melinda went upstairs to sort through the luggage she'd leave with Mrs. Collins, taking what she might need for a possible journey to Alaska and stuffing it into her valise. She added her small Bible and the knickers she'd planned to cut down for Evan. Who knew? She might need them herself. Mrs. Collins climbed the stairway to give her a small sewing kit, which went into the valise. She packed clothes into Evan's bag for his overnight stay in Seattle.

Mrs. Collins looked troubled when Melinda told her about the dream and her desire to warn Quin, but she didn't try to dissuade her. "Be very careful if you go, dear," she said. "Be sure to let your mother know where you are ... and me, too."

"I will, Mrs. Collins. You're always so kind! Thank you for your concern."

Then she bade the landlady goodbye and headed with Evan and the Swensons toward the big city of Seattle.

Seattle's pace seemed frenetic, after the quiet of the North Cascade mountains. Though the furor about the Klondike discoveries had died down considerably, the streets near the waterfront were still crowded with men preparing to journey north. Some were still heading for the Klondike, but most to the new gold rush on the Copper River. Outside the shops of outfitters, supplies were stacked on the sidewalks, everything from sacks of beans to racks of boots.

The group asked directions from a clerk standing next to his wares in a sidewalk display. "Office of *The Daily Dispatch?*" he repeated, and pointed up the hill behind him. "Follow this street to the second intersection, then go south two blocks."

The steep climb left them breathing hard. Melinda was glad to turn onto the level street that ran parallel to the waterfront. Between the intervening buildings she caught glimpses of the busy harbor, criss-crossed by the small boats of Puget Sound's Mosquito Fleet. They were the only way for passengers and commerce to get to many small settlements along the forested shores. Larger vessels of all descriptions lined the waterfront. Some seemed barely afloat, but stevedores and would-be-prospectors were loading them with sacks and bundles of supplies.

"Here it is, Mindy." Evan and Johnny had run ahead. Now they waited in front of a window with "Daily Dispatch" painted in ornate letters. Ole opened the door and held it while the women entered.

A grumpy-looking man with tousled gray hair and the stump of a cigar clamped between his teeth looked up from his littered desk. A brass plate on the desk read, "E. G. Bowden, Editor."

"What can I do for you folks?" he growled.

Melinda stepped to the counter and took a deep breath. "We're trying to find a man named Quintrell Chenoweth. We understand he recently took a position with your newspaper."

The man scowled from beneath bushy eyebrows. "And your relationship with Mr. Chenoweth?"

Melinda lifted her chin. "He's my fiancé."

Evan took Melinda's hand. "And he's my uncle."

The man's expression warmed a little. "Oh, yes. He told me about you. Miss McCrea, isn't it?"

Melinda nodded and introduced the others. "I recently returned from San Francisco, not knowing about his new job. He'd told his landlady that he might go to Monte Cristo on an assignment, but we didn't find him there. Then a letter he sent to San Francisco caught up with me. He wrote it while traveling to Valdez. I'm hoping you can tell us more."

"Hmmm. I'm not the one who hired him, but he'll be sending his stories to me." Mr. Bowden sounded friendlier now. He gathered some chairs from around the office and invited them to sit.

"I do know he outfitted himself with what he'll need to travel along with the gold-seekers: food, cooking utensils, blankets, etc. Plus, he was given an allowance to hire packers to help carry his stuff, or to buy a pack animal."

"How long do you expect him to be gone, Mr. Bowden?"

"As long as it takes to cover the story. Probably until late summer.

I'll show you the tentative route he planned to take."

Mr. Bowden riffled through the books and papers on his desk and pulled out a map. He spread it out and pointed to a body of water labeled 'Prince William Sound'.

"I say 'tentative,' because this is the trail most of the miners are using. There is a military expedition working at Valdez, planning to map out a new route to the Klondike, up north in Canada. But most prospectors heading for Valdez are hoping to find gold along the Copper River, without making that long trek to the Klondike.

"The Copper River comes through the mountains here," he placed an ink-stained forefinger on the spot, "and empties here into Prince William Sound, but it's almost impassable except when it's frozen. It runs through the interior in a big arc ... " He traced the river with his finger and stopped at the upper part of the curve. "The gold is supposed to be up here, in this area along the Copper River. Valdez is where the prospectors disembark." He put his finger at the end of an inlet of Prince William Sound.

"They then have to haul all their goods to the top of this glacier, then follow lakes and rivers into the interior until they reach the upper Copper River."

"What's in all that white space, Mr. Bowden?" Evan asked.

"Can't tell you. No one's mapped those places yet."

Evan's eyes widened. "Maybe my Uncle Quin is going there."

"Maybe," the editor agreed. "Maybe he'll send back tales that will make your hair stand on end. Maybe not. We haven't yet received his first story, though he should be in Alaska by now."

Melinda shivered, wondering whether it was just the difficulty of sending communications that had delayed the dispatch of Quin's stories, or if something had gone wrong. Recalling that awful nightmare, she hoped it hadn't been a presentiment of one of those tales. What she could do to prevent its fulfillment, she didn't know, but she made up her mind. She would follow Quin to Alaska. And somehow, she had to find a way to support herself while doing so.

By now, only a couple of hours remained before the busy downtown district would close up for the evening. They bade goodbye to Mr. Bowden.

As they walked back down the hill, she told Nell and Ole her decision. She could see the dismay on their faces, but they they didn't try any more to dissuade her.

They took Johnny with them into a store that carried restaurant supplies, and directed Melinda and Evan to a dry goods store down the street. Evan needed clothing for the rainy Washington weather if she didn't get back before fall, and she'd need some warmer things as well. She bought sturdy lace-up boots and thick woolen stockings for each of them, plus woolen knickers, a sweater and a coat for Evan.

She examined a long, heavy rubber poncho lined with soft fabric. She could wear it, or if she had to sleep on the ground it could double as a waterproof ground cover. But deciding it would be heavy to carry, she put it back on the shelf. Instead, she chose a coat of tightly woven wool. It would keep her warm and dry wherever she ended up. The total bill for her purchases made her gasp, but she handed over the money. The clerk wrapped the items in brown paper and tied the bulky parcels with twine.

As they stepped back into the street, one of Evan's packages slipped from his arms. He grabbed it before it hit the ground. "Mindy, I saw some canvas bags near the trunks and suitcases. They looked like the bags the sailors carried when they boarded our ship in San Francisco. Wouldn't it be useful to have something like that?"

"Why don't you show me?"

They returned to the store and he showed her the bags. "See? One could hold all these things and my satchel too."

"They're not too expensive. Let's each get one."

She paid for them and they packed their purchases inside. The double straps made carrying them easier.

They wandered down the street with their duffel bags, examining the supplies stacked outside the stores. A number of prospectors were selecting what they needed for their journey to Alaska. What, Melinda wondered, had Quin taken with him? What would she need for the same journey?

One establishment had a sidewalk display of portable stoves, metal dishes and pans, coffee pots and the like. She fingered a stack of metal pie pans. Five or six of those would be fairly light to carry. Through the open door of the shop, she could see sacks and bins of food supplies. Dried fruit, flour, lard, sugar ... how much of that would be needed to make lots of pies? One of those small iron stoves could hold two pies at a time. It came apart for easier packing, but it was heavy. She looked at a sturdy Dutch oven with a tight-fitting lid and little legs on the bottom. Maybe one could put a pie inside and set it down in the hot coals to bake.

Her mind buzzed with the decisions she needed to make. Intent on her inspections, she bumped into a tall person with a close-cropped, ginger-colored beard. Fiery hair curled beneath the brim of his bowler hat.

"Oh, I'm so sorry." She stepped back, tilting her head to look up at him. With his polished walking stick and well-tailored clothing, he did not seem like a typical prospector.

He touched the brim of his hat. "Quite all right, Ma'am." His voice sounded amused. "Do you intend to join the gold rush?"

Evan appeared at her elbow. He watched the man warily.

"No. But I imagine one could make a good living in Alaska offering the prospectors a taste of home cooking."

"You're probably correct." Freckled fingers tapped a tattoo on the head of his cane. "I myself have a business in Valdez. So far, my customers are mostly those on their way to or from the gold rush, but someday, I hope, the establishment will be part of an important city."

"A restaurant, Mr. ... ?"

"Cox. Ezekiel Cox, at your service, Ma'am."

She gave him her name.

"And who are you, my little man?"

Evan scowled. "My name is Evan. And I'm not your little man." Melinda sent a glance of surprise and reproof toward the boy. Such unmannerliness was not like him. But the red-haired man brushed aside the moment with a careless wave. "No, of course not. You look like you're a great help to your mom."

Neither Evan nor Melinda said anything to set him straight. She noticed that he hadn't answered her question about his business, either.

"Are you heading toward the Klondike, or thinking about Valdez?"

"Probably Valdez."

"Well, if you get to Valdez, look me up. I'd be happy to offer you a job. You'd make as much money or more working for me as you would trying to start a brand-new business."

"Thank you, Mr. Cox. I'll keep your offer in mind. Now excuse us, please. Friends are waiting for us."

As they lugged their duffel bags back toward where they'd left the Swensons, Melinda looked down at the small boy. "What's the matter, Evan? It's not like you to be rude."

Evan looked away. "I didn't like the way he was watching you, before you saw him."

"How was he watching me?"

"I don't know. But I didn't like it."

She squeezed his hand. Men were prone to be appreciative of attractive young women, and Melinda often found herself the subject of admiring glances. She found it sweet that the little boy felt so protective. He needn't worry. Even if she wasn't thoroughly in love with Quin Chenoweth, Ezekiel Cox was not her type. But it was good to have his job offer, *if* she ended up staying in Valdez.

The dream about Quin, though fading somewhat, haunted her, flashing into her mind when she least expected it. Maybe it *was* foolishness. But it seemed like a warning, a compulsion she didn't understand.

June 30, 1898

Quin lay down his pen and flexed his hand. The fingers injured in last summer's mine explosion ached. He pushed the tent flap aside to peer down the Valdez Glacier. A long procession of men and a few animals struggled upward through soggy snow. Though the rain had stopped, a cold wind gusted, swirling smoke from a fire smoldering in front of the tent. Wet boots steamed upside down on stakes near the fire. The two young men who tended the fire and the drying boots were too tired for the usual hijinks, after a day of slogging through knee-deep slush.

The two oldest members of the party had wrung out their soaked pants, socks, and long johns and hung them inside the tent to dry. Then they'd collapsed into their sleeping bags. Quin had changed his own wet garments for spare clothing. He planned to join his slumbering companions as soon as possible. Tomorrow they'd make another trip to bring up the last load of supplies. After that, they'd tackle the final and hardest stretch of trail left before the crest of the glacier.

He massaged his right hand, trying to reawaken the feeling in those fingers. Cold always brought pain from the injury he'd received in that not-so-accidental mine explosion at Monte Cristo, almost a year ago now. He and other miners had been trapped when Anton Cole's attempt to scare them had gone awry. He thought of the welcome he'd received from Melinda when they finally dug themselves out of the cave-in. He smiled at the memory, and picked up his pen. He'd write as long as the daylight lasted. He didn't want to miss a chance to send this dispatch to Seattle with the next mail carrier that came south over the trail.

" ... *Most of the Copper River gold-seekers have formed themselves into small companies for the assistance they can be to one another.*

I have attached myself to one of these. It includes a retired doctor from Pennsylvania, two young farmers from Minnesota, and a middle-aged miner who has prospected in Colorado, California, and Washington. Of the five of us, he is the one who is best prepared for the rigors of finding gold in this country.

I was fortunate to have procured a pack animal to carry my gear. Still, our group has spent several days getting our outfits over the ice of Valdez Glacier. What the horse can't carry, we haul on sleds, two hundred pounds at a time,

*up almost vertical cliffs where we have to chop footholds
in the ice and use ropes to hoist our sleds and equipment.
Between these cliffs, or benches, the going is easier, but
still constantly upward, 18 miles from sea level to 4800
feet. We look forward to reaching the northern, sunny side
of the pass.*

*Ahead lie raging rivers, swamps, and lands set aflame
by careless newcomers, according to discouraged miners
returning to Valdez over the route we are taking. Some of
them are ill with scurvy. Few have found any gold, but still,
they repeat rumors of wealth discovered beyond the places
they reached.*

*It is this reporter's advice to people still determined to
seek riches on the Copper River, and to those hoping for
an All-American route to the Klondike gold fields: take the
propaganda of the steamship companies with a liberal dose
of salt. Be well prepared, because it is a long, hard journey,
and some have not survived it.*

Quin hoped his plain stating of facts would help people avoid
suffering of the sort experienced by the returning miners he'd met.
He also hoped that if Melinda read this dispatch, it wouldn't make
her worry about him.

CHAPTER EIGHT

JOINING THE GOLD RUSH

Melinda was waiting outside the door of the Daily Dispatch when E.G. Bowden blew into the office from the back room to unlock the door the next morning. Surprised to see her there, he motioned her in.

"Mr. Bowden, at the risk of making myself a bother, I need to ask for a few moments of your time. You see, my friends must return to their home in Silverton today. I felt I should check with you once more for news from my fiancé before boarding a ship for Valdez."

"I told you yesterday that there'd been no word." He sounded gruff.

"Yes, I know. But I hoped maybe something came in after I left ... "

A rustle and thump of envelopes and packets hitting the floor sounded from the mail slot near the door.

"Postman. Early today." Bowden scooped up the morning's mail and leafed through it before tossing it onto his desk.

"You're in luck, Miss McCrae." He picked up a heavy envelope and slit it open. He unfolded several handwritten pages, muttering phrases aloud as he skimmed through Quin's first dispatches from Alaska. *"Men sick with scurvy. Not enough pack animals ... constant rain ... crevasses ... prospectors poorly prepared for conditions."*

He continued to skim, then handed her the last page. The ink had blurred a little where the paper had got wet. She could tell his hand had been hurting by the cramped, irregular writing:

" ... *gold-seekers have formed themselves into small companies ... I have attached myself to one of these.*

... spent several days getting our equipment over the ice of Valdez Glacier. We hauled our outfits up almost vertical cliffs where we had to chop footholds in the ice and use ropes to hoist ourselves and our equipment.

Ahead lie raging rivers, swamps, scurvy, and lands set aflame by careless newcomers ... Be prepared, because it is a long, hard journey, and some have not survived it.

Melinda handed the page back to the editor, taking one more glance at the familiar handwriting. She let her breath out in a grateful sigh. Quin was all right. At least he was when he'd written that story.

If she went to Alaska, could she really find him? And how would she explain herself to him if she did? What if he thought she didn't trust him to look after himself and felt humiliated by her following him? She put that thought out of her head. When he heard about the dream, of course he would realize she had to come.

She thanked Mr. Bowden and left the office. She needed time to think. When she reached their hotel, she did not go immediately to the suite where the group had spent the night, but instead went to the dining room where a few people were eating breakfast. The Swensons and Evan would be down soon. Meanwhile, she ordered coffee.

While sipping it, she thought about all those prospectors and their diet of beans and salt pork. Surely they would be willing to pay whatever she had to charge to make money on her cooking.

Maybe she'd work for Ezekiel Cox while amassing a small grubstake, enough money to set herself up in business. Perhaps that business could be a traveling restaurant. She could travel along with the gold-seekers and set up her restaurant at various places along the route. She would find Quin and warn him about the danger foreshadowed in her nightmare. By then she'd have earned enough money to return with him to Washington, where they could get married.

Now for practical matters. The Swensons had already agreed to let Evan stay with them. She checked the dwindling amount of money left in her purse. She didn't know what the fare would be to travel to Alaska. More than the price of the San Francisco to Seattle fare, surely. If it cost that much, she'd have to use her mother's money to buy the remaining supplies she'd need. She wouldn't have enough to live on for long, once she got to Valdez ... unless she took Mr. Cox up on his job offer.

"Lord, what do you want me to do next?" Her prayer was sincere. If God had warned her of danger through the nightmare, he surely would help her in carrying out her plan. The waitress refilled her coffee cup.

A couple of men entered the dining room and ordered breakfast at the next table. She couldn't help overhearing their discussion. One man apologized to the other for having to back out on their plans to sail to Alaska. He'd just received word that his wife was sick and he was needed at home.

"This really puts a crimp in my plans, too," the other man answered. "The Northward leaves this afternoon. I can probably find another partner, but not before the ship sails."

Maybe this was the answer to Melinda's prayer. Would the first man be willing to sell his ticket, maybe even at half-price? She could promise to send him the other half later. She screwed up her courage and stepped over to their table. She introduced herself, apologized for listening to their conversation, and asked her question.

Mr. Blackman was old enough to be her father, and he looked at her with fatherly concern. "Why do you want to go North, young woman?"

She told him about Quin and her plans to find a job once she got to Valdez, or to set up a business of her own that she could move from place to place.

"I could sell the ticket full fare," he replied. "The streets are full of people waiting for space on a steamer to Alaska. But I need to get home as soon as possible. Yes, you can have it, half the price now, the rest when you earn it. Are you interested in buying whatever of my outfit Pitts here can't use?"

He told her that he had a small tent and sleeping bag that he'd just bought yesterday, and best of all, a sturdy little pack horse.

"No," his partner said. "I'll buy the pack horse. I'll need him to carry the extra supplies.

"That's fine," Melinda said. "I wouldn't be able to pay for the horse right now anyway, but I'll gladly buy the tent and sleeping bag."

He told her his price and she counted out the money. He wrote out a receipt for her, with his name and address on it.

She heard familiar voices on the stairs. "Here are my friends. Thank you, Mr. Blackman."

Evan and Johnny clattered down the stairs ahead of Nell and Ole. Evan ran to Melinda and threw his arms around her waist. "I found your note, Mindy. I was worried about you."

Melinda hugged him. "I'm sorry you worried. I didn't want to wake you so early."

She turned back to the two men. "Where can we finish our transaction?"

"We'll be on the dock near the *Northward* before noon. The ship leaves at two o'clock."

Melinda was too scared and excited to have much appetite, but she ordered breakfast along with the others.

While they waited for their food, she told them about her talk with Mr. Bowden and what Quin had written in his dispatch. She told them she'd just bought a ticket to Valdez, plus some supplies.

Ole looked concerned. Nell let out a little involuntary sound of distress. "Oh, Melinda, how can you be ready so soon? Don't you think it would be better to wait for a personal word from Quin before taking such a step?"

"Perhaps, though that might take all summer. Don't you think finding someone willing to give me a ticket for half of what he paid for it, in such a serendipitous manner ... surely God must be leading me? Besides, I need a way to support myself until I find Quin."

She glanced at Evan, whose freckles stood out against a pinched and pale face. She put an arm around his shoulders. "It's going to be all right," she told him. "You and Johnny will have a wonderful summer. I'll find your uncle and come back as soon as I can."

Still looking worried, Ole went off to find a wagon to rent. They piled their purchases into it. The next few hours passed in a whirlwind of making lists, buying and packaging more supplies, and finally hauling everything to the wharf where the *Northward,* an old sailing vessel converted to steam power, waited. People were already boarding with boxes, bundles, dogs, and even sleds like the ones Melinda had seen outside one of the outfitter's stores. A crowd milled on the wharf: prospectors, a few women who appeared to be accompanying their husbands north, even a couple of families with children.

"See, Nell," Melinda told her somber friend. "Alaska can't be that wild or dangerous if women and children are going."

Nell summoned a smile. "I know you'll use good sense, Melinda. But please, will you write and let us know what's happening?"

"Of course I will. Evan, I will write to you, too. Every chance I get. Will you write back?"

He nodded, his eyes on a harried mother trying to keep track of four small children plus a baby while her husband carried their bundles onto the ship.

"Miss McCrea!" Melinda turned to see Mr. Blackman bent under a load of supplies. "Here are your new tent, sleeping bag, and a few other things I thought you might use. It's a very small tent, meant only for sleeping. There's a piece of canvas you can use as a rainfly." He deposited the bundles next to her pile of supplies. "This package is large, but lightweight." He showed her. "It's mostly dried fruit, and some evaporated vegetables you can use in stews."

"Thank you, Mr. Blackman. I hope your wife recovers quickly."

"Unfortunately, the doctor has his doubts." The man shook his head. "I wish you luck in your search, Miss McCrea."

He took his leave.

As Melinda and Nell wrote "M. McCrea" on waterproof tags and attached them to each of her bundles, Ole carried them up the gangplank to be stashed in the cargo hold by the deckhands on board. He saw to it that her personal things were taken to the compartment assigned to her.

Melinda looked around for Evan. He was sitting on his duffle bag in the wagon, looking forlorn. She climbed up to sit beside him. The boy turned his face away, but not in time to hide a tear escaping beneath his lashes.

"Oh, Evan. Please don't cry. You'll be just fine with the Swensons."

"I know, Mindy. But what about you? What if the boat should sink? What if you should get lost?"

"Sweetheart, bad things do happen sometimes. But you know, don't you, that Jesus is always with those who love him? He will be with me, and he will be with you, too."

"I want him to be with us together."

She smiled and lifted his chin, so he had to look into her eyes. "You will always be my Evan. Do you know that?"

"Yes." He sniffed.

"Always." She kissed him. "Now it's time for me to board the ship."

He dropped his head. "I'll stay here in the wagon."

Her heart clenched painfully at his distress. She hugged his rigid little body tightly. "Goodbye, then. Remember, I love you."

Melinda found her tiny, none-too-clean cabin near the bow of the Northward and checked to be sure the bag she wanted with her had been delivered. One of the first things she'd do would be to find a broom and some cleaning cloths. She looked out the smeary porthole.

Something seemed to be causing a lot of excitement on deck. She joined people at the rail who were watching a mule being hoisted from the dock. The big beast's legs dangled as his feet left the planks. His head drooped. He seemed resigned to what must have been a frightening situation. The long ears flicked nervously as his hoofs cleared the rail and he disappeared into the hold where the animals would be cared for.

Only one animal remained to be loaded. She saw Mr. Blackman's partner holding a pack horse's halter. She noticed the spatter of white spots over the brown rump as the animal danced in place. When a stevedore tried to loop the hoist's bands under its belly, the horse whinnied and shied away. Finally, two workers got them placed and the hoist began to lift. The horse heaved its body, trying to escape, and its hind legs slipped down to touch the dock. The workers yelled. One of them slapped the horse on the rump, making him lunge forward into the sling, and the hoist rose as the horse squealed and struggled.

"Poor thing," Melinda whispered. "I don't blame him for being terrified."

The animal continued to protest and struggle as it was lowered into the hold. Then deckhands covered the hatch. Others raised the gangplank, and loosed the hawser.

Had it been only six months ago that Melinda had stood like this on the deck of a ship backing out into Seattle's harbor? This time Quin didn't stand on the wharf, waving goodbye. She was sailing, not away from him, but to him, she hoped. And this time, no excited small boy stood at her side. Evan was down there on the wharf, waving with Nell and Ole and black-haired Johnny. Wasn't he? She remembered he wanted to stay in the wagon. There'd been such a flurry of goodbyes and last minute reminders she'd been afraid they'd raise the gangplank before she reached it.

The engine's sound changed and the ship began to move.

As the gulf between ship and watchers widened, Melinda searched the dock again, hoping to catch a glimpse of Evan. She hated that she'd had to uproot him from her mother's comfortable home in San Francisco. Now she was causing more disruption in his life. She caught a glimpse of the horse and wagon, almost hidden by the crowd moving away to the rest of their day's business. Well, Evan was in good hands. He'd soon be heading back to Silverton with the Swenson's.

For herself, she tried hard to hold on to her determination. She was determined to find Quin. Determined to make the most of her circumstances. Determined ... and scared.

CHAPTER NINE

DO SOMETHING, EVEN IF IT'S WRONG!

Though Melinda's cabin was cramped and not very clean, it did have two narrow bunks, one above the other, and a shelf which held a pitcher and washbasin. Hoisting her duffle bag onto the top bunk, she placed her hairbrush, small mirror, and toothbrush on the shelf. She hung her new coat on a hook so the wrinkles would shake out. She was ready for the voyage ahead, as soon as she swept the space and did a little scrubbing.

Melinda borrowed a broom and a rag for dusting from the steward. Back in her tiny compartment, even though the ship rocked and it was hard to keep her balance, she made up both bunks. She swept the space, dusted, and used a clean section of the rag and a little water from the pitcher to wash the inside of the porthole.

It had been a long time since breakfast and she'd missed lunch. She rummaged for a piece of the pilot bread she'd stashed in her bag while shopping that morning, and dropped it into her pocket. The hall outside her room opened to the stern. She climbed to the hurricane deck for a breath of fresh air.

Waves pushed against the hull of the boat and caused the rocking. They were crossing a wide expanse of water ... the Strait of Juan de Fuca, she realized. Whidbey Island lay to the east. She could see more land in the distance, both north and south. Buildings clustered along the shore of Vancouver Island to the northwest.

She was not alone on the deck. The mother with the large family sat on a bench next to the pilothouse, shawl pulled over the baby at her breast and looking exhausted. The two next youngest, a toddler and a four-year-old, clung to her skirt. Both were crying. The woman looked apologetic. "They're hungry," she said.

Melinda sat down on the other end of the bench and smiled at the little ones. "I have a piece of pilot bread in my bag. Could they have some?"

"Oh, thank you! You're a godsend!"

Melinda broke the hard disk and gave each child a piece. The older child squirmed onto the bench between the women. Melinda picked up the toddler and cuddled him in her lap while he sucked hungrily on the hardtack.

"You are a brave lady, to take these little ones into the wilderness. Are you and your husband joining the gold rush?"

"No. He sent machinery for a sawmill ahead to Valdez several weeks ago. He says there is a great demand for lumber to build the new town. We will be running the sawmill, or he will. Right now he's looking after our two oldest. As you can see, I have my hands full."

Melinda chuckled. "I think the wives always have the biggest jobs." They introduced themselves, and Mrs. Elizabeth Larson inquired as to Melinda's reason for going to Valdez.

"I'm looking for someone," Melinda said. "My fiancé, actually." She told the story to her new friend, wondering if her plan sounded foolish. "While I'm looking, I need to find a way to support myself. Fortunately, I met a businessman in Seattle who offered to give me a job once I get to Valdez."

"It's none of my affair, but please be careful," Elizabeth cautioned. "I hear that not all businesses in Valdez are the respectable kind!"

The creaking of the ship and people's voices in the hall kept Melinda awake a good share of the night, but she finally fell into a restless slumber. She awakened early, aware of a commotion on the deck. Pushing aside the drape over the porthole, she peered out at a group of deckhands crowded around something in the stern.

Through a gap in the wall of burly backs, she glimpsed hair the color of ripe wheat and the arms of a small boy clutching a duffel bag nearly as big as he.

She gasped. Evan! Without a doubt, it was Evan Chenoweth.

Quickly, she buttoned her shirtwaist and fastened her boots. She clamped her hat over her uncombed hair, grabbed her coat, and flew out the door. The deckhands had moved back, although one kept a firm grip on Evan's arm. "We've got ourselves a stowaway," he guffawed.

The boy looked disheveled, scared, ... and defiant. When he saw Melinda, he jerked free. He dashed across the deck and into her arms.

"Do you know this boy, ma'am?" growled the one who'd been holding Evan.

"Yes, I know him. But I don't know what he's doing on this ship!"

Another deckhand clattered down the stairs. "Cap'n Dowling says bring the boy to him." He reached out for Evan.

Melinda raised her chin. "I will take him, thank you. Please put his duffel bag outside Stateroom Twelve."

She grasped Evan's hand and marched him up the stairs to the pilothouse.

Outside the door she stopped and glared at the boy. "Suppose you tell me what you're doing here?"

"I'm going to Alaska with you."

"Oh, you are! Did you even think about how worried the Swensons must be?"

"They won't worry," he said with confidence. "I gave Johnny a note to give them after the ship left."

"But why, Evan? What am I supposed to do with you in Alaska?"

"Don't you remember, Mindy?" Evan looked less confident. "When we went to California, Uncle Quin told me I was to look after you. How can I do that if you leave me with the Swensons?"

Melinda's heart melted. Just then the door opened, and the captain of the vessel looked down at the boy. "Is this our stowaway?"

"I'm afraid so, Captain Dowling. I am Melinda McCrea, and Evan Chenoweth is my ward. He was supposed to stay with friends. I am as amazed as everybody else to find him on board the ship."

"Well, come in, both of you. Let's try to sort this out."

The pilot house was as neat as the captain was rumpled. But his questions to Evan were not unkind.

"How did you get on the boat without a ticket?"

"Everyone was watching a horse being loaded on the boat. So I just walked up the gangplank with the rest of the passengers."

"Hmmm. And what did you do then?"

"When I passed a boat on the deck, I saw nobody was looking. So I climbed in under the canvas cover."

Melinda interrupted. "That's where you stayed, all night?"

Evan nodded. "It was cold. And scary. I put my new coat on to stay warm, and used my duffle bag for a pillow."

"Young man, I should put you ashore and let you find your own way home." Melinda caught the glimpse of amusement in the Captain's eyes.

Evan glanced at the wild shoreline in the distance, fear blanching his face. Melinda stayed silent, letting Evan absorb the enormity of his predicament. Then she turned to Captain Dowling. "I'm so sorry. I haven't enough money to pay for another ticket. But may he stay with me in my cabin?"

The Captain regarded them soberly. He nodded. "One more question for you, Mr. Chenoweth. Why did you stow away?"

Evan repeated the answer he'd given Melinda.

"Hmm. You sound like a resourceful young man. You're a bit scrawny, but do you think you can make yourself useful around the ship? If your guardian agrees, you can work off the price of your ticket."

Evan looked up, his eyes hopeful. "Oh, yes. I could help the sailors with their work!"

"I was thinking more of you helping in the galley ... scraping dishes, peeling potatoes, that sort of thing. Could you do that?"

His face fell. "Yes, sir. Thank you, sir."

"All right. I'll tell Black Jack he's getting a new helper. Go to your room and settle in. Then report for work."

Blackjack? Wasn't that a gambling game, or maybe a weapon? What were they getting into? But Melinda kept her voice even. "Thank you, Captain Dowling, for being so understanding. He'll do his best."

The captain tipped his hat to her as they left the pilot house.

A chilly wind had come up. The ship plowed through white-capped waves. They had passed Vancouver Island during the night and were now crossing an expanse of open water, with no land visible to the west at all. This must be Queen Charlotte Sound.

She led Evan to their quarters. She poured water into the basin, splashed it onto her face and dried it, then told Evan to wash up and pay special attention to his grimy hands. While he scrubbed, she grimly brushed her hair and redid the twist at the back of her head.

"Are you mad at me, Mindy?"

She realized her jaw felt rigid, her forehead tense.

"Not so much at you, Evan. But I am upset. Who would ever believe life could get so complicated?" She ran a comb through his hair. "Ready to go to work?"

Evan followed her through the hall and into the dining room. The galley was a long, narrow space at the back of the dining area. They heard a clatter coming from behind the dividing wall. The cook, a very large man whose glistening blue-black skin contrasted with a white-toothed grin, looked up as they stepped into his workspace.

Melinda gave Evan a nudge. He moved forward a bit, looking scared. "Hello, Mr. Blackjack. I'm here to help you."

The cook looked him up and down. "I's just Jack. You the boy Cap'n tell me about?"

Evan nodded.

"Y'all don't look big enough to be much help."

"N ... n ... Yes, sir. I learn quick. I can help."

The cook poured hot water into a basin next to a dishpan full of soapy water and silverware. "Rinse the silverware in the hot water. Then dry them and put them on this tray. When you done, you can set them on the tables for lunch. You know how to set a table?"

"I think so. Grandma Rose taught me."

Melinda thanked the big man and left Evan to his task. He would learn lessons he'd not forget. The boat rocked and plunged. She wondered how the utensils would stay in place on the tables. The cook surely knew how to deal with that.

She entered her cabin and sat down on the bunk. Was her stomach feeling queasy? Maybe, but she refused to get seasick.

Evan wasn't the only one learning lessons. She couldn't really blame him for this latest complication to her predicament. She was the one who'd set off to find Quin in Washington, not listening to her mother's advice. She was the one who insisted on following Quin to Alaska.

Evan was just a little boy, trying to keep his promise to his uncle.

Something her stepfather, Jed Skinner, used to say when faced with decisions, popped into her head. *Do something, even if it's wrong.* The something Jed chose to do was often wrong. She thought about all the moves from one mining camp to another. When things were difficult, he chose to drown his troubles in drink. She and her mother also suffered from his poor decisions.

She wondered how Jed was doing now. He'd decided to abandon her and Rose in Monte Cristo and head for the Klondike. That decision had turned out quite well for her and her mom. When Grandma needed care, Rose had returned to San Francisco and continued her business as a seamstress.

In Monte Cristo, Melinda and Quin had fallen in love. After the November floods had destroyed the railroad to Monte Cristo, she'd worked for Mrs. Collins, their Everett landlady, while Quin helped make repairs on the rail line. When Grandma died at Christmas, leaving her some money for education, they postponed their plans to marry. Melinda and Evan joined Rose in San Francisco, while Quin searched for work that would support them. At last Melinda's dream of teaching was in sight.

Until the thief spoiled those plans!

She hoped Jed Skinner had found success in the gold fields of the Yukon. Wouldn't it be something if she found him instead in Valdez?

No, it would be better for all of them if he never came back into their lives. She could get along quite well without him, and so could her mother.

It did seem however, that he'd left her with an unhelpful legacy. *Do something, even if it's wrong.*

CHAPTER TEN

THE JOURNEY

Do something, even if it's wrong.

What should she do now, to make it right, or better, at least? There was no way to immediately assure Nell and Ole that Evan was safe. But she could write a letter to mail the first chance she had. She pulled out stationery and pencil ... she'd not brought ink because of the difficulty of carrying it with her. After explaining to the Swensons how Evan came to be aboard the *Northward,* she offered apologies for worrying them and thanked them again for all they'd done to help her. She began another letter, this one to her mother.

"*I know this whole idea must seem very unlike your responsible daughter, Mother,*" she wrote. With a wry smile, she put the word *responsible* in quotes. She told Rose about Evan's decision to join her, and how he'd become part of the ship's workforce as a result.

"*While I'm searching for Quin, I'm planning to provide a taste of home to gold-seekers tired of their own beans and bannock.*

The accommodations on this boat are not luxurious," she went on, "*But I've never seen more spectacular scenery. Steep forested slopes fall sharply into the ocean, both on mainland and countless islands, and to the east snow-capped mountains wall off the rest of the continent. I wish you could see it.*"

She heard a tap on the door. Evan poked his head into the room. "Mr. Jack said I'm done for now. I'm to go back in an hour and help him get ready for dinner."

"Why don't you lie down and rest for a while?"

"I'm not tired. Could I walk around the ship instead?"

"I'm ready for some fresh air too. Let's put on our coats, and I'll go with you." She put away her writing materials. Donning her new coat and tying a knitted scarf over her head, she locked the door behind them.

On deck, they saw that they had crossed Queen Charlotte Sound and were traveling in the shelter of islands once again. Billowing clouds crowded the sky and collided with the high peaks to the east. The wind had grown chillier. It stirred up more whitecaps. Passengers ambled around the decks or leaned against the rails. Most of them were would-be prospectors. The howling of dogs sounded from below decks, plus the occasional nicker of a horse. There were also some mournful bleats. Sheep? Goats? Would there be grass for animals in Valdez?

At the rear of the ship, they watched seagulls gliding above the wake. One soared past, turning a yellow eye to watch them.

"I think he remembers me, Mindy!" Evan told how Black Jack, whose name was really Jack Sebastian, had sent him out with a bucket of kitchen scraps to dump over the railing. Entranced, Evan had watched the gulls gather, wheeling and screeching and arguing over the receding bits of food.

"What else did you do to help?"

"I learned how to peel potatoes," Evan answered. "And I set the tables. Did you know the tables on this ship have little wooden rails around the edges so the dishes won't slide off?"

She smiled. "I did notice the rails. So that's what they're for!"

For the next couple of days, the weather remained cloudy and cool. Evan continued his work in the galley. Among the passengers, she'd been surprised to see Ezekiel Cox, the businessman she'd met in Seattle.

One evening, he sat down for dinner with her and other travelers. "We meet again, Miss McCrae," he said with a warm smile. "What do you and your young charge think of the voyage thus far?"

"It's been an adventure," she said, wondering how he knew that Evan was not her son, seeing as how she'd said nothing to disabuse him of that notion.

"Wait until you get to Valdez. You've seen nothing yet!"

She smiled politely. Mr. Cox proved to be a charming entertainer, regaling their dinner companions with stories of the soon-to-be city of Valdez.

Melinda got better acquainted with Elizabeth Larson, helping with the children when she could. When not needed in the galley, Evan played with her twins, who were a little younger than he.

"Nat and Nonnie want to show me their goats," he told her as she sat visiting on deck with their mother. "May I go?"

She glanced at Elizabeth, who smiled and nodded. "Fine. But come right back."

"With all these children, we thought we'd better take our own source of milk," Elizabeth said. "I wanted a cow, but of course, that would mean taking hay too. My husband says in such a rainy climate, we probably couldn't grow our own hay. Goats can eat almost anything."

Quin would know about that. She wished she could ask him so many questions. If only she knew he was safe!

Something thumped against the side of the ship. The engine's steady throbbing hiccuped. The ship slowed, then plunged ahead. The women exchanged glances, wondering. "Probably just a piece of driftwood," Elizabeth said.

The children returned from their excursion. "The goats have twin babies," Evan told her. "They tried to nibble my fingers!"

Although the group had been protected beneath the overhanging upper deck, the wind was rising. Rain blew into the sheltered space where they'd been sitting. Elizabeth took her five back to their cabin.

A gray-haired prospector sat nearby with his big black dog. Evan asked he could pet the friendly animal. Melinda left Evan and the prospector to their conversation and moved to the railing. She peered through the rain at driftwood streaming past, long strands of seaweed, even a few hewn timbers rocking in the water around them. Timbers? Where would those come from, in this wilderness? The ship appeared to be moving along a path of smooth water, with larger waves on either side. A tangle of rope floated by with other bits of civilized flotsam, a river of garbage in the middle of a choppy ocean.

Well, that was a puzzle she hadn't the knowledge to solve, and besides, she was getting wet. She hurried back to the drier space where Evan sat with his arm around the big dog's neck.

"His name is Bear, Mindy, and this is Bernie. Bernie for Mr. Bernard."

Melinda shook hands. She watched Evan stroke Bear's shaggy head, talking to him like an old friend. The big creature gazed into his face with rapt attention.

"I love that dog," Evan told Melinda when the prospector had taken his leave.

"I'm sure Mr. Bernard will let you visit with Bear again," Melinda said. "But don't you think you'd better wash your hands now, and get back to the galley?"

Evan scurried off, and Melinda found herself alone. The wind was blowing harder now. Whitecaps raced past. Another piece of driftwood thumped the bow and scraped along the side of the ship. She felt the ship change direction, attempting to get out of the current carrying all that trash.

They entered rougher water. Waves curled over themselves. Foam slid down their back sides. Spray blew from their tops. Then came an unearthly screech from the stern. The engine sounds stopped. The ship swung broadside to the waves. One of the deckhands working nearby grabbed a long pole and hastened with several others toward the stern.

Melinda clung to the railing as the *Northward* wallowed in the swells. Gray cloud tatters swept the churning surface of the channel ahead. Through a veil of blowing rain, an island loomed into view. For a moment shock froze her against the rail. She stared at wet black cliffs plunging into the sea. Streams of water poured from sources hidden in the clouds to join a network of rivulets and waterfalls cascading down the sheer rock.

A strong sense of deja vu swept over her. She'd seen these very cliffs in her nightmare! She strained to peer through the rain. Something moved against the vertical lines of falling water.

Only a seabird seeking its precarious nest. Other than that, only rock and water. No human presence. She turned away, stunned, and made her way after the deckhands.

A hush had fallen over the ship when the engine stopped. Now she grew aware of the cacophony of whistling wind, the roar of waves crashing against the cliff, gulls screaming, men shouting.

Melinda glanced starboard. Those black walls seemed closer than a moment ago. The waves were carrying them nearer the rocks.

What if the dream hadn't been about Quin at all? What if it had been a warning of the dangers waiting for the foolhardy, like herself? Because of her, Evan faced danger, too.

Her heart cried out. "Lord, forgive me. Help us!"

She must get to Evan, although she had no earthly idea how she could save him if the waves should break the ship against that strange, vertical island.

The ship slammed into a trough, causing her to lose her grip on the railing. She staggered across the deck, bounced off the outer wall of the dining room, and kept moving. Through a rain-spattered window she glimpsed a few people inside, their faces frightened. Where was Evan?

Deckhands were probing around the propeller shaft with long poles. The captain stood among them, yelling directions. Several responded, lowering the big anchor in hopes it would snag on the bottom and hold until the propeller could be freed from whatever kept it from turning.

Melinda struggled on toward the dining room entrance. The door burst open, almost knocking her over, as Evan rushed out, followed by the tall, red-haired figure of Ezekiel Cox. Looking frantic, Evan skidded on the wet deck as he turned toward the bow. Melinda grabbed him. He struggled to get loose, then saw who had him. "Oh, Mindy. Here you are! I saw you through the window and ... " He burst into tears.

She held him tightly. "I'm fine. We're both fine." She became aware of Ezekiel Cox close by.

"I saw the boy run past, but wasn't fast enough to stop him. It's dangerous out here."

Melinda wholeheartedly agreed with the last statement. Evan stared at the island looming ever closer. "What's happening, Mindy?"

"I think something is caught in the ship's propeller."

"The captain's got his hands full, whatever it is. He doesn't need passengers washing overboard. Let me help you inside." Ezekiel guided the two of them back along the wall to the door. Inside, they found a bench where they could watch the men working at the rail. She collapsed onto it gratefully, still clutching Evan.

"Thank you for looking out for us," Melinda said to Ezekiel when she caught her breath. "I saw a lot of garbage in the water, like a river of it, almost. There was rope and seaweed, and broken boards, even part of a chair."

Ezekiel nodded. "That was a rip. A current in the surrounding ocean that can go for miles. I noticed the garbage too. Maybe from a wrecked boat. There are a lot of unseaworthy craft trying to make it to Alaska."

The ship lurched as waves lifted and dropped it. Would the anchor hold?

They saw a burly seaman remove his boots and jacket and step into a kind of rope harness. Someone handed him a knife that he stuck into his belt. Someone else attached the harness to a sturdy rope and knotted it to a cleat on the stern.

Melinda held her breath as the brave sailor slipped over the railing and into the water.

"God help him," Ezekiel murmured. "They say that water is cold enough to paralyze a person in twenty minutes."

The captain leaned over, watching intently. Ezekiel left, but returned with Jack Sebastian, the cook. Jack carried a couple of heavy blankets. The two stood clutching the uprights on either side of the exit while the deckhands pulled the diver up and over the railing. Jack made his way to them with the blankets. The diver wrapped himself in one while another man climbed into the harness, grabbed the knife, and disappeared over the side.

Jack returned. "He says a rope done got tangled around the shaft."

Beyond the crush of men leaning over the railing, Melinda saw a length of frayed rope rise to the surface and float away. "Those are two brave fellows," Ezekiel commented.

The second man was down so long, Melinda feared for his life. Finally one of the watchers thrust a triumphant fist in the air. Others dragged the diver aboard, wrapped him in the other blanket, and helped both divers into the ship to get warm.

The engine growled into reverse. Soon its steady throbbing reverberated throughout the ship and a cheer went up from the passengers in the dining room. Sailors hauled in the dragging anchor.

Only then did Melinda stand and look out at the island. She gasped at their proximity to its looming cliffs. Those crashing waves might have reduced them to bits of wreckage like those that had nearly caused disaster to their ship. "Another few minutes and we'd have been on those rocks!" Her voice shook. Her whole body trembled. She collapsed back onto the bench.

Ezekiel sat down beside her, concern in his eyes. "It's okay. We're all right now," he said. He put his arm around her.

The stress of the past few days welled up inside. She found herself leaning into his chest. Tears came as his arm tightened. She felt him patting her back. It felt so comforting to be held like this. Almost as if Quin was here holding her.

But Ezekiel wasn't Quin. What was she doing?

She sat upright and pulled away. Her cheeks burned. "Again, I thank you for helping us, Mr. Cox." She stood up and grasped Evan's hand. "We'll go to our cabin now. Have a pleasant evening."

CHAPTER ELEVEN

VALDEZ

Melinda stood in a drizzle with the other passengers as the ship tied up to a makeshift wharf. So this was Valdez. She took in the collection of tents and shacks scattered along what might someday become proper streets. The crew lowered a ramp and began to unload the cargo. Carrying their duffle bags, Melinda and Evan followed the Larson family down a gangplank and along the wharf.

Finally! Back on dry land. Well, land, though not exactly dry. At the edge of the tide flat, mud sucked at their boots. Melinda searched for someplace where they could stack their bundles, once the crewmen unloaded them. She chose a spot beyond the tide line where rocks jutted out of the damp ground and set their bags down there. She left Evan to watch them and joined the passengers circling the piles of goods and baggage being unloaded on the wharf. Fortunately, her bundles were among the first to be unloaded. She lugged as many as she could carry down the wharf to where Evan waited. She checked them off her list and retrieved another load.

Nearby, Elizabeth Larson was trying to organize their belongings as her husband brought them to shore. At the same time, she was juggling the baby and trying to keep the other four out of the mud.

Melinda checked the last of her bundles off her list. She stood upright and stretched her back. Catching Elizabeth's eye, she reached out her arms for the crying baby. Snuggling the child against her shoulder, she raised her eyes to the mountains extending down both sides of Valdez Narrows. Low-hanging clouds hid their tops.

She turned to look inland. More mountains. The clouds parted momentarily, giving a glimpse of blue sky and glaciers spilling down from rocky ridges. Except for the level area where they had disembarked, they were hemmed in by rugged peaks. Several miles from where they stood, a jumbled mass of rock and snow curved out of sight beyond the shoulder of a hill. She realized that must be the terminus of the Valdez Glacier, the route the prospectors followed to reach the Copper River country.

Mr. Larson, who had walked off toward the settlement, reappeared with a horse and wagon. Elizabeth tucked her baby, the toddler and the four-year-old into the front of the wagon bed and put big sister Nonnie in charge of them. Nat helped his dad stack bundles and barrels in the back.

The deckhands finished offloading the cargo and were now unloading the animals. She saw Mr. Blackman's partner, Gus Pitts, go by. She waved and wished him luck. He was leading the packhorse with the spatter of white spots on its rump, the very same horse whose reluctance to board had distracted everyone and allowed Evan to slip unseen onto the ship.

Mr. Larson came down the ramp with their goats. Carrying the babies in his arms, he led the nanny and billy to the wagon and tied them to the back. Then he put the bleating kids in the wagon with his own children.

Elizabeth settled herself on the seat beside her husband. She called to Melinda. "Where will you stay tonight?"

Melinda looked around. She'd never seen another town like this, and she'd lived in several gold-rush towns over the years. Monte Cristo seemed positively civilized compared to this collection of board shacks and canvas tents. She saw nothing that looked like a hotel or rooming house here near the water's edge

"I have a tent." She tried to sound confident. "We'll find a place to set it up."

"My husband had time to put up only a one-room cabin. It's barely big enough for us, he says. But you are welcome to pitch your tent next to our place. You'll be safer there."

Melinda gratefully accepted her offer. Mr. Larson climbed down and tossed her bundles atop their load. She and Evan followed the wagon along the muddy street.

Evan's prospector friend, Bernie, called "Good luck!" as they passed. His big black dog carried panniers of supplies on either side, topped with pickax and gold pan. Bernie shrugged an even heavier backpack to his own shoulders. "I'm off to the Valdez Glacier," he told them as Evan gave Bear one last hug. "Maybe we'll meet up again."

Melinda slipped off her necklace to show Quin's portrait to Bernie. "This is Evan's uncle, Quin Chenoweth. Would you watch for him?"

Bernie pushed back his droopy felt hat and squinted. "Handsome young feller. Sure, I'll let him know you're looking for him if I see him."

They said goodbye. Ahead of them, the wagon turned a corner. She and Evan hurried after it as it headed toward a scatter of tents and shacks at the edge of the settlement.

At the corner, Melinda saw a building with ornate letters painted across the front, spelling out *Cox's Emporium*. That must be the establishment of which Ezekiel Cox had spoken. Just then, he came out the door and headed toward her. Melinda felt bedraggled in contrast to the dapper-looking man, but she pulled herself straighter and nodded.

"Well, Miss McCrae," he said. "What do you think of our little town?"

"Umm." She hesitated. "It has a lot ... of mud."

He laughed, then asked, "Is there any thing I can do for you?"

"No, thank you. The Larson's have a place where we can stay." That wasn't a lie.

"I've seen the Larson's place." He looked concerned. "It's not very big."

"We don't need a lot of room," she told him.

"I have rooms for rent at the Emporium."

She thought of her nearly empty pocketbook. "Thank you, but we'll be fine."

He looked at her quizzically. His eyes were a mixture of blue and green, she noticed. "I'm sorry if I offended you last night."

Uncomfortably, she remembered her hasty leave-taking. "You were just being kind. I wasn't offended."

"You weren't?" The blue-green eyes twinkled.

"No, but I'm engaged to be married, Mr. Cox."

"Yes. So I've heard."

He knew she was engaged, and still, he had hugged her, let her cry on his chest? Now she *was* offended.

But he didn't allow her time to dwell on it. "I'll let you catch up with your friends. Remember, if you want a room, or decide to take my job offer, stop by the Emporium." He seemed infuriatingly sure that she would come around.

When she caught up to the Larsons, she found their "place" was indeed small. One room, a door, a window. Through the door, Melinda glimpsed small bunks stacked against the back wall. A double bed frame filled the space next to the door on the left, on the right beneath the window a washstand, barrel stove, and tiny table took up the remaining wall space. The roof overhung a narrow front porch. The plank sidewalk continued along the street to a few other small cabins and tents.

She helped the Larsons unload the wagon, placing her own bundles at one side of the porch, while Elizabeth went to work spreading blankets on the bunks and putting the younger children down for naps.

With Nat and Evan's help, her husband brought planks and two-by-fours from somewhere behind the cabin. "You can use these to make a platform to keep your tent out of the mud," he told

Melinda. He took a handful of nails from his pocket and handed Evan a hammer. "You boys can be the carpenters."

With Melinda to supervise, the children laid three two-by-fours parallel to the walkway, then nailed planks side by side across them.

Evan wielded the hammer.

"Good job, Evan! Not a single nail sticking up to tear the tent floor!"

He grinned at her praise. "Uncle Quin taught me. I helped nail the floor in our cabin at Monte Christo."

"Let me try,"Nat begged. Evan gave him the hammer and helped him nail the ends of the planks to the last two-by-four.

Next, they set up the six-by-eight-foot tent, facing it away from the street. They staked the attached ropes to the ground beside the platform. It was barely tall enough in the center for Melinda to stand erect.

She wasn't sure what to do with the long piece of canvas the owner had called a rain fly until she looked at some of the other tents pitched along the street. The fly went over the roof to protect the tent. Mr. Larson helped her set it up with poles at the high points and ropes to stake it down.

He brought an old piece of canvas that she could use to cover their belongings. She tossed their duffels into the tent, along with sleeping bags and the sack of food she'd packed that morning, then piled everything else beside the tent flap and tucked the canvas around the heap. Elizabeth brought her some water and a kerosene lantern. She pointed out the outhouse in the backyard.

Melinda and Evan were set for their first night in Alaska, and just in time. The sky grew dark. The mist, which had turned to drizzle, became a steady beat on the canvas.

"Let's take off our boots, Evan, before we track mud all over our nice clean floor." They did so, then scrambled into their shelter.

Evan set their boots outside the door, protected by the rain fly. He pulled the flap shut and giggled. "This is fun, Mindy."

She wasn't convinced that she was having fun, but for Evan's sake, she could pretend. She nodded. "Wouldn't your Uncle Quin be surprised to see us now?"

"What's for dinner?"

"Well, we don't have a stove, so we can't cook. Let's see what's in the 'pantry'." She lit the lantern with one of the matches Elizabeth had thoughtfully provided and turned it low. She sat on her bedroll and pulled the food sack to her. "We have some jerky. I see some pilot bread, and some dried fruit."

"Is there anything to drink?"

"The water Mrs. Larson gave us. It's in the pail outside the door. Look! We get to use our new collapsible tin cups." She handed them to Evan. He unfolded them and pushed back the tent flap to dip some water.

Their simple meal finished, Melinda tied a piece of tent cord from one end of the ridge pole to the other. "I'll hang our coats over this so we can each have our own space," she told the boy.

Later, she lay in the dark, listening to the rain pound the canvas. She hoped that the water would not find its way through some tiny rip or hole to dampen them or their belongings. She shivered and squirmed, trying to find a softer, warmer place on the unyielding planks beneath her.

Where was Quin sleeping tonight? Maybe she'd even find him still here in Valdez. Maybe she'd even find him back here in Valdez again. She also hoped he would appreciate what she was going through to try to find him.

While she tossed and turned, Melinda pondered the idea of finding a job. They'd need money to rent a more comfortable place to stay while they were in Valdez. She needed money to feed herself and Evan. She'd need to buy more supplies if they should follow Quin into the wilderness.

The unreasoning fear that had propelled her to Alaska to search for her fiancé had subsided somewhat after the near-shipwreck in the waters of Prince William Sound. After all, they'd faced and avoided disaster in the very spot she'd seen in her dream.

But she still felt an urgency to find Quin, to warn him. About what? Perhaps it was foolishness. But she was here and so was Evan. Nothing to do for it now but to keep on pursuing the course she'd set. And to pray for wisdom. She'd done precious little of that. She tried to remedy that lack, and eventually fell asleep.

CHAPTER TWELVE

BECOMING A BUSINESSWOMAN

In the morning, Melinda began her job search. Elizabeth offered to keep Evan while she was gone. He could help entertain the children while she worked at making their one-room house more comfortable.

Melinda would ask about Quin while she searched. Of course, there was always Ezekiel Cox's job offer, she thought as she walked past his establishment. But she felt uneasy about any close association with him. The Emporium would be her last resort.

In addition to the Emporium, a few other sawn-lumber buildings, false-fronted like the businesses in Monte Cristo, were scattered along the street. Many establishments were nothing more than wood-floored canvas tents. Most had stovepipes poking at odd angles through the roofs. After last night's chill, she wished her little tent had room for a stove.

She passed a large tent on a wooden platform. It had board sides about three feet high, and real doors, front and back. Through the open front door, she saw copper boilers filled with water steaming on a stove. Two women who looked like sisters were scrubbing clothes against wash boards. She watched one woman twist the suds out of a pair of men's work pants, rinse them in another tub, twist again and stack with other wet items. A number of shirts already hung on lines behind the laundry tent. Lines zigzagged across the inside too, for use on rainy days.

The other woman stepped out to fetch an armload of split cottonwood from a pile beside the tent. Her calico dress was stained under the arms with sweat and her face glistened, but she smiled cheerfully at Melinda.

"Hello. Newcomer?"

"Yes. I arrived yesterday. How is business?"

"Can't complain." She gestured toward the piles of dirty clothes on the floor. "You can see a lot of people in this town are happy to have someone else do their laundry."

As they chatted, Melinda tried not to stare at the woman's red, rough hands. Laundry work was hard but honest. She might have to come back here.

She asked about Quin, but the women didn't know him.

Next she stopped at a couple of make-shift restaurants to inquire about employment, to no avail. She walked past a small church building under construction.

Near the church, a sign on a small plank building labeled it the home of the *Valdez Christian Endeavor Society*. This seemed to be a social center for the town, judging from the schedule of events posted on the door. Maybe someone here could answer her question about finding work. And maybe they'd know Quin. She opened the door and peeked in. A number of bearded, ragged men, probably returning prospectors, sat at tables, reading. She saw bookshelves with books, and a counter where a dark-skinned man with a blend of African-American Indian features smiled her way. "Melvin Dempsey, at your service. May I help you, Ma'am?"

She returned the smile. Back in San Francisco or even in Monte Cristo this friendly man would never be found in anything but a menial position. Alaska truly seemed to be a place of opportunity, for whoever wanted to reach for it.

She stepped to the counter. "My name is Melinda McCrae. I wonder if you might know my fiancé. His name is Quin Chenoweth. He's a journalist with Seattle's *Daily Dispatch* newspaper." She slipped the chain over her head and showed him Quin's tiny portrait.

"Oh yes. I know Mr. Chenoweth, although he's growing a beard these days. He came here to write and to interview people."

A surge of joy almost lifted her off her feet. Quin, here in Valdez!

But the man behind the counter continued. 'He left a few weeks ago with a party of prospectors heading toward Copper Center."

Disappointed, Melinda took her leave, forgetting to ask if Melvin Dempsey could suggest any jobs. If she was to find Quin, she'd have to follow him over the glacier.

The muddy streets had become busier. A number of the Northward's former passengers were hauling gear toward the glacier trail. Some had packhorses, some pulled loaded sledges through the mud, either by themselves or with the help of dogs of various descriptions.

From the direction of the glacier, a few dejected-looking men who'd found the odds too overwhelming trudged into town. She saw a business with a sign on the window stating "Goods Bought and Sold." A couple of returning prospectors came out of the shop, each with a few bills in hand. She supposed they'd just sold their outfits to buy tickets home, for much less than they'd paid for them, no doubt.

Streams flowing from the glacier cut through the outwash plain upon which the new community was growing. Groups of men were building dikes to protect the town. One man told her that sometimes the streams topped their banks and threatened to carry the buildings into the bay. Could she help build dikes?

A few uniformed soldiers worked around a complex of log buildings. This was the headquarters for Captain William Ralph Abercrombie's military exploring expedition. Quin had written about it in the dispatch Editor Bowden had shared with her. One cabin was used as a hospital for injured or sick prospectors, she learned from a former patient who was working off his bill in a fenced garden. He proudly pointed out cabbages, onions, potato plants, and what looked like kale, all of which grew well in the cool climate.

Mr. Larson passed with a crew of men and a horse and wagon, hauling machinery to the site of his sawmill. She waved, then decided she'd better get back to check on Evan. As she neared the Emporium, she noticed a building she'd not paid attention to yesterday. A sign on the door read "Mercantile."

A man walking ahead of her turned off and opened the door. The aroma of just-baked bread drew her in after him. The proprietress was just arranging six or seven still-warm loaves in a glass-fronted case. The man ahead of her was clean and neater than most of the prospectors who filled the town, but he looked ravenous at the sight and smell of the bread.

"Wrap one of those up for me, will you, Mrs. Olsen?"

"Ja, glad to. Aren't you doing your own baking these days, Mr. Flint?"

"I was mostly making biscuits to go with my stew." He glanced appreciatively at Melinda. "My little restaurant at the foot of the glacier is a good business, but I'm going to sell out. I'll be cooking next door to you, at the Emporium. I'm tired of stew and biscuits and smelly prospectors."

She decided she would use a few cents of her rapidly dwindling funds to buy a loaf of bread to treat the Larson family. They'd been eating pilot bread for a long time. She waited while Mrs. Olson wrapped Mr. Flint's bread in paper.

An idea began to grow in the back of her mind. She addressed the man.

"Mr. Flint, my name is Melinda McCrae. Excuse me for overhearing your conversation. I wouldn't mind running a little restaurant for a while. Would you consider letting me rent your place for a few weeks while you are looking for a buyer?"

"You? It's not like a regular restaurant, you know. It's just a tent, only big enough for my sheet metal stove, a work stand and shelves, and seating for about eight customers at a time. I have to cut my own firewood and haul it a couple of miles."

"Maybe I could trade home-baked goods for firewood," she mused.

"If I just served tea or coffee, and pie, I could take care of more customers."

"I suppose it could work." Mr. Flint looked doubtful. "But I'm a businessman, Miss McCrae. If I found a buyer who could pay cash, I would need to take the offer immediately."

"Agreed," she said. "Would you be willing to wait for the rent for a week, until I've had a chance to earn some money?"

The man smiled. "Unconventional," he said. "But you look trustworthy."

"Thank you, Mr. Flint. I'm sure you won't be disappointed."

As Mrs. Olsen wrapped her loaf of bread, Melinda noticed a bushel basket of past-their-prime apples on sale. They'd be still good for stewing. She asked for three pounds of apples, and paid for her purchases. The apples and the bread would help repay the Larsons for their kindness.

The possibility of having her own restaurant, for a few weeks at least, meant she wouldn't have to accept a favor from Ezekiel Cox. Foolishness? Perhaps. But he was a persuasive man. Even if his intentions were good, her heart belonged to Quin Chenoweth. She didn't want to encourage Ezekiel in any way.

Even if Quin had gone off to Alaska without being sure she knew he was going. Even if she now had to make her own way in this strange, wild country.

CHAPTER THIRTEEN

THE PIE PANTRY

Melinda stood in the middle of her new restaurant and wrinkled her nose. She'd just rehung the curtain to make the narrow sleeping space at the back of the tent a bit wider. She'd swept down the canvas walls and scrubbed the plank floor, but she couldn't get rid of the pervasive smells of bacon grease and unwashed bodies. Oh, well. Prospectors were used to that and she'd get used to it as well.

Evan piled another armload of firewood on the stack in the corner. Thank goodness the owner had left a big pile of split wood for her to start with. Mr. Flint had even left an ax. She'd seldom chopped wood, but she guessed she could if she had to. She did know how to build a fire. She lit one now. It was chilly here, with a cold wind blowing off the glacier.

Outside the tent, dogs barked. Someone new must have arrived in camp. The population of the facetiously named "Glacier City" changed daily as prospectors came and went.

The stove leaked smoke. Maybe the pipe needed cleaning. She pulled back the tent flap to let in some fresh air. Two new arrivals stood outside the restaurant, burdened with huge packs. A lightweight wooden sled held the rest of their supplies. One man seemed far too skinny to bear such a load, but obviously he was stronger than he looked. They were taking in their surroundings. The shorter, sturdier man caught her eye as she looked out.

"Afternoon, Ma'am. Any rules here say where we can set up camp?"

"No," she said. "Anywhere you find room is all right. I saw a couple of parties leave this morning. Just keep on going. You'll find their empty campsites, if someone hasn't claimed them already."

The thinner partner glanced at her. He seemed to start, then shifted away so that his drooping, black felt hat hid all but his scraggly mustache and chin whiskers. He looked like a dozen others in the camp. A shiver of something unpleasant went through her as she watched the two head in the direction of the glacier. The feeling didn't make sense.

The glacier's terminus, or the First Bench as it was called, towered above the camp. When they arrived that morning, she and Evan had seen men clambering upward on steps cut into the ice, uncoiling a long rope behind them to which they'd tied their loaded sled.

At the top of the bluff they'd drilled a hole for a post and attached a pulley. They threaded the free end of their rope through the pulley. Four or five men then grabbed it and descended the incline, dragging the sled and its load to the top. Since each person's outfit weighed between 1500 and 2000 pounds, getting all his goods to the top of the bench and then over the glacier proper took many trips and lots of cooperation.

For those lucky enough to have horses to carry their supplies, the route was even harder. The loaded pack animals had to climb the face of the glacier under their own steam. Their owners led them up a steep, slippery trail, around crevasses, between ice pinnacles and along sharp ridges. Shrill whinnies of fear often echoed from the wilderness of ice when the horses slipped and tumbled back down the trail.

Melinda shook herself and turned back to the tent. She hoped she'd be able to keep her restaurant long enough to earn what they'd need to return to Washington, especially if she couldn't find Quin.

"I'm hungry, Mindy."

"I imagine you are. You've really been working hard!" She gave the boy a quick hug. "I've got the pot on. As soon as the water's hot, I'll make some cocoa to go with our pilot bread. How's that?"

"Can we have peanut butter too?"

"Yes. Then I must mix up some pie crust. I'll bake pies this afternoon."   She sat Evan at the customer's table at the other end of the tent with his lunch. Nibbling on her own piece of pilot bread, she scanned her work area, pleased with her organization. Her counter top consisted of two extra wide boards laid together across a frame that supported shelves underneath for supplies. Wooden boxes stacked next to the frame held tin plates, cups, and forks. A dishpan, kettles, and pans hung from the tent uprights. There were hooks for her new dishtowels. She had a small table for dish washing. The fire in the cook stove crackled cheerfully.

What she didn't have was a rolling pin. There'd be no piecrust without that piece of equipment. She opened the big bag of dried apple slices that sat on the bottom shelf and let Evan help himself.

"You know that nice Mr. Bixbee in the tent next to us? Could you ask him if he would help you find a long empty bottle with a cork or a top? Tell him it's for a rolling pin."

Evan dropped the snack into his jacket pocket and headed out to find their neighbor. Melinda set a quantity of dried apples to soak, and lifted an oversized enameled mixing bowl from the shelf. She scooped lard, flour and salt into it and, using both hands, worked the mixture until she had coarse, even crumbs. Then she dribbled cold water in, mixing lightly until the dough clung together. "There," she told herself. "That will make six or seven pies, at least."

She poked her head out the door. Here came Evan, from the direction of the glacier. He carried an armful of bottles. A couple of prospectors passed her, going the other way with a loaded sled. "Afternoon, Ma'am," called one of them. "When are we going to get a taste of your wares?"

She smiled. "We open at two o'clock tomorrow."

Evan arrived with several bottles. One was long and straight-sided, just what she had in mind for her rolling pin. Another bottle had a cork that would fit the first.

"Where did you find so many?"

"Mr. Bixbee showed me where people throw their trash," he said.

Pouring hot water into the dishpan, she used a knife to scrape fine shavings from a bar of soap. She let Evan swish them into suds, then had him scrub the bottle, fill it with cold water, and cork it. He washed the others too, in case she might need them.

Meanwhile, Melinda floured a square of clean canvas to use as her pastry cloth and patted out the first round of pie dough. She dusted Evan's bottle in flour, then used it to flatten and enlarge the circle of dough. Fitting it into the pie pan, she exhaled a sigh of relief. Her makeshift rolling pin was harder to use than one with handles, but it worked!

"What can I do now, Mindy?"

"Why don't you take the bucket to the spring and get more water? If you fill the barrel, we can have baths tonight so we're clean for the opening of our restaurant."

Evan looked pleased at her calling it 'our restaurant'. He grabbed the bucket. As he hurried out of the tent, she warned, "Don't fill it so full it splashes on you."

While Evan worked at his task, she stirred flour, sugar, and cinnamon into the drained apples and filled the first two pie shells. She fitted the top crusts and fluted the edges, then brushed the tops with canned milk and sprinkled them with sugar.

She added more wood to the firebox and set the pies in the hot oven. By the time she'd prepared four more pies, she felt wilted. But the delicious scents of cinnamon and baking apples filled the tent. She patted the scraps into a ball, rolled it out and flipped the smaller round into a pie pan. She sprinkled it with sugar and cinnamon and put it in the oven to bake.

Evan came into the tent and told her, "People are standing outside sniffing the good smells." He saw her closing the door on the pie crust cooky and his eyes lit up. "Is that for me?"

"All your hard work deserves a treat, don't you think?" she said. "I hope we can sell all these pies. Six sounds like a lot, but if they're lining up already, I'd better make more tomorrow morning, just in case."

She drew the curtain across the back corner of the room, next to the stove. "Evan, would you sit at the table and tell anyone that tries to come in that we're not open until tomorrow? I'm going to wash my hair and get my bath while the next pies are baking."

She dug clean clothing out of her duffle bag. She even found an apron Nell had given her as they were leaving Silverton. Dear Nell! How had she known she'd need such a garment? Before pies three and four finished baking, her hair was clean, she was clean, and she was dressed in clean clothing. It felt wonderful! She'd wash their dirty clothes tomorrow, after the customers had gone. She lugged her bath water away from the restaurant and dumped it.

Returning, she rummaged beneath the platform where their tent and other belongings were stored. She pulled out their sleeping bags. They'd still be sleeping on a board floor tonight, but they'd be warmer than they were in their own tent at the Larson's.

She found Evan working with a piece of board at the table. He held it up for her to see. He'd outlined the side view of a steaming pie and above it lettered the words, "Melinda's Pie Pantry."

"It's perfect! Thank you, Evan. Where did you ever find paint?"

"It's shoe polish." He held up a bottle labeled *Arabian Elastic Waterproof Shoe Polish*. "Mr. Bixbee ordered two bottles from Sears Roebuck and gave one to me. He said we should use it on our boots. It helps make them waterproof."

"You're very creative. Who else would have thought of using shoe polish as paint? And Mr. Bixbee was very thoughtful to think about waterproofing our boots. I think when you finish your bath, you should take him the first piece of pie, don't you?"

They hung the sign outside the tent, then she helped Evan wash his hair. Next, while he scrubbed in the makeshift bath corner, she put the final pies in the oven to bake.

She thought of Quin and wondered where he might be now. Maybe he would return to Valdez within the next couple of weeks.

She should have money saved by then. If he didn't return, she would try to follow him. Or would he be impossibly far ahead of them?

Melinda woke at daybreak the next morning. She tied on Nell's apron, stirred up the fire, and set a pot of oatmeal to cooking for their breakfast. The camp had been noisy all night with people and their animals coming and going, packing their goods onto the glacier before the day's warmth turned the snow to slush. Soon Glacier City would quiet down while men rested for their next onslaught on the bench.

She worked quietly so as not to wake Evan. He was trying so hard to do his part. She must tell him how glad she was to have him with her, even if his presence had been unforeseen. So far the prospectors had been perfect gentlemen. She was sure having a child with her made them even more respectful. And he was a big help.

She got out a sack of raisins for raisin pie, and tossed a handful into the oatmeal. Evan would like that. Then she stirred up another bowlful of piecrust.

By 1:30, the last pies were cooling. She'd tidied the restaurant, made a giant pot of coffee, set out her stock of plates and forks and cups, and had a dishpan of water warming on the stove, plus the teakettle full of hot rinse water. Evan could help keep up with the dirty dishes. She opened a tin of canned milk and set it on the table for the coffee, poured the big potful into smaller pitchers to stay hot at the edge of the stove, and started another pot.

She parted the tent flap and peeked out. "Oh, goodness!" She gasped. "Evan, there are dozens of people waiting out there."

Quickly she folded and tore a piece of brown paper into squares. She asked Evan to write numbers on them from one to ... how many? "Twelve pies, six pieces each," he calculated. "Seventy-two!"

The table could hold eight people. He took the numbered slips outside and passed them around. At two o'clock, Melinda tied back the tent flaps. The men closed in, joking, laughing, looking hopeful. She took a deep breath and welcomed them, explaining that she only had one table, but there was plenty of pie if they didn't mind waiting their turn. She invited those with numbers one through eight to come in and sit.

The next three hours passed in a whirl of serving pie, pouring coffee, ushering one tableful of customers out as soon as they finished and welcoming in the next set. Most customers left extra coins. Some offered to trade a load of firewood for a whole pie, a bargain since the trees were so far away. She gladly accepted their offers.

"We meet again, Miss McCrae. I see you've recovered very well from the voyage!" It was Gus Pitts, the former partner of Mr. Blackman, the man who'd sold her his ticket on the Northward. Gus told her he'd joined a group who would be relaying their goods up the glacier on sleds. He planned to take a helper and travel ahead of them with his packhorse to Lake Klutina. There he'd get a head start on building a boat for the rest of their journey.

The two prospectors who'd asked where they could camp that morning sat down at the other end of the table. The skinny one grabbed his fork and dug into his piece of pie. Those around him bantered, but though his eyes darted from one person to another and all around the room, he had little to say.

While the men at the table finished their coffee, Melinda asked Gus if he'd heard how Mr. Blackman's ill wife was faring.

"No," he said. "I imagine he's got his hands full."

She walked to the entrance with him. "Well, if you contact him for any reason, please tell him I hope to have money soon to send him the remainder of his ticket's price."

"I will," he said. He thanked her for the pie and stepped out to the street, where he'd left his packhorse tied.

"He's a pretty little animal," she said, admiring the shiny brown-black coat and the white spots sprinkled like stars over the hindquarters. The horse shied nervously when the men came out of the tent. He bobbed his head and flicked his ears, as she remembered him doing when the crewmen had hoisted him onto the Northward. Gus might have trouble taking such a nervous animal over the glacier, she thought, but he didn't seem worried. She turned back to prepare for the next group of customers.

By the time the last prospectors headed back to their campsites, her feet and her back ached. She was drooping, but pleased. At this rate, she would not only be able to send Mr. Blackman what she owed, they'd have what they needed to live on while in Alaska plus a start on what return fares to Seattle would cost.

Early that morning she'd set a kettle of beans to simmer on the back of the stove, adding molasses, dried onion, and bacon. She dipped some out now for their dinner. They split the piece of apple pie she'd hidden away earlier.

Evan yawned, then savored his last bite of pie. "This is *so* good, Mindy. I think lots of customers will come back for more."

"You know what that means, don't you?"

"What?"

"I must start on tomorrow's pies."

Wearily, she rinsed her dishes and cleared her workspace. When she turned around, her helper was slumped over the table, fork in hand, sound asleep.

CHAPTER FOURTEEN

CODE OF THE NORTH

"Mindy, have you seen my boot polish? I left it right there on the bottom shelf so I could waterproof our boots this morning."

Evan had finished hauling in the day's firewood and had topped off the water barrel behind the tent. He'd cleaned his boots and Melinda's, while she worked on the day's baking. Melinda looked where he was pointing.

"I haven't seen it, Evan." She moved the pots and pans so they could look behind them. Evan squatted down to peer under the shelves, then looked on the other shelves and in the boxes next to them. He rummaged through his duffel bag and inspected his sleeping space.

"It's gone. Why would someone take my bottle of shoe polish?"

"There must be an explanation," Melinda said. "This country is lacking in many social graces, but there's one thing in its favor. People don't steal, especially the prospectors. Their very life depends on what they carry along with them."

"Well, Mr. Bixbee gave the polish to me so we could keep our feet dry, and now it's gone!" Evan scowled.

"Tell you what," she offered. "I'm sending a list of supplies we need to the Mercantile today. Why don't we add boot waterproofing to the list? Even if we find Mr. Bixbee's polish, we can always use more later."

Evan wrote it on the list. Then, at Melinda's suggestion, he put his boots on again and went out to find someone going to Valdez for another load of supplies. He'd ask them to drop the list at the Mercantile, and someone from the store could bring more flour, lard, maybe some eggs. And boot polish.

Melinda hoped the delivery would come by tomorrow. She only had flour left for two or three more batches of pie crust.

That afternoon, fewer customers came in. There was an uneasy undercurrent to their talk. No one seemed to be joking as usual. Were they tired of her wares, or worse, was something wrong with her cooking?

Gus came in, his face dark with anger.

"Gus, what's the matter?" she asked. "Has something happened?"

"Yes, something happened," he snapped. "Sorry, ma'am ... it's not you. Someone stole my packhorse last night. Right out of the corral where everyone keeps their ponies."

She gasped, thinking of Gus's pony, with the distinctive white spots spattered across his rump. "That's terrible. But I'm sure you'll find him soon. He should be easy to identify."

"Nobody has seen him in Valdez." Gus gulped the last of his coffee. "Several of us are taking the glacier trail right now. We're traveling light. If someone has taken him onto the glacier, we'll soon catch up. If ever there was a place for Miner's Justice, this is it!"

Melina shivered. She knew what that meant. The culprit would have a trial, with the other prospectors as judge and jury. The consequences of a thievery verdict were severe. Death, or at the least, expulsion from the ranks of the miners.

Gus was gone for several days. Rain fell almost constantly. By now, Evan had his new bottle of shoe polish, so he and Melinda kept their feet drier when they left the tent.

Gus and his companions came back soaked and discouraged. They'd passed a number of parties with pack animals, but no pony with distinctive white spots on its rump. No one they'd talked to had seen such an animal either. Gus gave up his plan of going ahead to build a boat. Instead, he would help his party sled their goods in relays over the glacier. Together, they'd build their boat after they reached the Klutina River.

As the days passed, Melinda fretted. Quin didn't return, and there was no word of him. Each day undoubtedly was taking him farther away from her and perhaps, closer to the danger she'd dreamed about.

Meanwhile, the changing population of three hundred people or so in the tent city waded through a morass of mud and water. It became impossible to keep the floor clean. She prayed for the rain to stop. Word came that softening snow on the glacier was making travel more difficult. At the same time, blizzards caused misery near the summit, fifteen miles away. Many would-be prospectors gave up on crossing the glacier.

One discouraged man traded his sled to Melinda for a half pie. A bargain, she thought, if she was to try to cross the glacier herself. Not only would the sled carry supplies, she could bring it inside her tent at night and one of them could sleep on it, instead of on the ice or snow.

A few days later, their prospector friend, Bernie, hobbled back into Glacier City. He'd gotten his feet wet on the return over the glacier and frostbitten his toes. Bear whined joyfully when he saw Evan. He rose on his hind legs, his tail whipping his whole body, and plopped his front paws on the boy's shoulders. In the onslaught of the dog's delight, Evan fell to the floor. He wiped away happy tears as he hugged the big black creature.

"Those two really love each other." Bernie grinned. Looking around the tent, he commented, "I see you've set yourself up a nice little business."

"Please, sit down." Melinda indicated the bench by the table. "I'm running the restaurant only until the owner sells it. If Quin hasn't come back by then, I plan to go looking for him."

"Just you and the boy?" Concern furrowed Bernie's wrinkled brow when Melinda nodded yes. He sat thinking. "I can't give Bear up for good, but he'd be some protection for you if you're set on finding that man of yours. He could help pull the sled, or carry some of your supples."

He told them that stories of gold along the Copper River were greatly exaggerated. He'd decided to prospect near Valdez, instead, as soon as his toes healed.

"You'd really let Bear go with us?"

"Yes, if you're determined to cross the glacier. By the way, I talked to several people who'd seen your fiancé, but I didn't catch up with him myself."

"You did!" Melinda's heart leaped. "Did they say how he was?"

"He was fine when they saw him. They said he asked lots of questions and took lots of pictures."

He was still all right! She chuckled. "That sounds like Quin. Thank you, Bernie, for inquiring."

Melinda agreed that boy and dog belonged together, and having the dog's help pulling the sled *could* be a lifesaver. But how could she take on the responsibility of a dog as big as a buffalo and just as hairy? She patted Bear's head. "He's such a big dog. Doesn't he eat a lot?"

Bernie told her he had traded with Indians along the way for dried salmon for him to eat. "I'll leave what is left so you won't lack for dog food for a while. He knows how to catch rabbits, too."

Evan's grin spread ear to ear as he promised to take good care of Bear. "We'll bring him back when we find Uncle Quin," he said.

Melinda made coffee for Bernie while Evan helped him unload the packs Bear had been carrying. Bernie hung the sack of dried salmon inside the tent, out of reach of other dogs, and unrolled another bundle.

"It's a wolf skin," he told her and Evan. "I bought it from an Indian trapper, but I don't need it anymore. I used it like a shawl when the weather was cold or wet." He fitted the skin of the head over Evan's head, like a hat, with the rest of the skin like a cape around his body. "Like this, see? At night, I slept with it between me and the cold ground."

Melinda and Evan stroked the fur. The long hairs of the neck and back felt stiff, but beneath them was a thick layer of softer fur.

"That underfur makes the skin warmer than any blanket," Bernie said. "and rain runs right off these long guard hairs. If it's all right with you," he turned to Melinda, "I'd like the boy to have it."

It would add a few pounds to the load they must carry, she thought. But it was big enough for Evan to sleep on and would keep him off the floor at night. Or off the ice, if they ended up camping on the glacier.

"Are you sure?" she asked. "Won't you use it when you're prospecting?"

"I already have a claim near Valdez. First thing I'll do is build me a cabin there, with a sturdy bunk. I won't need it."

Melinda offered Bernie a piece of pie. While he enjoyed it, she wrote another list. She asked him to take it to the Mercantile, and filled a canvas bag with enough coins to pay for her order, plus some extra for his trouble.

As Bernie hitched his pack to his shoulders and slogged off through the drizzle toward Valdez, Melinda noticed that the aroma of wet dog had permeated the restaurant.

She suggested to Evan that he make a place for Bear to sleep under the tent platform. Bear could be a guardian to warn away any intruders at night. Now to build up the fire and let the scent of baking pastry overpower the less pleasant smells of wet, unwashed men and dog lingering in her Pie Pantry.

The next day, shortly before noon, a man led a packhorse down the difficult trail descending the face of the glacier. He tied the animal to the tent platform and poked his head inside.

He introduced himself as Jackson Miller, new mail carrier between Valdez and Copper Center. "The guys on the trail are all talking about the best pies anywhere in Alaska, right here in Glacier City. I see your sign says you don't open until 2 pm, but I'll be long gone by then. Any chance that I can trade a letter for an early spot at your table?"

"A letter? You have a letter for me?"

"Aren't you Miss Melinda McCrae?" He rummaged in his pack and handed her a battered envelope. Quin's handwriting! She collapsed onto a bench, clutching the letter to her heart.

"I can see you're Miss McCrae," Mr. Miller observed. "Does that mean we can make a deal? I'll pay, of course."

"Oh, yes! What kind would you like? I made dried peach and apple both today."

"Peach, please."

She cut the pie and brought him a double-sized piece, along with coffee.

"Did you see him, Mr. Miller? How did he look? Is he all right?"

The mailman laughed. "Yes, I saw him. He looks fine. And yes, he's all right. He's a bit hirsute. We do get attached to our whiskers, here in Alaska! But he's hale and hearty, and he can't wait for the day a certain Miss Melinda McCrae returns from San Francisco. He'd been carrying the letter with him, he said, hoping a mail carrier would come along. The last one decided to go prospecting and mail delivery has been haphazard since then."

"But if he thinks I'm in San Francisco, how did you ... "

"I collected various bits of gossip between here and where I saw him in Copper Center. Then I put them all together with a bit of deduction, and found you! Of course, I don't know what you're doing here, and it's none of my business."

He lifted an eyebrow in her direction. She squirmed. "It's a long story, Mr. Miller. Thank you for the letter. It means the world to me to know he's all right."

Even as she said the words, she realized Quin had been fine when the mail carrier saw him. But where was he now? Anything could be happening. The nightmare flashed again through her head. Why did the premonition of danger keep returning?

CHAPTER FIFTEEN

PACK HORSES AND PROBLEMS

All afternoon, Melinda's hand kept straying to her apron pocket, just to feel that the precious missive was still there. After the mailman left, she hadn't had one moment to sit down and open it. Finally, she served the last piece of pie, bade goodbye to her final customers, and closed the tent flaps after them. Postponing preparations for the next day, she told Evan he could go play with Bear for a while. She poured herself a cup of coffee and sat down to read Quin's letter.

July 10, 1898

My dearest Melinda,

I'm sitting on a sun-warmed rock above my camp on the Klutina River, watching the rosy light of evening fade. I'm missing you more than I have words to tell!

Daylight lasts a long time this far north, so until the breeze dies and the mosquitoes come out, I shall sit here and pretend we are together. I'll imagine my arm around you. I'll steal a kiss or two, and we'll talk about our hopes and dreams for the future. You can tell me about San Francisco, and I'll tell you all about my adventures in this beautiful, wild land. Doesn't that sound grand?

A lot of men turn back before making it this far. I'd never recommend the glacier crossing, but we made it safely, and also down the river. (We travel by boat when the current allows.)

This river is shallow, but dangerous. In places we've packed our goods overland and lined the boat down. We learned to do that early on, when we got caught in rough water. I nearly lost my outfit to the river. Some items did get swept away from us, but I kept my camera and equipment safe. I'm grateful the upper Klutina is less than thirty miles long.

I'm staying in camp for a few days to catch up with interviews and writing, while my party prospects up a couple of side streams. I talk to travelers every day, both those trying to return to Valdez and those continuing on to the Copper River. Some of them are young and vigorous, but many should be home in their rocking chairs. Their stories are all pretty much alike. They are willing to face incredible hardships for one chance to make good.

A couple of those discouraged prospectors are camping with me tonight. I'm sharing my food because they capsized and lost their supplies. I hope they make it back over the glacier.

We'll travel on when my friends return, although they might strike it rich and decide to stay. I don't expect that to happen!

Well, dear girl, I will seal this with a kiss and my love. When we meet the mail carrier on his way from Copper Center to Valdez, I'll send it with him. If you have received my letters, you know you can write to me at Valdez. It's been too long since I've heard from you.

Greet your mother for me. All my love to you and Evan, Quin

P.S. It's July 26. I've arrived in Copper Center and have just met the mail carrier. He'll get this to Valdez, where he'll mail it on to you. I'd hoped to find a letter from you waiting there, but no such luck. All is well. I have

visited several mining claims near this settlement. This is
beautiful country. I wouldn't mind settling here if you were
with me.

All my love, Quin

She read the letter twice, imagining herself with Quin as he
wrote. Then she refolded it and put it in her apron pocket to be
read again later. Why had he not received the letters she'd sent
him since they left San Francisco? With all that could happen
along the way, she shouldn't be surprised that mail could go astray.
She'd write another letter to send when Jackson Miller returned
on his way back to Copper Center.

Quin missed her too! How she wished he would come hiking off
the glacier on his way back to Valdez and find her here at the Pie
Pantry. What a marvelous reunion they would have!

Emotion threatened to overwhelm her, but the work wouldn't
do itself. She shook herself, stoked the fire, then mixed batter to
top a big pan of cobbler. Beyond the tent walls, more than the
usual bustle echoed in the street. Busy as she was preparing for
tomorrow's customers, Melinda took a few moments to peer out
through the drizzle and the fog rolling off the brink of the glacier.

The commotion was caused by a procession of skittish pack
horses clomping through the muck. Dogs barked and men shouted.
Soldiers and a few civilian packers clung to the reins to keep the
horses from bolting.

She had seen some of those soldiers in Valdez. They'd told
her that the commander of their exploring expedition, Captain
William Ralph Abercrombie, had sailed back to Washington State
in search of pack animals. Evidently he'd found them, because
there he was, walking at the head of the column. He was a fortyish
man in a rumpled uniform, hat pulled down over his ears, a pipe
sticking out of his breast pocket.

Prospectors crossing the steep passes beyond Skagway and Dyea
complained mightily about paying duties charged on everything

they hauled into Canada. In response, the American government had sent an expedition, this expedition, to find an all-American route to the Klondike.

But even before that, steamship companies were playing up rumors of gold on the Copper River. Melinda had seen the resulting excitement in San Francisco and then in Seattle, as people clamored for passage to Valdez. That's why Quin was in Alaska.

By the time Abercrombie's expedition reached Valdez, they found themselves in the midst of hundreds of gold seekers already going to or coming from the Copper River by way of the glacier. Some had even found their way through Alaska's Interior to the Klondike.

Abercrombie decided that exploring without pack animals wasn't possible, so he returned to Washington State in search of horses. From the number of animals (including mules, burros, dogs, even goats) already crossing the Valdez glacier, Melinda doubted he'd found any pack horses left in Seattle.

That had been the case, so the Captain crossed the Cascades to Eastern Washington. There he bought forty ponies from the Yakima Indians. These were the ponies he'd purchased. Finally the expedition was ready to attempt the glacier crossing.

Dogs barked, a burro brayed. A prospector, his felt hat dripping rain, hooted from the sidelines. "Aren't you army guys a little late? We've been using this trail for months!"

To Melinda's surprise, a young woman about her own age led one of the animals, a paint pony who not only bore loaded panniers but dragged a sled full of equipment as well. The barking dogs made the pony dance and toss its head. The woman spoke soothingly to the nervous animal and it calmed.

The expedition members headed for an empty area behind the tents lining the opposite side of the street. She watched for a while as a temporary encampment began to go up.

Later that afternoon, the woman she'd seen, Lillian Moore, stopped by to get acquainted. Melinda liked her immediately.

Lillian, from New York City, had just completed her education at Vassar. "I pooled my resources with twenty other women," she said. "We hired a schooner to take us around the horn of South America."

"Goodness! That took a lot of courage," Melinda said.

"Look who's talking!" Lillian swept her hand around the "restaurant."

The rest of the women had continued on to steam up the Yukon to the Klondike, she said. Although Lillian planned to do some prospecting, it was obvious that she was more interested in adventure than in finding gold. Why she'd diverted to Valdez, Melinda didn't ask, but Lillian volunteered that she'd met Captain Abercrombie and his horses. He'd noticed her skill in handling the half-wild animals and invited her to accompany the expedition across the glacier.

"I've always liked working with animals," she said. "Did you know that originally the government planned for the expedition to use reindeer as pack animals? Now that would have been an experience!"

"Reindeer!" Melinda exclaimed. "I've never even seen one. Do they live around here?"

"Not that I know of. These were shipped from Norway. Five hundred of them! The expedition was supposed to use some for pack animals and take the rest as food to miners who were sick and stranded in the Interior last winter. But reindeer eat lichens, and the voyage to Alaska was long and stormy, with no lichens. When the ship finally reached Haines, the reindeer were too weak to go any farther."

Melinda laughed. "I *am* sorry for the reindeer, but leave it to the government to come up with a plan like that!"

Although Lillian had already put in a full day's work, including setting up her own campsite, she was still bubbling with energy. "I'm going to take a hike up the glacier to see what we're facing," she told Melinda. "Want to come along?"

"I have to finish tomorrow's pies," she said. "Otherwise, I'd go. Please come back, though, and tell me what it's like."

When Lillian stopped by later that evening, her energy was noticeably less. Her hair straggled in damp strands from beneath her drooping hat. Soggy skirts clung around her ankles. Melinda had her sit near the warm stove and served her a piece of tomorrow's cobbler.

"Well?"

"Even though daylight lasts a long time this far north, I couldn't see much because of the fog. But it won't be an easy journey," the other young woman said. "The trail is a mess after all this rain, big rocks on top of ice. Steep, slippery slopes. Up on top it's nothing but slush." She took a large bite of the pastry. "Mmm. This is good."

"It's going to be hard on the pack horses," she went on. "I need to get back to camp and see if I can help. A farrier is trying to shoe them now. They've never been shod, but Captain Abercrombie said that needs doing before we take them up over the ice. Would you like to come with me and watch for a little while?"

"Let me put my boots on," Melinda said. "I need to check on Evan's whereabouts, anyway. He's probably visiting the horses." She laced her boots, grabbed her coat and hat from their nails on the tent frame, and followed Lillian outside.

At the camp, the horses crowded to the back of a makeshift corral, as far away as possible from the watchers offering unsolicited advice. Several soldiers had been assigned the job of helping to shoe them. They caught and led a sturdy dun out of the corral. It side-stepped and kicked when the farrier tried to lift its foot. The man cursed, wiping mud splatters out of his eyes. He told his helpers to topple the horse onto its side. It gave a terrified whinny as it crashed into the mud. One man held its head down, another sat on its rump.

"Oh, the poor beast," Melinda sympathized. She felt sorry, too, for the men who had to wallow in the mud alongside the horse.

Captain Abercrombie had stopped to watch. He heard what Melinda said. "It has to be done, Miss," he told her. "That ice would be pure purgatory for an unshod horse."

"I understand," Melinda answered. "And it's Miss McCrae, Captain Abercrombie. Melinda McCrae."

"I'm glad to meet you, Miss McCrae. One of my men brought me a piece of your pie. You're offering a comforting service to these people so far from home."

Melinda thanked him. Then she spotted Evan in the circle of watchers. She made her way over to him. "I'll need your help soon, Evan. When this horse is shod, come on home."

She made her way through the tents and across the muddy street. A packhorse loaded with boxes and bags stood outside the Pie Pantry. To her surprise, the man holding the reins was Ezekiel Cox.

"Don't tell me you are going prospecting, Mr. Cox!"

"Ezekiel, please, Miss Melinda, and no," He gestured toward the glacier's terminus. "I'll leave that jumble of ice and rock to others. I intend to make my fortune with my brains, not brawn. I'm here with the supplies for our little business."

"*Our* little business?" Those three words made her mental antennae bristle. What did he mean? And why should he take the time to walk all the way from town with her supplies?

"Where do you want me to put these bundles?"

Melinda glanced at the loaded horse. "They can go under my work counter until I have time to put them away," she said, tying back the door flaps and preceding him into the tent. She hung up her damp coat, added wood to the fire, then arranged the bags and boxes so they'd not be in her way.

"What's a man got to do to get a cup of coffee and some of that wonderful pie?" Ezekiel asked.

He'd certainly earned a free piece of pie for his long walk and his help, but somehow she felt suspicious. And a little contrary.

"The coffee's free. It's still hot, but it's rather stale. The pie costs a nickel."

He placed a dime on the table. She handed him a tin saucer with some still warm pie. She cut it larger than usual to assuage her conscience, then poured him a cup of coffee. She placed the canned milk beside it and narrowed her eyes.

"What did you mean, '*Our* little business,' Mr. Cox?"

Ezekiel looked slightly embarrassed. "Let me explain."

He told her again that he planned to influence the development of the new town of Valdez. One way to do that was by investing in new businesses to serve the potential city on Prince William Sound.

"That's why, when the Mercantile's owner, Mrs. Olson, decided to return to Seattle because of a family tragedy, I offered to buy the business.

Since I'm now the owner, I took the opportunity to fill your order."

"But why would a busy man like you not just hire someone to deliver it? And why should owning the Mercantile involve you in my little business?" Even as she asked the question, she suspected she knew the answer.

He gave her an engaging grin. "Perhaps I had an ulterior motive."

"Mr. Cox, you know I'm engaged to be married."

He waved away that pesky idea. "I like your independent spirit, Miss Melinda McCrae. You and I could go far together."

We're not going anywhere together, she thought, but clamped her lips against the retort.

"I appreciate your thoughtfulness." She emphasized the last word. "Thank you for delivering my supplies."

Turning to the washbasin, she washed her hands and tied on her apron. "I must finish the baking for tomorrow's customers," she said. "I'm sure you can find your own way out."

Ezekiel stood and took a step toward her. "There's something else I should tell you."

Her hands in flour, she stared at him. "What's that?"

"Mr. Flint, the previous owner of this business, has also decided to leave Alaska. He sold this restaurant to me."

Well. That was convenient. For Ezekiel Cox.

"Don't worry. Nothing needs to change. Or, if you prefer, my offer of a job at the Emporium still stands."

Melinda thought of the fancy lady at the Emporium who seemed to be on such good terms with him. What kind of job did he have in mind? She asked him.

"A much easier job than you're involved in right now, I assure you." He glanced at her work-roughened hands. "A job where those pretty hands can stay soft and smooth." His smile, she thought, seemed more like a barely disguised smirk.

Melinda didn't even stop to think.

"Mr. Cox, I'll give you two days to find my replacement. Then I am leaving. Now, if you'll excuse me, I have work to do."

CHAPTER SIXTEEN

ON THE GLACIER

Though July had blurred into August a few days ago, here at the foot of the glacier, summer seemed far away. After bidding goodbye to her last customers, Melinda fastened a piece of cardboard over the "Pie Pantry" sign. It read, "Closed Until Further Notice." As Evan washed and dried the remaining dishes and pans, she tidied the restaurant and packed food and cooking supplies.

"What are we going to do now, Mindy?"

She glanced up. His face mirrored her own uncertainty, but she tried to make her voice confident for his sake.

"Miss Moore told me that Captain Abercrombie and his men are leaving early tomorrow to cross the glacier. We'll follow along behind the expedition. The soldiers will help if we need them. When we get to the settlement at Copper Center, I'm hoping we'll find your uncle."

Even to her it seemed a sketchy plan. Evan seemed to think so, too.

"Then what?"

Then what, indeed? "Why, don't you think it would be fun to all come back to Valdez together?"

Evan nodded, but still looked doubtful.

What in the world had she gotten herself and the boy into? She couldn't shake the feeling that Quin needed her, or would need her. But was that truth, or just imagination? The frightening nightmare, which had faded with all the activity of the past weeks, came back to mind, clearly. Quin crossing that precarious cliff, Quin falling into the pounding surf. What had made her think she could affect the outcome of whatever risky situation he faced, anyway?

Even so, she had to put distance between herself and Ezekiel Cox. Probably it was only her imagination, but a different kind of risk seemed to hover there.

Well, no time to ponder all that now. If she and Evan were to stick close to the protection of the expedition, they must be ready to leave at dawn.

She sent a quick, but heartfelt, prayer heavenward. "Lord, I'm scared. Give me courage. Guide us, every step of the way."

She'd washed and dried their laundry after she'd given Ezekiel Cox her notice. Evan had treated their boots with his new bottle of water repellant wax stain. Now, well before daylight, she stirred up the fire, then dressed in layers of woolen clothing over a set of long underwear. The glacier would be cold and damp. She roused Evan, who put on the warm garments she'd laid out for him. They sat down to oatmeal and cocoa, probably the last hot meal they'd have for a while.

She filled a cloth sack with hardtack, dried fruit, jerky, and tea and stored it inside a cooking pot. She put it with the duffle bags, firewood, and other belongings they'd haul on the sled. Bear's packs included extra food and water. While she filled their back packs with other necessities, Evan tossed dried salmon to Bear. He wrestled the sled out from under the restaurant platform.

The sky lightened as the rain ceased, but fog billowed down over the brow of the glacier. Other people were out and about. She heard shouts and whinnies as Abercrombie's expedition moved the horses toward the ice. Lillian led one of animals. She saw Melinda loading the sled and waved.

Ahead of Lillian, people and horses struggled up steps cut into the sides of the maze of crevasses fracturing the terminus. A horse nickered fearfully, then slipped and tumbled back down the trail. Its handler shouted for those nearby to come to his aid. The packers ahead of Lillian flung the reins of their horses to her. She held at least four, stamping and snorting, while their handlers went to the aid of the fallen packhorse.

By the time the line was moving again, Evan had harnessed Bear to their sled. Melinda hefted her own pack onto her back, and closed the tent flaps. She looped a rope at the front of the sled over her shoulders. While Evan pushed and steered with the gee pole, she and Bear pulled, maneuvering the sled through the muddy street.

Melinda glanced back at Evan. He was straining as hard as she. So was the dog. This was work! And they'd barely begun. "Once we're on the glacier, this will be easier," she assured Evan. She hoped she was right.

Ahead of them, heavily-laden men struggled upward. The whinny of a horse echoed from the mists above. They stepped off the trail to catch their breath as other people moved past them. How would they ever get their sled and equipment over that jumbled, almost vertical wall of ice, even with Bear's help?

Then she heard someone calling, "Miss! Miss!"

Looking around, she saw a couple of men beckoning from a level spot at the foot of the glacier. One of them gestured toward the sled. "Do you want us to hoist your outfit to the top?"

Gratefully, they hauled the sled over to the men. Evan unhitched Bear. The men attached the sled to a long rope that disappeared up the face of an incline and looped around a block and tackle. One of them shouted, "Ready."

At the top, five or six men grasped the other end of the rope, just as Melinda had seen people doing when they first came to Glacier City, and started down the steep slope. As they tugged, the sled moved up the incline toward the surface of the glacier. The men who'd called to them followed along, balancing it.

Melinda and Evan scrambled after them. Even though Bear stayed near enough that she could steady herself by grasping a handful of his thick fur, her long skirt kept tripping her. She stopped long enough to hitch up the top of her skirt, tucking some of the fabric under her waistband to make the front shorter. She'd do something later to make foot travel more practicable, she resolved. A shout from above told her that the sled had safely reached the top of the bench. By the time she and Evan caught up with it, people below were preparing another sled for the upward journey while a couple of returning prospectors were securing their own sled and equipment for the trip down the incline.

They thanked the men who'd helped them. Then she and Evan dragged their sled off to the side. A vast expanse of ice stretched up the valley until it curved around a mountain. It extended to the mountains on either side. Closer at hand, confusion surrounded them. People were coming and going. Piles of unguarded supplies dotted the ice. They saw two people, a husband and wife, loading some of their belongings on a sled. They covered the remainder with canvas, leaving the stack behind until they could come back for another load.

Watching them, Evan commented, "Aren't they afraid someone will steal their belongings?"

"People have to trust each other in a place like this," she reminded him. *Although not everyone is trustworthy,* she thought, remembering that someone had stolen Gus's packhorse. Someone had even taken Evan's boot polish. Undoubtedly Evan was thinking of the incidents, too. She remembered the severe punishment meted out for such crimes by the other prospectors, if and when perpetrators were caught.

They watched the couple join a line of people heading toward a switch-backed trail close in to a mountainside. The wife went ahead, pulling the sled, while the man pushed.

That trail led to the steep second and third benches. Melinda wondered if the benches formed when the river of ice that was the glacier broke over precipices beneath the surface. It made sense.

Far away across the ice, she made out a line of horses and packers coming onto the glacier. Abercrombie's expedition? She wondered if Lillian was among them. If so, she and Evan should be trying to close the distance between themselves and the expedition. But the horses were moving much faster than they could travel with their load. Her plan to keep up wasn't going to work.

She turned to the boy. "Evan, we need to find a place to leave some of our gear. We have too much to haul all at once."

Leaving clothing, some of the firewood, and bundles of food she tucked a canvas over the pile. Trusting they'd find everything undisturbed when they returned, they set out with a much lighter load. This time she pushed and steered from behind, while Evan and Bear pulled.

Dark peaks loomed through the clouds. Ice and snow spilled down the divides between the peaks and met the ice flowing toward Prince William Sound. One of those divides opened to the Copper River country, but where their trail would take them, she couldn't tell from here. Wherever it went, Quin was up ahead. What adventures might lay ahead before they caught up with him?

By the time they'd climbed the switchbacks close to the mountainside, the sun broke through the clouds to announce midmorning. They came to a group of people resting on their sleds. They stopped too, and drank from the canteen they'd filled with good spring water that morning. One man pointed to snow piled at the base of a steep cliff, not far from the trail. "That's from the snow slide that came down last April and buried everyone camping here."

Melinda gasped. "Was anyone killed?"

"They dug most of them out, bruised but okay, although they lost ten burros. Then in May, melting snow uncovered three men who'd died."

She glanced ahead at the broken face of the second bench, and above it, the third. It would be a steep, difficult climb. But she was eager to get away from the avalanche area. "Let's go," she said to Evan.

The top of the third bench was only about two miles from where they'd started at Glacier City that morning. Though they carried no stove or heavy axes, shovels or equipment like most others, dragging the sled through the softening snow was exhausting work. To reach the top required three block and tackle assists from helpful fellow travelers.

In places slush had melted into deep puddles. Water ran over their boot tops. Melinda could feel icy water sloshing around her toes.

Other people had piled their goods at the top of the third bench while returning for their next load. They found a packed down spot of snow where someone had earlier pitched a tent, and deposited their burden there. They too started back for another load. All day they worked.

Evan didn't complain. But when they got the final sled load to their camping spot, he collapsed atop the sled, panting. Melinda looked at him with alarm. His face was flushed, his eyes swollen and teary.

"My eyes hurt, Mindy. And I can't feel my toes!"

She helped him remove his boots. His woolen stockings were wet through, as were his boots. Her feet were wet too, but she must set up camp before doing anything about that. She pulled some stockings and a pair of pants from Evan's pack and had him put them on. She unloaded the sled, except for his bed roll, and had him lie down, his head on his bed roll, with Bear at his feet. She covered him with his wolf skin.

"Put your feet in Bear's fur to get them warm." She dribbled water onto her handkerchief and made a cold compress for Evan's eyes. His cheeks were hot and flushed, but his forehead felt cool. Sunburn, she realized. Her cheeks, too, felt hot. The sun had reflected fiercely from the snow whenever it came out. "Try to take a little nap," she told him.

What needed doing first? A fire. It wouldn't do much to warm them, out here in the open, but they needed to dry their boots. Where had she packed their shoes? She found them, and put

Evan's on the sled for when he wakened. She gathered some flat stones that the glacier had carried down and built a small fire atop them. Angling some sticks of firewood into the snow, she hung his boots and wet stockings to dry.

She heaped her kettle with clean snow and set it near the fire to melt while she set up the tent the best she could, the open door facing the fire. She hoped the wind wouldn't blow hard that night. Others around them also set up camp, while many continued to pass by. She'd heard that the foot of the fourth bench was eight miles farther on. That meant several trips back and forth before they'd be on the main glacier. Now she felt sure they'd never catch up with the military expedition. If they were going to cross this glacier, they were on their own.

In the tent, she sat on her bedroll while changing into dry socks and her shoes. By tucking her skirt into her waistband, she'd managed to keep it fairly dry. Now she used the little mending kit Nell had given her to hem it shorter.

She checked Evan's boots and hung hers to dry near his. The big dog stretched and greeted her with a questioning "Woof?"

Evening had come, but the whiteness around them reflected the remaining light. The air grew colder. Around them, smoke puffed from stovepipes protruding through roofs of bigger tents. She wished they had a sheet metal stove like other people were using.

She gently shook Evan's shoulder. "Bear is hungry. Can you wake up now and feed him?"

Evan's eyes were swollen nearly shut. Groggily, he put on the shoes she handed him. She gave him the bundle of dried salmon and told him it would be safer from other dogs if he kept it in the tent at night.

Then she bent to the fire. Their first dinner on the glacier would be rehydrated vegetable soup, with some jerky tossed in, and hardtack. Nourishing, if not delectable.

She realized that Evan was probably suffering from a case of snow blindness. Would it get worse? And what could she do about it?

CHAPTER SEVENTEEN

LOST ON THE ICE

Melinda woke with a groan. Every bone, every muscle in her body cried out. The sled beneath her felt hard as a slab of stone and as cold. The darkness in the tent showed only the vaguest of shapes. The mound at her feet moved, then "woofed."

Sounds of people moving around outside had wakened both her and Bear, whom she'd brought inside to share his body heat. She stayed in her sleeping bag a while, working stiff fingers, toes, ankles. She squirmed to loosen her back muscles and warm up a little. Did she really want to follow through with this wild plan? Only their first night on the trail, and already they'd nearly frozen. If Evan's eyes had not improved, how could she take him any further? Her own eyes felt painful.

At least there'd been no rain on the tent last night. She would slather their faces with petroleum jelly this morning and be sure they kept their hat brims down to shade their eyes. She'd seen some people yesterday with soot smeared across their cheekbones. They must have been trying to ward off snow blindness. She could try that, too.

She laced her boots, then pulled on her heavy coat, gloves, and hat and stepped outside. A deep breath of frigid air brought the tantalizing smell of coffee from a neighboring camp. Hurriedly, she laid a small fire atop last night's ashes, then picked her way to an area of clean snow. Packing her kettle full, she carried it back to the fire. She would start the morning with hot coffee, too. In the pre-dawn dimness, other campfires glowed along the trail, where other travelers were preparing for the day.

Glimmers of lantern light below marked Glacier City. Beyond, where Prince William Sound reflected the brightening sky, lamps were being lighted behind the windows of Valdez.

While the snow in the kettle melted, she dragged the sled outside to sit on. She ground a handful of beans in her small coffee grinder, tied the grounds into a square of cloth, and when the water boiled, she dropped them in. While the brew simmered, she mixed flour, salt, and baking powder with water. She didn't have jam or syrup, so she tossed some dried blueberries into the batter. While the skillet heated, she called, "Time to get up, Evan." He poked his head out.

"How are you feeling this morning?"

"I'm sore all over," he answered. "But my eyes feel better. Thank you, Mindy."

The cold compress must have helped. There was so much that could go wrong in this wild country. She felt very much like an unprepared cheechako, a newcomer. "You're welcome, Evan. And let's thank God, too," she said. "He's the one who helps us."

She flipped a hotcake onto Evan's plate and sprinkled a little sugar over it. "Eat it quickly, before it gets cold," she told him. While her own cooked, she poured coffee into their cups and added sugar and powdered milk to Evan's. She caught the gleam of his teeth as a grin spread across his sunburned face. The coffee made him feel very grown up.

After breakfast, Melinda retreated to the tent to roll up their sleeping bags. She heard the ring of a familiar voice.

"Are you here?"

Melinda scrambled out to greet Lillian Moore with a hug. "Did you come all the way back just to find us?"

"Yes, although it didn't take long with nothing to pack, or to lead."

Melinda offered her the last of the coffee. "How are you doing with the horses?"

"I'm doing fine, but this is frightening for them, poor wild things. They have a terrible time getting up the steep, broken places. Sometimes they slip and roll back down the trail. Sometimes one breaks through a snow bridge over a crevasse hundreds of feet deep. Then it just hangs there by the forefeet, not daring to move, until the men get its pack off and ropes on it to pull it out. When that happens, I have to hold the horses for the men who are helping the horse in trouble. After all that, they're tame enough!

"The expedition is camped several miles up the glacier, so I thought I'd come back and check on you before we get up on the fourth bench. We're over the terminus of the glacier now. There's a steady rise of about 1900 feet over the next eight miles before we reach the fourth bench. There'll be crevasses to cross or avoid. But if you stick to the trail you'll be okay."

Melinda shuddered. "Hear that, Evan? No exploring on your own for you or Bear."

Lillian glanced at their outdoor fire, which even on its rock foundation had melted the surrounding snow until Melinda had to kneel and reach down to her kettle and frying pan. "That fire couldn't have kept you very warm last night."

"It didn't, but sleeping on the sled helped a lot. Evan slept on his wolf skin. Were you warm enough, Evan?"

"I got a little cold."

"The higher we go, the colder it will get," the other young woman said. "I'm told storms can hit any time of year. I wish you had a little stove like I have." With her hands she shaped a box about the length of a stick of firewood. "It has metal legs that fold down and a little stovepipe. Just a tiny fire keeps the tent warm, and I can cook on it, too."

"Maybe someone coming back to Valdez will have one he'd part with. It would certainly be a godsend."

"If I come across someone like that, I'll be sure to send him your way," Lillian assured her. "The Expedition will be ready to leave so I've got to get back now. Be careful, both of you. I'll keep watch for you along the trail. I hope we'll meet again!"

She watched Lillian stride away, passing others who were already pulling sleds or leading pack animals toward the fourth bench, and wished she were as brave as her friend. She turned to look back the way they'd come yesterday. People labored back and forth along the trail, moving their caches of supplies over the glacier. It was light enough now that she could pick out "The Pie Pantry" tent at Glacier City. She could clearly see Valdez, too. A just-docked ship was discharging another load of hopeful gold seekers. Giving up the idea of keeping close to the protection of the expedition, she resigned herself to crossing the glacier with Evan on their own.

If they were to reach Twelve-mile camp today it would mean a round trip of sixteen miles. Eight miles to the base of the fourth bench and eight miles back here. It would take more than one such journey to get all their goods to the camp at the foot of the fourth bench. She decided not to try for Twelve-Mile camp, but to stop somewhere in between.

"We'll leave our tent and bedding for last, Evan, in case we need to sleep here tonight. I'll load the sled with some of our goods. Will you put these things in Bear's packs?" She pointed to a pile of food, extra socks, and other small items.

Using charred wood from the now dead fire, she smeared soot under Evan's eyes, and under her own. Immediately, the snow's glare softened. She tucked the bit of charcoal under one of the bundles on the sled for future use. Filling the canteen with water, she tied it around her waist. Then they turned their faces to the trail and plodded off.

For the first half-mile they made slow progress. The first time they pulled off the trail to let someone pass, their sled ran up on a hummock of ice and nearly tipped over. Whoever pushed from behind soon learned to run ahead when needed to balance the weight. The first time Evan pushed, he ran the sled into Melinda's heels. "Not so fast," she remonstrated. "We have a long way to go yet. Don't wear yourself out."

The uphill slog soon had them puffing. They stopped frequently to catch their breath. Finally they reached the first large camp, called Five-mile Camp, and cached their belongings.

There were more caches than tents, Melinda noticed, because they were so close to Glacier City. Some people brought their goods this far, then returned to spend the night at Glacier City, where they had plenty of wood and water.

Returning for the next load, Evan hopped a ride on the empty sled. He hung on, shouting with glee, while Bear loped ahead, pulling. Melinda ran behind to steer. They made another trip, then one more. On the last trip, they took tent, bedding, and the remainder of the firewood. They pitched their tent and built a fire so they could cook a hot meal.

That night Evan slept soundly in spite of the cold, but Melinda wakened often to deep rumblings and crackings echoing through the ice. Once she even felt vibrations. The glacier seemed like a great living beast slumbering beneath them.

They woke to heavy fog. The eerie voices of neighbors echoed through the cotton batting surrounding them. Melinda cooked a pot of oatmeal with raisins. They ate half of it, saving the other half to reheat for supper. Then, as the fog began to thin, they loaded the sled. She didn't want to waste a single hour getting over this frightening, icy obstacle that lay between her and Quin.

Dogs barked and packhorses nickered, as if picking up the sense of haste felt by the people in the camp. The temperature was dropping again. Was a storm on the way? Nothing to do now but push on up the trail to Twelve-mile and set up camp before the weather worsened.

Melinda rummaged through their duffle bags, looking for their warmest clothing. "See if you can find your scarf and mittens, Evan." She looked for her own and found them.

"Remember, you gave me this last Christmas?" Evan said, winding the brightly striped scarf around his lower face and neck. "You made one almost like it for Uncle Quin."

Pulling on her mittens, she smiled. "I wonder if he used it when he crossed these mountains."

"Probably he did. I wish he was here now to help us," Evan said.

Oh, me too, Melinda thought. But aloud she teased, "If he was here, do you think we'd be climbing this glacier?"

At the last minute, she added the tent, some firewood, and their bedrolls to the sled. If the weather worsened and they had to camp in place, they'd have shelter at least. She hoped they could get all they were leaving on the second load and not have to make a third trip. When Bear saw her tie the canvas over the load, he leaped up, ready to go again. The three of them set off. Their sled felt much heavier this time. Certainly their backpacks were heavier, or maybe the wind slowed them down.

Several individuals slogged downhill, detouring around them. One haggard man stared vacantly. He coughed and spit, then staggered on. She wondered if he'd make it back to Valdez.

Around noon, the wind lessened. Cold settled over the glacier like a heavy blanket. They came to a group of four men huddling around a tiny sheet metal stove like Lillian had described, brewing coffee.

She raised a hand in greeting. One man called out, "If you have cups, we'll share our coffee."

"Thank you. That's very generous of you." She and Evan hauled their sled to where the men rested. Bear flopped on the snow. They pulled their folding cups from their pockets and introduced themselves.

The man tending the fire grinned at her, then at Evan. "This is pretty powerful stuff. Might stunt Shorty's growth."

Evan grinned back and took a cautious sip of the brew in his cup.

Melinda took a taste of hers and tried not to make a face. The coffee *was* powerful. But it was hot, and the men's kindness warmed her heart.

"How is the trail ahead?" she asked.

"It will be tough going, especially for two such unlikely-looking prospectors," one of them remarked. "It's cold. We came through wind and drifting snow that could have blown us off the trail." That was worrisome news.

"You want to stay away from the crevasses, too. Fall into one of those and no one would ever find you."

"We're not prospectors," Evan told them. "We're looking for my Uncle Quin."

Melinda described Quin and explained that he was writing about the gold rush.

"We haven't seen him," said the oldest man. "But we were checking out rumors of strikes up some of the creeks and could have missed him. Finally decided to give up because we were running out of food. We'd thought we could live off the country if necessary, but all these cheechakos have cleared out most of the game."

Melinda told them about Abercrombie's expedition and that she had hoped to catch up with it.

Their party had passed the military expedition near the summit, they said. It was a long way ahead of her by now.

She eyed their small stove. "How much is a stove like that worth? I'm hoping we'll meet someone who wants to sell theirs."

"We have a bigger one." The first man indicated his sled with a jerk of his chin. "Okay if we give them this one?" he asked his companions.

No one objected, so he emptied the coals out of it. While it cooled, he pulled a few lengths of stovepipe from his load, and helped Melinda stow them and the stove on their sled. She thanked them and offered payment, but they refused her money.

The oldest of the men watched with concern. "Young woman, that's a pretty rough trail for you and the boy. Why don't you turn around here and travel back to Valdez with us?"

Give up now, after all they'd gone through to get this far? What if she turned back and then found that Quin really had needed her?

The older prospector saw the struggle in her face. "At least, try to join another party going your way. There's safety in numbers."

Melinda felt grateful for his concern and told him so. "We *will* join another party, if they'll have us."

She wished the men godspeed. Hitching themselves to the sled once more, Melinda, Evan and Bear trudged on up the glacier.

The trail curved upward, steeper and more rutted. She made sure not to stray from it, as she'd been warned that the trail made a big curve to avoid an area full of crevasses. Cold wind gusted over the ice. Melinda pulled her scarf over her nose and glanced at her companions. Bear strained hard, his tongue lolling out of his mouth. His breath puffed out in clouds. Evan staggered, his head drooping. He looked exhausted, poor child.

"Let's stop and rest for a few minutes," she suggested, steering the sled off the trail.

Bear dropped to his belly, panting. Evan said nothing, just plopped on the sled. Melinda rummaged in her backpack for some of the jerky and hardtack she'd packed earlier. When she turned to offer some to Evan, he was hunched over his knees, his head on folded arms. Asleep.

She chewed on a piece of jerky, not hungry but knowing she needed the strength of food to carry on. She tossed some to Bear as well. Should she wake Evan or give him a few more minutes to rest? They could keep from freezing in this wind only if they kept moving.

She heard voices through the blowing snow, footsteps crunching. Another party, coming up behind them.

She couldn't really see faces, the five people were so bundled against the wind. But one was another woman. They told her they were the Prosper family and welcomed her to travel with them until they got to Twelve-Mile Camp.

The party kept moving. She roused Evan and urged him to chew on the jerky while they pulled the sled. The few minutes rest had revived both him and Bear. The three of them threw all of their energy into hauling the sled. Snow fell harder. The people ahead grayed into shadows. The snow and wind muffled the sound of their sleds.

The wind no longer blew straight at them. First it howled from the left, then from the right. The shadows ahead disappeared completely. She listened, but could no longer hear the sounds of sleds or voices. The wind shifted to shove at their backs. *If we just let the wind push us,* she thought, *we'll get there.* They stumbled along, snow clinging to their clothing and eyelashes.

Bear seemed nervous. He kept pulling to the right. She told him sternly to stop. The snow grew deeper, the visibility so poor she could no longer see where people had walked ahead of them. She could scarcely feel her hands or feet.

She wished the Prosper family would slow down a little so they could catch up. She watched for Twelve-Mile camp, or for travelers coming down the glacier. But they saw no one. Anyone with sense had probably stopped to wait this storm out. She stopped for a few moments to pull Evan's wolf skin from the load. She put the skin of the head over his knitted cap like a hood and pulled the rest around his shoulders so it hung down like a cape. Strips of hide hung loose on the shoulders. She tied them together under Evan's chin to keep him warmer. "Now," she said. "You look fierce as any wolf!"

He grinned weakly. After what seemed like hours, Evan asked, "Melinda, are you sure we're still on the trail?"

What could she say? Suddenly, she was no longer sure of anything.

Especially when she realized that the snow-cloaked shapes looming ahead through the falling snow were boulders ... huge rocks that might have rolled down a mountain. They shouldn't be near a mountainside if they were still on the trail, should they? Terror clawed at her throat. She'd heard of people getting lost on the glacier and wandering for weeks.

With a sinking heart, she realized it was growing dark. It was too late in the day to retrace their steps. They'd have to wait for daylight, and try to survive the night in the storm. Evan shook with fear and cold. They needed shelter. Fast.

Dear God, what do we do now?

She took a deep breath and tried to sound cheerful. "Evan, are you ready for another adventure? See these big rocks right here?"

She stepped over to two huge boulders. They leaned against each other, forming a shallow, cave-like space. The snow in the space seemed level, and big enough for their tent.

"Tramp the snow down here for our campsite. That will help you warm up. I'll get the tent ready."

"I don't want any more adventures." Evan's teeth chattered, but he went to work. Melinda helped him finish, then together they struggled against the wind to erect the tent. They pushed the sled inside and spread Evan's wolf hide beside it. Melinda set the little sheet metal stove on the piece of tin the prospectors had given her, and pushed the stove pipe sections together and into place on the back of the fire box. The last section of stove pipe fit neatly through a reinforced flap in the roof.

While Evan piled the kindling and firewood near the stove, she got a tiny fire crackling. She set the morning's leftover oatmeal in its pot on the stove to heat and packed snow into another pot to melt. She'd use some of her homemade cocoa-sugar-dried milk mix to make them some hot chocolate.

Evan fed Bear, who curled up next to the tent. "Can't Bear sleep in the tent again tonight?" he asked.

Melinda didn't mention the first reason she preferred to leave the dog on guard outside the tent. Bear could warn them of any danger approaching in the night. She gave her second reason to Evan. "We'll be warm enough with our little stove, but Bear has such a thick coat he'd be uncomfortable. Besides, there's really not room with the stove and wood in here."

By the time they'd eaten, darkness had fallen. The wind still howled, making the canvas ripple and flap. The snow continued, but the boulders protected them from the worst of it. Melinda melted snow to refill their canteen. She tucked Evan into bed on the sled, where she usually slept, then rolled out her sleeping bag on his wolf hide so she could more easily add wood to the fire throughout the night.

Then she crawled into her own sleeping bag. "God, keep us," she prayed, thinking about the uncertain night ahead and the equally worrisome tomorrow.

CHAPTER EIGHTEEN
A CLOSE CALL

After rousing frequently throughout the night to add fuel to the little stove, Melinda became aware of dim light filtering through the sides of their tent. The overhanging boulders had sheltered them from the worst of the wind last night, but the canvas above her head sagged alarmingly under the weight of fresh snow. Crouching on her bed, she pulled on her outer garments, then rolled her sleeping bag and checked for embers in the stove. The fire had gone out not long ago. The stove wasn't quite cold. But she wouldn't build a new fire now. If the weather allowed, they must try to find their way back to the trail.

Grabbing her frying pan to use as a snow scoop, she crawled outside. A hummock near the tent exploded in a shower of crystals as Bear leaped up, shook himself, and stretched.

She took a moment to gaze around. The clouds had lifted. Snow no longer swirled. A vast empty sheet of ice and snow extended in all directions, except for the mountain wall looming behind the jumbled boulders where they'd camped. Nothing moved, anywhere. Had they wandered to the edge of the world? No, she decided. They might be somewhat lost, but surely they could find their way back to the trail now that the storm had stopped.

As she brushed snow off the tent, Bear, nose to the surface, zigzagged down the slope up which they'd come last night. Was he sniffing out their own trail? She realized she should have paid attention to his attempts to guide them last night. He was their only hope now. She called him back to the tent and rewarded him with a piece of dried salmon.

Evan poked his head out of the tent. "Wow!" He exclaimed, scanning the empty scene around them. "Where are we?"

"We lost the trail last night, but I'm sure Bear can help us find our way back," she said, forcing herself to sound confident. "Let's get ready."

As she packed the stove, she took a piece of charred wood and blackened their cheekbones to guard against snow blindness.

When the sled was loaded and they'd eaten some jerky, Evan picked up his loop of rope. He turned to Melinda, who had harnessed Bear between them. "Mindy, don't you think we should pray before we start out?"

"You're absolutely right, Evan." She reached for his hand. "Would you like to ask our Heavenly Father to lead us?"

Evan bowed his head. "Dear God, thank you for taking care of us last night and for our tent and food and fire. Now will you please take us safely to the trail? Thank you, and Amen."

"Amen," Melinda echoed, smiling at his simple faith. "Shall we go?"

Bear seemed eager to pull. He bore right, down the slope. It seemed to Melinda that they should be going left, since they must keep climbing to reach the glacier's summit. But the big dog had been correct yesterday. So she and Evan followed his lead.

After quite a distance, she looked back. The boulders where they'd stopped were scarcely visible, just a lumpy area in the glacier's white blanket. As she slowed, Bear paused, then nudged Evan in a direction that would lead them more steeply downslope.

He must be trying to head back toward Valdez. "No, Bear. This way." She tugged him more to the left.

Bear whined, swung his furry head to look downslope, but obeyed.

They were coming to an area of broken ice. Perhaps an old avalanche? Surely they could find a path through it. She stopped the sled and climbed a hillock.

Now she could see the problem and her heart nearly stopped. Before them lay a deep chasm in the ice. Smaller canyons branched off, and others snaked away in the distance. She could hear water rushing far below, at the bottom of the one in front of her. She could also see that there were areas where snow had filled in the crevasses, forming bridges, some of which had slumped as the snow rotted. Some still looked firm and crossable. She saw what seemed to be a shortcut through the crevasses. It could save them hours of walking.

Evan climbed up to stand beside her. "This looks scary, Mindy. Those men who gave us the stove said to keep away from places like this."

"I'm pretty sure I see a way through. We'll go back if we can't make it."

As she returned to the sled, she devised a plan. She would tie one end of her rope to the sled and take the lead. When she was sure the ice was safe, she'd call Bear to follow. Evan would come last, pushing.

She explained her plan to the boy. "If anything happens, get off the snow bridge as fast as you can," she told him.

Evan looked frightened. "But what about Bear and you? And the sled?"

"Don't worry. I'll stop if it looks dangerous."

She pulled one of the tent poles from the load to use as a probe and led the way toward the snow-bridge ahead of them. Up close, she could see how snow had melted away from beneath, making the bridge thinner at the edges. They would have to stay in the center so they wouldn't break through, but it seemed plenty wide enough.

What would Quin Chenoweth say if he could see them now? She felt the incongruity of the situation. She'd started out on this journey, believing he was in danger, believing he needed her. Now she needed him. No, what she needed right now was her heavenly Father's guidance. But they'd already asked for that. It seemed that all she had was a little boy and a dog.

The snow squeaked beneath her boots. She plunged the pole into the snow on either side as she stepped onto the bridge. It felt firm, so she walked a few yards further, testing with the pole. She leaned into her rope. "Come, Bear. Push, Evan."

Every few steps, she stopped and probed again. Now the chasm yawned on either side of them. Its walls were sculpted in beautiful curves, the ice glowing an unworldly blue. Bear whined. Evan looked frightened.

"Don't look down. We're almost across."

She turned forward, stepping a little to her left. Her foot broke through the crust with a sickening jolt. She felt herself slipping toward the edge and threw herself forward on the snow, digging in hard with her pole. The sled bumped against Bear, who braced himself to keep it from moving further.

"Evan, go back!" she shrieked. Instead, the boy ran to the front of the sled, grabbed her rope, and pulled with all his strength. Feeling the tug of the rope, she squirmed on her stomach toward the sled. As she did, she heard chunks of ice ricocheting off the sides of the crevasse. Only by God's grace, she thought, was she not among them.

Together, she and Evan pulled the sled backward, off the snow bridge. Then she fell to her knees and threw her arms around both the big dog and Evan, tears of relief and gratitude cold on her cheeks. "Bear, you're the smartest dog in the world. And Evan, you're the bravest boy I know!"

They'd been trudging downslope for what seemed like hours, heads hanging and eyes squinted against the brightness of the snow, when Bear paused in his pulling and "woofed." Melinda looked up. In the distance, black dots moved up and down the glacier like ants following a scent. The trail! A couple of dots were moving their way. Someone looking for them?

"Good boy, Bear. You saved us!"

A surge of energy filled all three. They rapidly closed the gap between themselves and the searchers, who turned out to be 18-year-old Lafe Prosper and his hulking younger brother Jake.

"Are you all right?" Lafe called.

"We're fine."

"We missed you before we got to Twelve-mile Camp, but we couldn't find you in the storm."

"Ma sent us to look for you," Jake added. "She sent food."

"Thank you for coming. And for bringing food. We didn't have much breakfast," Melinda told them.

She pulled out the little stove and some firewood and asked Evan to fill the kettle with snow to make tea. While waiting for the water to boil, they told the brothers of their adventure, and how Bear had tried to keep them on the trail. She said as little as possible about the near-disaster on the snow bridge. "I've learned a lesson," she said. "After this, I'm going to pay attention when Bear tries to tell me something."

While they shared the biscuits and cheese the young men brought, she asked what led them and their family to Alaska.

The brothers told her that the Prospers had intended to farm, not prospect, when they left Wisconsin. But they'd found the Northwest in the grip of recession. It was a bad time to start a farming venture. Then their old neighbor, Conner Gilvray, joined them. He was excited about the proposed all-American route to the gold fields. They soon caught his enthusiasm and decided to go together. They hoped to travel farther north to the Klondike. But first they planned to prospect along the Copper River or its tributaries.

They'd emptied the coals from the stove as soon as the tea was brewed. Eager to get to Twelve-mile Camp, Melinda jumped up to put kettle and stove back on the sled. Evan had fallen asleep atop the load.

"If you'll walk behind and steer, Miss McCrea, we'll pull the sled and let him sleep for a while," Lafe suggested.

So the party started out, the brothers pulling, Evan asleep atop the bundles, and Melinda plodding behind with Bear. When they reached the trail and its upward slope, Evan woke and hopped off. He joined Melinda behind the sled, pushing. With the strong young men to help, they passed many people struggling with their supplies up the glacier. Sooner than she'd dared to hope, the camp loomed ahead.

Jake lumbered off to let his parents know they'd found the missing travelers, while Lafe helped them set up camp.

When the shadows from the surrounding peaks lengthened, Jake returned. "Ma says you're to come eat with us," he announced. "We're having venison stew. She said bring your bowls and spoons."

Melinda gladly followed the brothers past other tents and caches to where the Prospers and their friend Mr. Gilvray had set up two large tents, with their supplies stacked between them. Smoke trickled from the stovepipe of the largest tent. Caroline Prosper pulled back the door flap to greet them. She was a couple of years younger than Melinda's own mother, with the same kind, reassuring presence. With her emphatic voice and energetic movements, Melinda doubted anyone got away with much nonsense in her household.

"Come in, come in, you two." She pulled them inside. "Are you all right? No frostbite or anything? Do you know you are responsible for the first sleepless night I've had in a long time?"

She paused for Melinda's assurance that they were fine.

"The wind and snow made it impossible to see anything last night. We kept shouting back to you, and thought you were right behind us, but when you didn't come into camp, we knew you'd missed the trail. It was terrible to think of you out there in that storm, not knowing where to look for you!"

"I'm sorry, Mrs. Prosper. I was pretty worried myself."

Benjamin Prosper wiped his glasses on his shirttail and put them on again. He was thin and round-shouldered, not nearly as hearty as his wife. "Let me take your coats. It will be plenty warm in here when the boys and Conner come in."

Melinda shoved her scarf and hat into the sleeve of her coat, her mittens into the pockets, and handed it to him. He hung it on a hook on the tent frame and did the same with Evan's wraps.

Melinda looked around. "The stew smells wonderful!"she said to Caroline."Your tent is a palace compared to our little shelter. You have so much room!"

"I'm using some of the venison we traded for in Valdez," Caroline said. "And thank you. I'm thankful for the space."

She cooked in the area next to the entrance. Pans, dishes, and sacks of food were arranged in stacked open boxes near the sheet metal stove; like Melinda's but larger. Two wood and canvas folding cots formed an "L" against the back and the other side wall. They'd piled firewood outside the door.

"Do you have a jackknife?" she heard Benjamin ask Evan.

"Yes." Evan pulled his prize possession out of his pocket and handed it to the man, who picked up a slender stick of kindling wood and made a downward cut along one edge, leaving the shaving attached to the stick.

He examined the knife's edge. "Hmm. Do you have a sharpener?" When Evan told him "no" he took a small whetstone out of his pocket and showed him how to use it.

With the knife properly sharpened, he showed Evan how to turn the stick around, making shavings up each corner. While Melinda helped Caroline Prosper finish dinner, Evan turned his stick into a mass of curly shavings. "Now," said kindly Benjamin, "You have a magic fire starter. And you have something to do when you run out of entertainment." Evan grinned with delight when he told him to keep the whetstone, saying he had another.

While Melinda stirred the pot of stew, Caroline lifted the lid on a cast iron skillet. The mouth-watering scent of freshly baked biscuits filled the air. She poked her head out the door. "Jake! Lafe! Conner! Dinner time!"

The three came from the other tent, stomping snow from their boots and filling the remaining space with jostling and joking. They took seats on the boxes and bundles lined along the opposite wall. Benjamin sat on one of the cots with Evan next to him, leaving the remaining cot for the women. He asked a blessing on the food, then Melinda helped Caroline Prosper dish it out and pass the plates around.

"Thank you for helping us, all of you," Melinda said, her heart full of gratitude. She smiled at their new friends. "You are a blessing." She dipped the edge of a biscuit into her stew. "What a feast! And to think, we're enjoying it halfway to heaven on a frozen glacier. Never in all my life could I have imagined myself in a place like this!"

Clear, windless, and cold enough to keep the snow solid underfoot. A good day to retrieve the rest of their goods, Melinda thought as she built a fire in the little stove next morning.

The Prosper family planned to spend the day hauling their gear to the summit of the glacier, but Melinda and Evan still had another sled-load of supplies to fetch.

After a quick breakfast, the two of them hitched Bear to the sled and started down the glacier to Five-Mile camp. On the first downhill stretch, Evan hopped on the empty sled while Bear pulled and Melinda ran behind, steering.

"Your turn, Mindy," Evan offered after a while. They exchanged places. As the slope grew steeper, the sled picked up speed. Evan lost his grip on the gee pole.

"Slow down," she yelled.

But the sled had already run away from the boy. Melinda had no way to steer or slow the sled. It caught Bear and scooped him up with her.

She grabbed the rope attached to the front and rolled off into the snow. The sled's momentum yanked her along until she managed to dig in her heels. Then it slowed and stopped, the astonished dog still aboard and tangled in his traces. Evan ran to brush her off, while she loosened her scarf and dug snow from around her neck.

"Are you all right, Ma'am?" A couple of prospectors laboring uphill grinned.

Embarrassment reddened her cheeks beneath their soot smears. "Perfectly all right. Thank you."

At the camp, they found their cache undisturbed. They transferred the remaining goods to sled and backpacks.

"When's lunch?" asked Evan.

"Put some dried fruit in your pocket to munch on. We should try to go at least two miles before stopping again." It would be easier for all of them if they could break the journey into smaller segments.

She could almost feel her tongue lolling out like Bear's when they finally arrived at Twelve-mile Camp, weary from the seven-mile uphill struggle. Leaving the load on the sled, Melinda started supper while Evan let the Prospers know they'd returned.

They rolled out early the next morning, eager to reach the summit of the glacier. Around them, prospectors were moving up the last steep section, which rose at an angle of 45 degrees to meet the sky. Some must have started out long before daylight. From a distance they looked like little black flies clinging to a wall.

Melinda found Caroline loading bundles onto a sled. "I'm thankful the weather is so nice," she commented. "Everyone says this last section to the summit is the hardest part of the trail." She looked up at the glistening sheet of snow and ice, estimating the distance to the top at about three-fourths of a mile. "I wouldn't want to climb that in a storm like we had the other day."

Caroline tossed her a corner of the tarpaulin she was tying over the load. "Makes my knees ache just looking at it," she said. "Tuck this under, will you please?"

The Prosper party had been foresighted enough to bring their own pulley and a thousand feet of rope. When they'd finished with the last load yesterday, they brought the rope and pulley down with them.

Now Evan scrambled to join Lafe, Jake, and the older men as they stretched the rope up the slope to a stake they'd planted yesterday. Fastening the pulley to the stake, they threaded the loose end of the rope through. The women attached the sled with its two-hundred-pound load to the other end. The men grabbed the free end and Evan found a grip as well. They started down, hauling on the rope. The sled moved upward. Caroline and Melinda accompanied, in front and in back, steadying it to keep it upright.

Then the men climbed back to where they waited, planted the stake farther up the mountain and began the process all over again. Meanwhile, other prospectors wrestled their own sleds, with lighter loads, by hand up the trail.

Finally, after moving the sled in shorter stages, they stood at the five-thousand-foot summit of the glacier. The men had climbed up and down that wall of ice the equivalent of three times to bring one loaded sled to the top. They would have to repeat the journey several more times to get all their goods to where they now stood.

But they weren't thinking of that now. All of them were gazing in awe at the top-of-the-world views that stretched in every direction.

Though Melinda's leg muscles ached, she felt triumphant to have come this far. She gazed at the expanse of ice spilling down the other side of the mountain, and now called the Klutina Glacier. It continued for another ten miles. Far below it gave way to the forested Klutina Valley, where summer reigned. Somewhere out there, she hoped to find Quin.

Facing back the way they'd come, she caught her breath. The coast lay far below. Though a bulge of mountain hid part of the glacier, she saw Valdez clinging to the edge of Prince William Sound. In between stretched eighteen miles of snow and ice. A long streak of humanity wound its way toward where she stood. *Well, not all are coming this way*, she amended the thought. *A lot of those people have already been here and are going back.*

Quin had stood on this same summit. What had he thought about this amazing sight? And where was he now?

CHAPTER NINETEEN

THE INTERIOR

They worked hard for the remainder of the day. Finally all their goods were at the top of the pass.

Again, Melinda turned from the panorama spreading below their lofty vantage point, wondering when they'd return to the village clinging to the edge of the Sound. So far as she knew, any other points of non-indigenous civilization were hundreds of miles across the wilderness; at Dawson City in the Klondike, maybe, or the old Russian town of Sitka. Or at Cook Inlet, which had had its own gold rush a couple of years ago.

Copper Center and the possible presence of Quin would be civilization enough for her. She let her imagination run across the miles to where the Klutina and Copper Rivers met. If she knew where to look, she might see the place from here. Would she even recognize Quin? His face by now would be hidden under a beard like those worn by most of the men in this country. But nothing could change those smiling dark eyes and the way he looked at her.

She touched her throat, where the heart-shaped locket with his portrait hung. She smiled back into those eyes almost every night before she went to sleep.

"Mindy, can we camp here?" Evan leaned against their sled, his arm around Bear's shaggy neck.

Sleeping here at the top of the world would be an unforgettable experience. However, the wind had sprung up. A thick mass of clouds blowing in from the ocean threatened another storm.

"Let's see what the Prospers want to do," she answered, making her way to where they were re-arranging supplies on their sleds.

Their companions did not think it wise to risk being caught in such an exposed place if it stormed. They were preparing to take as much as they could carry down the Klutina side of the glacier to where projecting cliffs could shelter them from the wind. They'd collect the rest of their supplies the next day, then relay them down to the timber where they planned to build a boat.

With gravity to help and the wind at their backs, she, Evan and Bear set off with their laden sled, following the Prosper party. By the time they'd made their way past the upthrust cliffs, sunset glowed pink on the glacier. The world below lay in shadow.

They found themselves in a sheltered cove, bare of snow, where rocky outcrops alternated with patches of tundra. Here, only a light breeze tickled their faces. Low bushes grew everywhere, laden with green blueberries. Close to the base of the cliff where the heat of the sun concentrated, a few were were ripe enough to eat.

Evan and the teens abandoned the sleds and ran to stuff their mouths. As the parents unloaded their sled, Caroline laughed.

"Come back, you boys. We have to set up camp before dark!"

Melinda looked around. "This is like heaven, compared to where we've been," she announced. Tonight they'd sleep warmer, and maybe tomorrow they'd be traveling away from the mountains.

While Evan searched for bits of deadwood for their fire, she erected their tent in a cleared spot that had obviously been used by previous campers. Then she built a fire in the stove with Evan's wood, heaped a kettle with snow from the glacier, and set it to melt. She'd make soup for everybody tonight from dehydrated vegetables, rice, and bouillon cubes, while Caroline baked the biscuits. Maybe once they were in the woods, they'd find game to add to their diet, although with all the travelers who'd passed this way already, she doubted they'd find much.

Darkness had fallen when they finished eating and went to bed.

In the gray light of early next morning, Lafe, Jake, their father, and Conner Gilroy headed back to the summit with the sleds. By the time Melinda and Caroline had breakfast ready, they heard the returning brothers whooping as they flung themselves atop their loads and coasted their sleds down the glacier to a stop several hundred feet from the edge of the cove. The older men followed more sedately with the remainder of their goods.

"Goodness!" Their mother scolded good-naturedly. "How's a body to hear themselves think with all that racket?"

"It's fun, Ma!"

Lafe punched his brother in the shoulder. "It's better than sledding behind the barn back in Wisconsin, right, Jake?"

The tents were already down and folded, and stacks of hotcakes kept warm on the stove.

"Coffee's ready," Melinda said. The menfolk grabbed cups and tin plates while Melinda poured coffee and Caroline plopped hotcakes onto each plate. The women served themselves and found a couple of boulders to sit on.

Melinda bowed her head for a quick word of thanks for food and safety and the untamed world spread out before them. She turned to Caroline. "I am so grateful to you and your family for letting us travel with you. We'd never had made it this far without your help."

"You are helping us, too," Caroline said. "You and Evan are a civilizing influence on these boys of mine, and you certainly do more than your share of the work."

Melinda hoped that was true, although as far as she could see, Lafe and Jake were as civilized as any other young men their ages.

Back on the glacier, the downhill slope and the wind at their backs made sledding easier. That changed when they reached the terminus. They picked their way through the jumble of tumbled rocks and ice, everyone joining together to move the sleds past the obstacles.

At the foot of the glacier, meltwater poured from beneath the ice to form the headwaters of the Klutina River ... shallow, but wild, swift and growing larger as other streams added their water. They followed a well-trodden path along the river until they came to a place where others had forded. A trail worn into the bank opposite led into some spindly trees, where the walking undoubtedly was easier than the trail on their side. That rocky path led along the edge of a precipitous drop into the river.

"I'll check it out." Jake Prosper, the biggest and strongest among the group, picked up a sturdy stick.

"Be careful, Jake," Melinda worried. "It's so full of silt you can't see the bottom."

"It must be okay if others have crossed here," he said. He waded out into the current. By midstream, the water pushed above his knees. He struggled to stay upright. Suddenly, he howled, lost his balance, and toppled. His stick went racing away.

Caroline screamed as the swirling water tumbled her son over and over down the river. Melinda forgot to breathe, so sure was she that he would drown. Then he slammed against a boulder where he clung, coughing and choking.

Lafe had grabbed a rope when Jake went down. He scrambled after him, made a loop, and tossed it to his brother. Hand over hand, he hauled the sputtering, shivering young man ashore. Quickly, his family wrapped Jake in a blanket.

He examined a bruise forming on his left shin. "That water carries big rocks like they are pieces of driftwood," he said. "I felt one hit me. That's what knocked me over!"

Probably those who crossed here had horses, like Lillian and the Abercrombie expedition, Melinda thought. Or maybe they crossed early in the morning, before melt water increased its flow.

Whatever, they'd been defeated by a twenty-foot wide creek. What could they do now? The larger timber was still several miles downstream. The banks of the creek were of loose rock, and dropped sharply into the water. They'd have to do as people ahead of them had done: cache their supplies, leave their sleds, and take only what they could carry to where they planned to set up camp.

Unloading their sled at the top of the bank, Melinda divided their belongings into smaller loads for herself, Evan, and the dog to pack. She helped Evan drag the sled and remaining supplies to where rocks jutted out of the hillside and shoved them underneath. They'd need the sled for the journey back over the glacier, whether or not they found Quin.

For their first trip, she tied her sleeping bag to her pack, with the tent on top. She loaded Bear with the small stove, stovepipe, and the hatchet, while Evan carried his own pack and sleeping bag. Using the tent poles as walking sticks, they started after the Prosper family. They stepped carefully along the narrow trail, watchful not to misstep and tumble into the river below. The loose rocks made walking difficult. Before they'd gone very far, Melinda felt her boots rubbing uncomfortably on her feet.

They passed a grove of stunted spruce trees with a few tents scattered among them. Men who'd spent days on the glacier were resting around fires built with the plentiful dry wood.

Beyond their camp, mottled brown-and-white ptarmigan flushed from the trail to perch in tree branches. She grabbed Bear's collar just in time to stop him from bolting after a long-legged snowshoe hare, also still wearing remnants of its white winter coat. The dog couldn't have caught it, loaded as he was with his packs. But rabbit stew would have tasted good tonight. Or fried ptarmigan, for that matter.

While Melinda persuaded Bear that following the rabbit was not a good idea right now, she became away of a high-pitched whine close to her ear. Then something prickled her forehead. She slapped at it. Her hand came away with a splotch of blood and the remains of a mosquito. Prospectors had warned them of mosquitoes big enough to attack full-grown dogs and she'd smiled at the joke. Well, here they were, boiling up from the underbrush, buzzing around Bear's face as well as her own.

They plodded along behind the Prospers, everyone swatting mosquitoes away. Farther down the valley, about twelve miles from the summit, their stream joined another at a level area scattered with trees. They'd reached Twelve-mile Camp. Benjamin said it was also called Forest Camp, to distinguish it from the camp called Twelve-mile on the glacier.

Many of those already camping there called out a welcome, or at least raised a hand in greeting. They seemed a friendly lot, maybe because women like Melinda and Caroline were rarities on the trail.

Melinda noticed that one man, thin and sullen in appearance, scarcely looked up from his fire. His drooping, rusty black hat hid most of his features, except for thin, scraggly whiskers hanging from his chin. Something about him seemed familiar. Maybe it was his surly attitude. She made a mental note to stay away from him, and to keep Evan away from him too.

They set up their tents in a pleasant spot at some distance from the other campers, though closer to the sullen man than she'd prefer. They rested a bit, then tramped back to the glacier for another load of supplies.

Long before she limped back to Forest Camp, the blisters on her feet had broken. Evan had blisters too. He'd tried removing his boots to go barefoot, but whenever the breeze died down, the mosquitoes descended in whining swarms to attack any exposed skin. They were accompanied by small black flies called 'white socks' that painlessly bit out tiny chunks of flesh, then flew away before their victims became aware of them. The insects left any exposed skin speckled with itching red welts and trickles of blood. One of the white socks left a painful swelling on Melinda's wrist, another on her temple.

Back in camp, Evan whipped out his jackknife to make a fire starter, while Melinda hurried to collect fallen branches. They lit a fire among the rocks near the creek and hovered close while the smoke discouraged the tormenting pests. Melinda took off her boots to cool her feet in the creek. Evan did the same.

Caroline came from her tent to check on them. When she saw their blisters, she disappeared. She came back with gauze, adhesive tape, and also some mosquito netting. She showed Melinda how to sew it to the brims of their hats, then tuck it into their collars to keep the mosquitoes from their skin. "The bites won't itch as much if you don't scratch them," she said. Then, examining their blisters, she asked, "Do you have any petroleum jelly?"

Melinda found her small container of the greasy substance. Caroline had her dab it over their blisters, then taped the gauze in place.

"You'll be good as new in a few days," she said. "We're going to stay here a while. The menfolk plan to build a boat to take our supplies on to the lake."

"A boat? Can we ride, too?" Evan asked.

"Well, they'll carry your belongings." Caroline glanced at the Klutina River, which continued to grow larger with every glacial stream that joined it, then churned its way down the mountain more powerfully than ever. "I, for one, plan to walk!"

The Prospers, like many other parties, had brought a whipsaw to cut lumber from the spruce trees that grew in the valley. Up and down the stream, people worked in pairs, sawing boards. Then they hammered them together to make boats in which they hoped to ride to Lake Klutina. After that, they'd have an easy twenty miles to the outlet of the lake, where the Klutina River again flowed on to join the Copper River at Copper Center.

Meanwhile, they heard some returning prospectors talking about the Copper River valley. They'd found no nuggets lying about waiting to be picked up, they said. Most of the country was geologically wrong for gold. Those vaunted nuggets were simply the pipe dreams of ship owners and businessmen who were trying to wring money from people gullible enough to fall for their tales.

"I think those men are giving up too soon," Conner Gilvray said as they sat beside their campfire one night. "Anyone knows you don't find gold lying around on top of the ground. You have to look in the creek beds, not where the bedrock is buried far beneath the surface."

"I agree," Benjamin Prosper replied. "We never thought this quest would be easy."

Melinda thought about her own quest. Finding Quin had turned out to be not easy, either. Although she had asked those who'd been in camp longest, as well as more recent returnees, she found no one who knew anything about Quin Chenoweth.

Had he gone on to the Klondike? Or maybe he'd already returned to Seattle. *Lord,* she thought, *I guess I ran ahead of you. What should I do now? Stay with the Prospers, or go back?*

Their sullen neighbor was still camped nearby, but he kept to himself and she did not talk to him. A bony packhorse was tethered near his tent. The horse favored one leg. Somehow he'd been injured. Maybe his owner was waiting for the leg to heal before going on to the Copper River. A ragged blanket lay cinched across the horse's back and over his rump. Was it an attempt to protect him from the pesky flies that tortured all of them when the breeze ceased blowing, or was it for another purpose?

The animal had nibbled all the vegetation within his reach. Why, she wondered, did the man not let him graze in one of the nearby patches of grass?

Sometimes the horse whinnied plaintively and bobbed his head to one side. It was a peculiar habit. She thought of the frightened animal belonging to prospector Gus, the horse that had protested so vigorously being hoisted onto the ship Northward. He'd bobbed his head the same way. She'd been watching the distraction along with everyone else when Evan had slipped aboard to stow away.

Later, the same horse had been stolen while Gus was preparing to cross the glacier. That horse was the same dark color, although it had distinctive white spots across its rump. What, she wondered, might be hidden under that blanket? It was none of her business. But her curiosity was working full speed.

Evan also had noticed the neglected animal. "That man doesn't take good care of his horse," he told Melinda. "He's not at his camp right now. Could I pull some grass and give it to him?"

"I'll go with you," she said. They each gathered an armful of tall grass from a sunny spot near the river, and making sure the owner was nowhere near, they dropped it in front of the horse. He attacked the pile ravenously. While Evan stroked his neck, Melinda flipped back a corner of the filthy blanket.

No markings. The animal bobbed his head in that peculiar manner as he chewed a mouthful of grass. Melinda ran her hand against the hair's direction, and noticed something. Under the hair shafts, white spots splashed the skin. The base of the hairs growing from the white spots were also white, or a very light brown, like they'd been dyed. The connection popped into her head. Evan's lost boot polish! He'd used it like paint to make her restaurant sign. And it had gone missing the same night the horse disappeared.

She dropped the blanket back into place, and turned toward their own camp. "Come on, Evan. Let's go."

"Why are you snooping around my camp?" A growl. Malevolent.

A chill shivered down her spine.

Chapter Twenty

WENTZEL

Melinda whirled to face their glaring neighbor. Despite her fright, she kept her voice under control. "Your horse is starving. We simply brought him some grass to eat. Why don't you let him graze over there where it's growing?

"What I do with my property is my business," he snapped. "I'll thank you to mind your own."

Well, Melinda fumed upon reaching their camp, *if he's a thief, it's my business to do something about it, isn't it?*

But what? It would come down to her word against his. And what if someone else was the thief? The man could have purchased the horse. If she accused him, the consequences might be serious. What if he was innocent?

However, it wouldn't hurt to get the advice of people she trusted, like the Prospers and Conner Gilvray. She got her chance after supper that evening when Lafe and Jake invited Evan to go fishing with them. As soon as they headed for the river, she asked Caroline if she could talk to her and the men privately,

"Of course," Caroline said, lifting her eyebrows. "Come into the tent," she invited, and beckoned to the men to join them. "Melinda wants to talk to us," she said. "Would anyone like more tea?"

The men held out their cups to be refilled, but Melinda shook her head. Her stomach felt knotted. She took a deep breath and told the three what had happened with their neighbor that afternoon. "He seemed very angry. Why would he be angry unless he's hiding something?" She told about the disguised spots on the horse's back. "I'm sure he's the same horse that disappeared just before we started across the glacier. And though there's nothing to distinguish the man from lots of others, I think he was the same one who was in my restaurant the night Evan's shoe polish disappeared, just before someone took Gus's horse."

No one said anything as they thought over Melinda's story. She hated the role she was forced to play. But she needed good counsel.

"It's odd," Benjamin said. "Several of us were discussing "Miner's Justice" just this morning. It came up because a couple of fellows stopped here recently with a sad story. Their party had actually made a strike in the Copper River country. They had found enough to make mining it worthwhile. Two of them were taking what they'd mined to Valdez, planning to buy winter supplies. Evidently they celebrated on the way out and spoke a little too freely. When they sobered up the next morning, the gold was gone.

"Everyone who's heard the story is on the lookout for a stash of gold the owner can't readily explain. If it's found, too bad for the thief! People here have to make their own laws. And they have no sympathy for someone who steals what might mean life or death for someone else."

"I tried to get acquainted with the neighbor you're talking about," Conner Gilvray said. "I managed to find out that he goes by the name Wentzel. He stays to himself, lurks in the shadows more or less. Some people call him 'Weasel' behind his back."

"I heard he had a partner, but they broke up," Benjamin added.

Caroline sniffed. "Hmm. Wonder why?"

"He's not a very pleasant person," Melinda said. "But what do you think I should do, if anything?"

"Well, for starters, you and Evan need to stay out of his way. If he's up to no good, we don't want him getting suspicious of you."

"You're right, Mr. Prosper. But that poor horse doesn't deserve to be starved like that. I think he's been beaten, too. I saw scars on his neck."

"We'll talk to Wentzel. I don't know why he's hanging around so long, but we'll keep an eye on him."

The next day, Melinda noticed the still-blanketed horse had been staked out in a lush patch of grass a short way from his owner's campsite. Later, she saw a knot of men near the river in animated discussion. Now and then, someone glanced toward the camp. The man nicknamed 'Weasel' seemed aware of the watchers. He stuck close to his camp.

Melinda spent part of the afternoon doing laundry at the edge of the river. When her hands were numb and almost blue from the icy water, she wrung out the last item and sat back on her heels, listening to the noisy song of the river.

Further upstream, Evan watched Benjamin Prosper and his sons whipsaw lumber for the sturdy, flat-bottomed boat they planned to build.

She beckoned the boy to come help her carry the clean garments back to their camp, where they shook out the wrinkles and spread them over bushes to dry in the sunshine. She flapped a wet shirt at Evan, sprinkling him with droplets of water. He giggled and flapped his garment at her.

She glanced past Evan's shoulder. Wenzel stood motionless among the trees. He was glowering. At them? She felt a shiver run through her as their neighbor abruptly turned his back.

CHAPTER TWENTY-ONE

MINER'S JUSTICE

It took a long time that night for Melinda to fall asleep. Though they'd smoothed the ground beneath the tent before setting it up, she discovered a rock the size of a hen's egg lying beneath one hip. She squirmed away from it, only to feel another pressing into her shoulder. She sighed. Oh, for the comfortable feather bed she'd enjoyed at her mother's home in San Francisco. Or the one at Mrs. Collin's boarding house in Everett.

The breeze from the mountain died down. She heard an owl who-whoo as it ghosted through the trees, searching for nocturnal prey.

Listening to the nearby creek soughing against the rocks, she turned her thoughts to her heavenly Father. Finally sleep came.

She woke with a start. Moonlight filtered through the canvas above her head. What had wakened her? *It's going to be one of those nights, she* thought grumpily. Then she heard it again. Furtive scrapings, a soft thump.

She sat up, careful not to awaken Evan, squirmed out of her sleeping bag, and slipped her boots on. Wrapping herself in her shawl, she peeked past the tent flap. In the splashes of moonlight she saw Bear, lying alert at the end of his rope. He flicked his ears at her but kept his eyes on their neighbor's campsite. Creeping to him, she put her arm around his neck. She felt the intensity of his attention, and followed his gaze.

Something moved among the trees surrounding Wentzel's campsite. A flash of moonlight reflected off a shovel blade. She heard the stamp of a hoof. Wentzel's horse bobbed his head and snorted under what appeared to be a load of bags and bundles. In the middle of the night? Why was Wentzel digging?

Mosquitoes whined about her ears. She felt a small sting, then others. It took all her will power not to slap at them. Bear thrust his head forward, intent on the man's actions. Now he'd stooped and was brushing dirt from something. He lifted a small, heavy object. Metal, she thought. A box? A can? He hefted it. She heard a faint rattle of something like pebbles.

He seemed to be smoothing the disturbed dirt with the shovel. Then the shadow that was Wentzel moved to the horse, stuffed the container deep into one of the packs and added the shovel to the load. He swung his head toward the neighboring campsites then, watching and listening.

When he turned in her direction, Melinda crouched lower and held her breath. Not until she heard muffled footfalls move cautiously away did she venture a look. Sure enough, Wentzel and the packhorse were leaving, carrying something he obviously didn't want anyone to know about. Bear whined softly.

She patted him. "Shh. Stay, Bear."

Keeping her tent between herself and the man, she peered toward the glacier trail. Wentzel was probably out of earshot now, but she tried not to make any noise as she darted to the Prosper's tent and tapped softly on the side of it. "Benjamin!" she hissed. "Caroline! Wake up."

When she heard them stirring, she crossed to the other tent and woke the occupants. "Hurry, Wentzel's getting away," she whispered when their heads popped out.

His dad sent Lafe to wake some of the other men. He and Conner Gilvray questioned her.

"He had his horse loaded and ready to travel. I saw him dig up something small and heavy. He hid it in one of the packs."

Nobody said the word "gold," but Melinda knew the story of the miners' missing treasure was on all their minds. Even if the container held no gold, she was confident that the mistreated horse had been stolen. Things wouldn't go well for Wentzel if the prospectors caught up with him.

Her stomach twisted. How did she end up in the middle of this, anyway?

As she heard Lafe returning to their campsite with other men, she crawled back into her tent, folded the shawl she'd been wrapped in, and pulled on her skirt and jacket.

Evan turned over and asked sleepily, "What's happening, Mindy?"

"I'm just getting up early. Go back to sleep. You don't have to get up yet."

He yawned. "All right."

Back outside, she and Caroline listened as the men discussed in low voices the best way to proceed.

"If Wentzel knows we're following him, the first thing he'd do is get rid of the evidence."

"No way to keep him from hearing us on that narrow trail."

"Maybe there is." It was Lafe's voice. "Remember, Jake, when we were out scouting for more timber? How we circled around that first hill and came out on the glacier trail? It's starting to get light. If we go right now, I think we can get ahead of him. Sort of hide in ambush."

"Is there a place wide enough where we can surround him?"

"Yes," Lafe said. "Where we came out, the trail was back from the edge of the bluff far enough that we could hide in the brush on all sides."

"What if he's armed?" Caroline worried.

"I've got my shotgun," said one of the prospectors.

"Me, too," said another. "Let's go."

"God keep you," Caroline whispered, giving each of her sons and her husband a quick hug.

The women watched until the men reached the hill and turned off the trail, making their way single file cross-country behind Lafe and a man with a shotgun. Then they lit a fire and started a big pot of coffee.

Melinda and Caroline took their coffee cups to the edge of the trees, where they could more easily watch for the men coming back, and sat down on a fallen log. A breeze came up with the rising sun, encouraging the mosquitoes to seek shelter in the moss and bushes. Melinda didn't really want coffee, but it gave her hands something to do as they waited.

"It sounds strange to say this," she said to her friend, "but I hope, I truly hope, there's a good explanation for what Wentzel did. I hope my suspicions about the horse are wrong."

"You saw what you saw, Melinda. It's not normal for someone to act like he did."

Melinda answered with a little shriek. Something soft and wet had poked her in the ribs. She heard a giggle.

"It's just Bear, Mindy."

"Evan! Don't sneak up on people like that!"

"I didn't sneak." Evan looked insulted. "I got up and nobody was around. So I came to find you. Why are you out here?"

"It's okay." She put her arm around his waist and squeezed. "Come, sit down with us and I'll tell you why we're here."

She told him about their neighbor's doings early that morning and the men going after him. "If they find him, there'll probably be a trial. I don't want you to be there, Evan. You and I will find something else to do."

"As will I," Caroline said. "It might be unpleasant business."

Bear turned to stare up the mountainside. Melinda squinted in that direction. "They found him."

Someone who looked like Lafe led the packhorse down the trail. Others surrounded a man in a droopy felt hat, stumbling along with hands tied behind his back. Even from this distance, he projected an air of bravado. As the group came closer, his gaze took in Melinda and Evan. He sent her a look of pure malevolence.

Without a doubt, he blamed her for his situation. But how could he know?

"Stinkin' spy!" He spat the words. Oh. He'd seen her inspecting the horse's back, that's how. He knew she'd connected him with the missing animal.

One of the guards gave him a shove. "Shut up. You'll get your chance to talk."

The group moved to a clearing near the river. One man tied the rope that bound Wentzel's hands to a tree, while another relieved the horse of his burdens, including the ever-present blanket. The man swore, and motioned others to look at the creature's back. Benjamin rummaged through one of the panniers, then the other.

Wentzel sat on the ground, fulminating at the men around him. "Leave my property alone! What gives you the right to chase a body down and steal his belongings?"

Benjamin ignored him. He turned and held up a small metal container. Unscrewing the rusty lid, he looked inside. He nodded, letting her know her suspicions were correct.

She might be a 'stinking spy,' but perhaps those miners would get their hard-won gold back. Suddenly she felt a lot less burdened.

Melinda poured coffee into the cups the searchers brought to Caroline's tent. Though the sun was just tipping the far mountain peaks, Forest Camp had awakened. Word spread quickly and men gathered for the trial in the nearby clearing. Melinda wanted Evan away from there before proceedings began.

"Evan, you and I are going fishing today," she said.

"But I want to see what ... "

"No, we don't need to see what goes on. We can hear about it later."

Evan didn't look happy, but then he thought about going fishing. "Okay," he said. "Can we take a picnic?"

"Yes. You can put our breakfast in a bag." She took a sip of her cold coffee. "Find our hats, and be sure to take your knife and extra hooks and lines. We'll have a fish fry tonight!"

Evan ran off and came back, ready to go fishing.

"Lead the way, Evan."

"Wait," Caroline said. "Where will you be?"

"Lafe and Jake took me to a nice place around that first bend in the river," Evan said. "I think Mindy will be able to catch something there."

"Right," Melinda smiled at his unconscious superiority.

As they started off, she glanced back. Solemn prospectors crowded the clearing. They faced Benjamin Prosper, and the still-shackled Wentzel, who stood staring back at them defiantly. She shivered. Didn't he realize what waited if he was found guilty? He'd do well to act a little bit penitent.

She followed Evan along the riverbank for about a quarter mile, until they came to the sharp bend where she knew several boats had come to grief. A ledge of rock jutted up from the river bottom there. She could tell that high water often covered the ledge. Cobbles had caught in crevices where the speeding river had whirled them round and round, grinding out potholes in the ledge. Small rocks still lay in the hollows, waiting for the river to rise again to continue their work. On the downstream side of the exposed ledge lay a large, quiet eddy of water where fish could lurk.

Evan used his jackknife to cut willow poles, while she searched the shallow water at the edge of the stream for caddis-fly larvae. At Silverton, they'd dug earthworms to use for bait, but Evan told her Alaskan fish liked these little creatures, which crawled the stream bottom protected by armor of their own making.

They assembled their fishing poles and tossed out their lines. Then Evan unpacked their breakfast, a couple of last night's biscuits and an assortment of dried fruit. She asked God's blessing on the food and for guidance for the men sitting in judgement on Wentzel this morning. She also asked for Quin's protection, wherever he might be.

"Do you think Uncle Quin might have stopped here?" Evan asked.

She looked up at the tree-crowned bluffs across the narrow river, and the blue, blue sky above them. "Maybe. Maybe he even caught some fish for his breakfast."

"Oh! I got one!" Evan grabbed for his pole as it went sliding across the rocks. He caught it just in time and jerked the line. In moments a nice trout lay flapping at his feet.

Though Melinda didn't feel like celebrating, she cheered his catch. Soon she felt a tug on her line as well, and Evan cheered and clapped as her smaller fish landed near his.

They were interrupted by Jake's shout.

"Melinda, the miner's court wants to ask you some questions." He clambered down to the rocks where they stood. "Mom says I'm to stay with Evan."

Dread clutched at her heart. She'd hoped she wouldn't have to be involved. As for Jake, he didn't look happy about missing the trial. She knew he'd prefer to be in on the excitement.

She thanked him, handed him her pole, and trudged back to camp.

She felt the tension at the miner's court as soon as she reached the clearing. Wentzel, no longer bound to the tree, but with hands still tied, stood defiantly facing the jurors. Benjamin called her to stand beside himself and asked, "Do you promise to tell the truth and nothing but the truth?"

"I promise," she answered, avoiding the angry eyes of the defendant.

"We have inspected the horse's hide and come to the conclusion that his identifying markings have been covered over with some kind of dye, just as you told us." Benjamin said. "Can you tell us what made you check for that?"

"I was just curious, wondering why the poor animal had to wear that filthy old blanket all the time. I was running a little pie shop at Glacier City when a prospector's horse disappeared. At the same time, a bottle of shoe polish on our shelf went missing. The stolen horse had distinctive white spots on his back. I guess I was looking for those spots when I looked under the blanket."

"Yes. Well, the blanket hid more than a paint job." Benjamin gestured toward the pack horse, nibbling grass at the edge of the clearing. Melinda gasped. The hair had nearly been rubbed off its withers. Knotted scars ran across the bare spots. What kind of man would mistreat an animal like that?

"I told you how it happened ... " Wentzel interrupted.

"Yes, you've already had a chance to explain," Mr. Prosper said. "Now, Miss McCrae, please tell us what you saw the defendant doing this morning."

She described the noises that woke her before daybreak, the horse loaded and ready to travel, and how she'd watched Wentzel dig something from the ground.

"What did he dig up?"

"It looked like a metal jar or can, about this big." She measured with her hands. "He put it in one of horse's bundles, and then led him toward the glacier trail."

Wentzel slumped to the ground, his air of bravado gone.

"Was that when you called us?"

"Yes."

Benjamin held up a dirty metal jug. "Was this what he dug up?" He handed it to her.

She hadn't expected it to feel so heavy. She shook it slightly and heard the contents rattle. "It was still quite dark, but I think it is."

"Read what's scratched there, on the side."

Melinda turned the jug so she could decipher the two words scratched into the metal. "It's a name," she said. "Jack Scan ... Scanlon."

One of the jurors leaped to his feet. "I know Jack Scanlon," he said. "Jack was one of the two prospectors who came through here minus the gold they meant to take to Valdez."

"Will you swear to that?" Benjamin Prosper asked.

The man stepped forward and raised his hand. "I swear that Jack Scanlon told us his gold had been stolen."

"You have heard the testimony of the witnesses," Benjamin said to the jury. "Is there anything else that should be said before you render a verdict?"

Melinda looked at the ashen face of Wentzel. A pitiful specimen of humanity if there ever was one. Had anyone ever loved him? Yes, God loved him, unlovely though he was. Didn't everyone deserve a second chance?

"I have something to say." She was as surprised as anyone by the words that burst forth. "I know thievery can't be tolerated on a frontier like this. But will hanging this man make us the better for it?"

She saw second thoughts cross the determined faces of some of the jurors. They began to argue among themselves, and she turned away. "May I be excused now, Benjamin?"

"Wait until the verdict is reached."

Reluctantly, she sat down on a stone and watched the discussion. Finally the men returned to the places where they'd been sitting. One, elected as foreman, stepped forward.

"We have a verdict."

"Stand, Mr. Wentzel." Benjamin took his elbow and urged him to his feet.

"Proceed." He nodded to the foreman.

"Guilty, as charged."

"Recommended sentence?"

"In deference to Miss McCrae's plea, his life shall be spared. But, because of his cruelty to a helpless animal, he must run a gauntlet of his peers who will inflict the same kind of punishment this horse received.

"He will be allowed to take only the blanket which hid the afflictions of this animal, and a small bag of food. Once through the gauntlet, Mr. Wentzel is free to run for the pass and to head for Prince William Sound. People will follow to be sure he gets started. If he makes it, we hope he will decide to reform himself. If he doesn't make it, then it's a well-deserved end to his story."

Wentzel stood speechless, shivering with dread, while the group split up and went to cut long, limber willow saplings. Someone brought a cloth bag with food in it. Someone else folded the filthy horse blanket and dropped it at his feet.

The men lined up in a double row, brandishing their sticks. Benjamin untied Wentzel's wrists and told him to take the blanket and the food and run for his life. The man went down on his knees, blubbering. "It's certain death! I'll never make it over the glacier with no outfit."

Someone shouted, "It's more of a chance than you deserve, you scum."

"C'mon, coward, or we'll come get you."

Melinda saw him take a deep breath, grit his teeth, and plunge toward the double row of men, into a melee of swinging sticks, grabbing hands, howls of pain. A couple of times he went down and scrambled back to his feet.

She saw him emerge from the other end of the gauntlet, running crouched over with flailing limbs, the worn soles of his boots slapping the trail. Another picture flashed through her mind. She herself flung to the ground. Through a forest of people's legs, someone ran in a crouch, shoe soles flapping, limbs flailing. A skinny, unkempt person who had just stolen her school tuition. A man who'd watched her leaving the bank and recognized her when he saw her again at Glacier City, though she herself had never seen his face. Beyond a shadow of a doubt, she knew. That person and Wentzel were one and the same.

CHAPTER TWENTY-TWO

QUIN

More than a month before Melinda's arrival at Forest Camp, Quintrell Chenowith had left that place with his packhorse and several companions. As he hiked along the upper Klutina River, he took photographs for the paper and interviewed people coming and going. The trail was narrow and rocky. In places it skirted along the bluff, with scarcely room for two people to pass each other.

In one of those spots, he stepped to the outside of the trail with his horse to allow someone to pass. A rock rolled under his foot. He felt sharp pain as his foot skidded over the edge. He threw himself forward. Above his head, he heard the packhorse snort, but it didn't panic. The traveller saw him fall and dragged him to safety.

The foot hurt--oh, it hurt! But he could move it. It was probably just sprained, he thought, but what would he do now? Sitting on a rock uphill of the trail, he removed his boot. The ankle had already turned blue and puffed up.

"Here, take my bandana," said the passerby. "It's none too clean, but you can fold it diagonally and wrap your ankle. That will give you a little support." He handed him his walking stick to use.

Quin thanked the man. He unloaded most of his horse's bundles and left them beside the rock. He'd send his companions back for them. Then he climbed on the horse's back and set off toward Peninsula Camp, where he'd been ever since.

Now, it was mid-July. He remained at Klutina Lake while his friends prospected along a stream coming down from the mountains.

Before he started his next dispatch, he would write to his fiancee. If Melinda missed him half as much as he missed her, her mind and prayers would be with him, despite her busy schedule there in San Francisco. He wouldn't tell her about the sprained ankle, though. That would only worry her. Besides, it had nearly healed.

Leaning on his stick and carrying his portable writing desk-- really just a thin, lidded box--he climbed to a sunny spot above the lake and looked around. What a wonderful contrast to the dark, closed-in mining tunnels where he'd spent so many years of his working life! Settling into a niche in the rocks, he retrieved pen, paper, and ink from the box and began his letter.

Klutina Lake, Alaska
July 10, 1898

My Dearest Melinda,

What I wouldn't give for one of your newsy, loving letters right now. But those letters are probably piling up at Mrs. Collins' boarding house and I won't see them until I return from this adventure in Alaska. I hope mine are reaching you, my love, although mail service here is very irregular.

He looked up from the paper, scanning a view worthy of an artist's painting.

I wish I could share this beautiful place with you! I'm camped in a spot that surely must be as close to heaven as any God ever created. The waters of the lake are blue and cold and full of fish. Fresh breezes sweep our campsite free of the voracious mosquitoes that rise in clouds most places. Wildflowers and ripening berries cover the hillsides. I'm reminded in many ways of the mountains at Monte Cristo. Klutina Lake lacks only your presence to make it the perfect resting spot.

Right now I'm hearing the shouts of people near the lake. They are sawing lumber or hammering boats together. But I'll be walking with my packhorse, all the way to Copper Center.

My fellow sojourners are torn between prospecting here or continuing toward the Copper River. I believe if there was gold to be found here, we would be hearing the sounds of a great city a-building, rather than those of saws and hammers fashioning craft to carry their owners down the Klutina.

You would understand my appreciation of this place, Melinda, had you journeyed over the Valdez Glacier with us. Suffice it to say it was the strangest, wildest, most uncomfortable journey I've ever undertaken. We fought rain, snow, wind, and sleet! That was in addition to ice, slush, and crevasses. I am young and strong, with a packhorse to carry my equipment and supplies, whereas some of my companions are much older. They had to make many trips back and forth over the glacier in order to get all their supplies this far.

I will write more soon. Now I must pack photo negatives and write a dispatch so they'll be ready to go along with this letter when a mail carrier comes by. Know that you are always in my thoughts. I look forward to the day we shall be joined in the blessed estate of matrimony and separated no more!

Your loving future husband,
Quin

Melinda sat alone at Forest Camp. The brilliant early August sunlight had somehow lost its sparkle. Though leaves were showing the colors of autumn, the vivid carmines and golds seemed dull.

She couldn't dismiss the image of the scrambling, cringing form of that pitiful thief and the switches whistling through the air. She wanted her mother. She wanted Quin!

All of the men had left the clearing now, and sounds of saws and hammers started up again. A couple of miners had followed Wentzel up the trail to make sure he kept going. She hunched on her rock, feeling relief that Wentzel was gone, yet grieving her part in his downfall.

Caroline grasped her shoulder. "Melinda, snap out of it. You saved his life, you know. Maybe he'll take this second chance you were responsible for. Maybe he'll change his ways."

Melinda looked up, Caroline's face blurred by her tears. "Thank you. It's good of you to say that."

Caroline sounded like she was scolding one of her boys. "Don't you see how the men are watching you? Your grieving bewilders them. You know they had to do something!"

Melinda sighed. "Yes. I'm sorry." She straightened her shoulders and stood up. Then she told Caroline the rest of the story.

"He's the man who stole my money in San Francisco," she said. "I'm sure he recognized me, but I didn't realize who he was until I saw him running away."

Caroline gave a start. "Then he really got off easy." She put her arm around Melinda's waist as they headed back to the tents. "All the better that he's gone!"

"Yes." Melinda laughed a little. "If not for Wentzel, I'd never have met you. I'd never have come to Alaska. I'd still be waiting for Quin in San Francisco!" *And,* she thought, *I'd be very close to becoming a teacher!*

The Prosper party had gone back to work on the sturdy boat they were building. Jake and Evan returned to camp with several more nice fish and cleaned them before joining the boat builders. The women decided to pick blueberries for cobbler to go with the fish fry.

The cobbler was so successful that in the following days, while the men finished the boat, the women picked berries and turned them into more cobblers in Caroline's oven. Unsuccessful prospectors heading back to Valdez shed a little of their discouragement when they smelled the aroma. Most were broke, but managed to find the price of a piece of cobbler.

A few were ill with scurvy. Caroline made sure they knew berries would help. Many of them were city people and afraid to try unfamiliar foods for fear they were poisonous. They'd subsisted on beans and salt pork, not realizing that natural foods full of the vitamin C that could prevent scurvy were all around: moose meat, greens, even spruce needle tea.

It became Evan's task to move Wentzel's stolen horse from one grassy glade to another, and to lead him to the river to drink several times a day. Melinda could almost see the hollows between the creature's ribs filling out. One night after the day's work was done, Conroy Gilvray mentioned the horse's increasing strength.

"We need to get him back to Valdez, before winter sets in," he said. "How about if we cut enough of that grass by the creek to make hay? We could send him with someone returning to Valdez, with hay for the trip. The military expedition could keep him until the owner shows up."

A few days later, the horse set out on the trail, loaded with hay and a few items belonging to the men who'd agreed to take him to Valdez. Evan had scrubbed at the boot polish staining his rump with soapy water. The white spots had reappeared.

New gold-seekers continued to stream through Forest Camp. At the river's edge, some of them hastily knocked together boxy craft that Benjamin Prosper said would probably fall apart before they made the thirteen miles to the lake.

They had watched one of those boats collide with a submerged boulder before reaching the first crook in the river. It floated downstream in pieces. Chagrined, the owners salvaged what goods they could and spread them along the bank to dry. Then they'd started the journey to Klutina Lake on foot, carrying what they could on their backs.

When they finished their boat, the Prosper party dragged it to a quiet eddy of the river, tied it to a tree, and sank it so the water would swell the wood and seal the seams. In the morning they emptied and refloated it, checking for leaks. When they found none, everyone helped break camp and load their goods into the boat. Melinda, Caroline and Evan filled their packs with sugar, flour and other foods that needed to stay dry. They filled Bear's pouches as well.

"Please, can't I ride with the men?" Evan begged.

"Don't you remember what happened to Jake when he tried to wade the river?" Caroline told him. "He's bigger and stronger than most men, but he couldn't get out without help. And the river here is fiercer and wider."

Evan looked pleadingly at Melinda. "No, and that's that," she said.

The corners of his mouth turned down, but he said no more.

The men tied down the load and climbed in, each grabbing a long pole which they'd use to push themselves away from obstacles in the river. "Untie the rope, Evan," yelled Benjamin. "We're off!"

Disappointment still on his face, Evan did as asked. They shoved out into the current, which caught the boat and whirled it, dipping and bobbing, out of sight before the women and Evan had even shouldered their packs. They tucked the mosquito netting hanging from their hat brims securely into their collars and started along the riverside trail, Evan and Bear in the lead.

They caught up with the boat within half a mile. It had hung up on a gravel bar in the middle of the river. The men, barefoot and with pants rolled up, were out in the icy current, pushing with all their might to shove the craft into deeper water. Suddenly it broke loose and the men leaped back aboard. Away they went again, using their poles to avoid colliding with boulders or logs or even upright trees where the river had overflowed its banks.

Along the way the walkers passed piles of salvaged goods from boats that had come to grief. Grim-faced owners were trying to dry them or going back and forth on the trail with belongings on their backs. A few had hired pack horses to help.

Another boat careened past, barely avoiding tree roots protruding from the eroding bank below them. Evan noted the terror-stricken expressions on the two men trying to guide the boat. "They don't look like they're having much fun," he commented.

Melinda swung her pack to the ground and rolled her aching shoulders. "Aren't you glad you're on solid ground?"

"Mr. Prosper's boat is bigger and stronger," he said stubbornly. A few moments later the boat they were watching tried to skirt a whirlpool and got caught. The men paddled frantically to avoid being sucked down as the boat whirled around the edge. Finally they broke free and shot toward the rapids downstream.

In late afternoon, the little party was still struggling along the trail. "Bear is tired, Mindy. Can't we stop?"

She glanced back at the boy, no longer in the lead. His face looked hot and sweaty beneath his mosquito net.

Caroline stopped walking. "These pests are biting through my clothes," she said. "We need to get where we can build a fire. One good thing is that we've not come across our boat, and the river is calmer here. Maybe they've made it to the lake, and are setting up camp for us!"

They trudged on for another mile. Suddenly Bear yipped and plunged ahead to greet Lafe and Jake, hurrying toward them.

"We made it, Ma," called Jake. He reached them, and shouldered his mother's pack.

Lafe took Melinda's from her, and jibed at his brother. "You almost didn't make it! You fell out of the boat."

"I didn't either fall out. I was trying to keep us from crashing into a boulder, and the pole broke!"

"Lucky Pa grabbed you as you went under."

"Yeah, Man! That water was cold!"

Their mom wiped away tears of relief and hugged both her sons. "Praise God, you're safe!"

Melinda relieved Evan of his smaller pack. For the first time she realized the apprehension Caroline had been hiding behind her cheerful chatter along the trail. From the look on Evan's face, she could tell he was rethinking his disappointment at missing the boat ride.

Grateful for the help with their burdens, they followed Jake and Lafe toward Peninsula Camp.

The men had already set up Melinda's small tent and the larger ones in a cluster near the lake. She rolled out their sleeping bags, arranged their belongings as best she could, then fixed a quick meal of pilot bread with peanut butter. She tucked Evan into his bed, then collapsed on her own.

She woke to sunlight seeping through the canvas. The tent rippled above her head. Must be a little windy, she thought. Good! No mosquitoes for a while. Evan snored softly. She dressed, brushed and pinned up her hair, and aching in every muscle, pushed back the tent flap and slipped outside. Bear stretched and wagged his tail. She scratched his head and looked around.

This camp consisted of several dozen tents scattered across a peninsula which jutted out into a sparkling, beautifully blue lake. The ground was mostly clear of the thick brush that would hold swarms of mosquitoes such as had plagued them yesterday. A few blackened snags stood sentry. Obviously a wildfire had burned here. A cool breeze blew from the direction of the glacier.

This was a good place for a camp. Most everyone bound to or from the Copper River had to come this way. Had Quin stopped here?

Hopefully she'd get news about her fiancé soon. Maybe he'd even return before she had to make a decision about going on or giving up.

Lake Klutina, according to some she'd talked to, was about twenty miles long, an easy trip for a boat. After that, they'd travel by river for many miles. Or by foot through swamps and forests.

She'd like to stay right here. Fireweed and lupine were blooming everywhere. Close to the tent, a few lingonberries reddened. Nearby hills rose to meet the peaks of the Chugach Range. She remembered the berries they couldn't stop to pluck yesterday as they plodded over those foothills. Blueberries, sweet black raspberries and red ones, tart currants, wild strawberries ....

Caroline Prosper stepped out of her tent with a couple of kettles. Melinda waved hello, grabbed her own kettle, and followed Caroline to the bank of a small stream which emptied into the lake. They dipped their containers full, then Melinda splashed her face with the icy water. "Whew! That woke me up!"

Caroline laughed, and washed her own face. "I could have slept all day," she said. "But the men were up early, off to see what they can find out about mining prospects around here. They're eager to get started. It will soon be mid-August and winter comes early this far north."

"Will you go with them while they prospect?" Melinda asked. Pushing on into the wilderness without the Prospers' company was an alarming thought.

"If they make a strike, I'll join them and do the housekeeping chores so they can put in as many hours working as possible. Until then, I'll stay here and make some money with my cooking. You saw all the berries yesterday, and I might be able to catch fish in the lake.

"There are rabbits and other game too," Melinda added. "I thought I'd stay here, too, until a mail carrier comes through from Copper Center. I'm hoping for word about Quin before going any further. I could help you for a while, if you like."

"That's a wonderful idea," Caroline said. "You ran that little restaurant at Glacier City. We could do something like that."

Carrying their water, they returned to their tents.

Melinda set up her stove on a spot of bare ground and kindled a fire. She added dried beans to the kettle and set them to simmer with a piece of salt pork. She sliced a couple of pieces to fry for breakfast and made Johnny cakes to go with it. The aroma drew a sleepy Evan out of the tent. He said little while savoring the crispy-edged Johnny cakes, delicious even without syrup or honey. Then he looked around at his surroundings and grinned. "Bet there's fish in that lake."

"Maybe you can catch our dinner for tonight."

"Yeah!" He chewed on his slice of fried salt pork. "Do you think the people here are all going to the Copper River country?"

"Some are. Our men plan to prospect here first. And some, like that man over there," she nodded toward a ragged figure near a well-worn tent, "are going back over the pass."

"I guess he didn't find any gold."

"No, probably not." She watched the stoop-shouldered man puttering over a small cookstove. One of the legs was missing, she noticed, but he had stacked flat stones in its place to level the rusty relic. The scents of coffee and wood smoke floated over to their camp, but he seemed to have no food to go with his brew. She flipped the last Johnny cakes onto a third tin plate, added the last slice of salt pork, and picked up her cup.

"Do you want to come with me to say hello, Evan? I'm going to see if he'll trade me a cup of his coffee for these Johnny cakes."

"Yes, but can I have one of those for Bear?"

Bear had been drooling as he watched them eat. He caught the cake Evan tossed him and swallowed it in one gulp. He strained at the end of his rope, hopeful for another.

Their neighbor, who said to call him Mathias, was happy to make the trade. He wolfed down the Johnny cakes almost as fast as Bear had swallowed his. Melinda wondered if he was out of supplies. He was terribly thin, his face haggard. He appeared much too old to attempt the trek back over the mountains, though his voice sounded younger.

"Are you traveling alone?" she asked.

"Yes. My partner drowned when our boat capsized on the way to Copper Center."

"Oh, I'm sorry."

"I lost almost everything, though I managed to salvage this cookstove. It was too heavy to float away. I had to turn back. This whole gold rush is one big fraud, anyway."

Evan tugged at her elbow. "Mindy, ask if he's seen Uncle Quin."

The man looked down at the boy. "Is that what you and the young lady are doing here? You're looking for someone?"

"My fiancé," Melinda said with pride. "His name is Quintrell Chenoweth. He's a journalist, writing for the Daily Dispatch. He's carrying camera gear and talking to people about their experiences."

"He's very tall," Evan said. "About your height."

Melinda smiled. The prospector was only average height, but then, to Evan he probably looked tall. "He has dark eyes and dark wavy hair," she added.

"I did meet someone like that," he told them. "But it was nearly a month ago. In fact, I met him at the camp at the other end of this lake. He had a packhorse, and left ahead of me, so I never caught up with him again."

A month ago! Where might Quin be by now?

CHAPTER TWENTY-THREE

PENINSULA CAMP

Mathias handed the plate back to Melinda with thanks.

"You're welcome," she said. "Thank you for the coffee. How long do you expect it will take you to get back to Valdez?"

"Oh, a day to Glacier Camp, then if my luck holds, maybe two days on the glacier. I'll take the canvas rain fly for shelter, and leave the tent here. I don't have much else to carry."

"What about your stove?" It had a small oven. Caroline could make good use of that, she thought.

"No use for it any more. Do you want it?"

"My friend and I hope to make some money cooking while her family is prospecting. We'd love to have it."

She didn't want to appear nosy, but had to ask. "Do you have food?"

"Not much. But I can make it for three days."

She thought for a moment. She didn't have that much food herself, but she could give him some of the beans that were simmering in the kettle right now, and there was pilot bread, and a little dried fruit left.

She studied his tent. "Would you trade me that tent for some food? We can use it while we're here. I'd offer you our small tent, but we'll need it for the rest of our journey."

The man's face lit with a faint smile. He agreed to the trade. "I'm leaving first thing tomorrow. I have some rabbit snares to check today, and I hope to catch a fish or two before I go."

She hastened over to tell Caroline about her bargain.

"I have a little money left," Melinda said. "I'll give him something extra for the tent so he can buy a meal or two when he gets to Valdez. If he wasn't broke, he wouldn't be so thin."

When Caroline heard about the stove, her eyes lit up. "I can give him an extra blanket," she said. "He'll need more than a piece of canvas to stay warm on the glacier."

Their own menfolk came back to camp just before sunset, having followed a promising creek up into the hills. They'd panned out a few flakes of gold and were eager to continue their explorations.

"We didn't see anyone else on that creek," Benjamin told them. "We want to spend a few days there."

"Fine," his wife told them. "You and the boys chop a big pile of firewood and Melinda and I will earn a little gold ourselves while you're gone."

The men set to work cutting up some trees scorched by the earlier forest fire.

Their neighbor returned mid-morning with a number of snowshoe hares he'd captured in his snares. Evan helped him skin and clean them. He gave a couple to Evan for his help. When Melinda saw them, she immediately thought of the Cornish pasties that Quin had shared with her when she first met him in Monte Cristo. There wasn't a lot of meat on each rabbit, but cut into small bits and mixed with rehydrated vegetables, it would make a good filling for the pocket-sized pastries.

She went to work, while Evan accompanied Mathias to the lake. The man had dried some fish to take on his journey. He told Evan how he had done it. He showed him the rack he'd made, in an open spot where the breeze would blow the flies away. Evan could use it to dry fish for Bear.

Caroline asked the men to build a work table outside her tent. They planed off three sides of some four-foot poles and laid them next to each other across a frame, using cord to lash them together. It wasn't the most level of surfaces, but by spreading a floured piece of canvas on top, Melinda made a place to assemble her pasties.

Mathias's three-legged stove sat near her tent, smoke puffing from the stovepipe.

Fellow campers stopped by to comment approvingly on the prospect of eating something other than their own cooking. But Melinda's pasties would mostly go with their menfolk tomorrow. She'd give some to their neighbor, as well. She patted out a round of dough, placed a mound of vegetables and meat in the center, and sprinkled it with salt and pepper. Then she folded half the round over the filling and crimped the edges together. She slid the first pan of four pasties into the oven.

By the time the golden pasties were cooling under a cloth at one end of the table, Melinda had another batch ready for the oven.

"Look what I caught, Mindy!" Evan appeared beside her, holding up a fish half as long as he was tall. "It's a pike! He almost broke my line. I had to go in after him!"

She glanced at his wet pant legs. Mathias grinned behind him.

"Goodness!" she exclaimed. "That's a monster!"

"Pike are bony, but very good eating," said their neighbor. "Come on, Evan, I'll show you how to skin and fillet it."

But Evan had noticed what Melinda was baking. He licked his lips. "Pasties! My favorite!"

Melinda cut one in half. Steam curled from the filling. "Here, half for each of you. Careful. It's hot!"

They took her offering and went back to the lake to clean the several fish they'd caught. Later, Melinda saw Evan standing on a stump next to the rack, hanging strips in a row to dry. His pike would be their dinner.

The next day, the Prosper menfolk and their partner Conner Gilvray rowed away early for the creek where they hoped to strike it rich.

Their neighbor Mathias swept out his tent with a spruce branch, said goodbye to Evan and the women, and started up the glacier trail with pasties in his pockets and some of Melinda's beans in his kettle.

Melinda and Caroline set about readying their restaurant. Evan had noticed the boat builders trimming the branches from the trees they cut to whipsaw into planks. He dragged some fresh branches to camp and used the hatchet to trim them. He piled the bushy ends on the floor of their neighbor's old tent, as he'd seen some of the men doing. Now he and Melinda had evergreen-scented mattresses of springy boughs to sleep on. He cut the leftover wood to add to their firewood pile.

"That boy is worth his weight in gold," Caroline told Melinda.

"Yes, he's wonderfully responsible for only eight years old," she replied, smiling as Evan seemed to grow a couple inches taller at her words. She wished Quin could see how well his nephew had adapted to this life. For that matter, he'd probably be surprised that either of them had made it this far. Well, she admitted to herself, it wasn't her own efforts. God had sent people to help, over and over.

She said as much to Caroline. "I'm so grateful for you and your family. You had more than enough to do without helping us."

"We're here to help each other," Caroline replied. "Besides, you're not that much older than my boys. You're like a daughter and a good friend all in one."

The two of them moved the work table and the stove to sit between two trees near Mathias's tent. If it rained, they could rig a canvas awning overhead.

When neighbors found out about the planned restaurant, two of them offered to saw a log into rounds. They rolled them up the slope for customers to sit on.

"We'll keep our menu simple," Caroline said. "We can cook rice or beans. We have dehydrated potatoes, and some dried vegetables. There's fish from the lake. Someone might bring in game. And we can make berry cobbler. That's easier than pie."

Limited though their offerings were, the women immediately had all the business they could take care of.

In the mornings, Evan and Melinda picked berries on the slopes above camp, while Caroline did the day's baking. Each evening Caroline counted the day's earnings into two piles. Melinda cached her share in her backpack.

Despite feeling an urgency to continue the search for Quin, Melinda enjoyed the stay at the lake, especially when, a few days later, a group of boisterous young people rowed up the lake. Cheerful voices rang out as they unloaded their boat and set up camp. These were adventurers, not the usual older, discouraged men giving up on their last hope to make it good. Among the voices, she heard a woman's laughter. She recognized that laugh!

She ran to greet Lillian Moore, who was delighted to find Melinda at Peninsula Camp. Lillian introduced her to her party. "I've got a claim staked," she said. "I even found a little gold. But when my friends decided to head back, I came along. I can always continue mining next spring."

"What happened to Captain Abercrombie's expedition?"

"We had a frightful trip over the glacier. It's not a practical way to reach the interior."

Melinda already knew that.

"Captain Abercrombie sent some of the men back to Valdez to work on a trail through Keystone Canyon. He went on to Copper Center, planning to split the group again there for more exploring. When my friends wanted to prospect along the Klutina, that's when I decided I'd do the same."

Melinda looked at her carefree friend in amazement. "You're so casual about it. Aren't you ever afraid?"

"Of course. Sometimes. You can't take anything for granted out here in the wilderness."

Lillian began a tale of their return after several weeks of staking claims. "The woods are burning," she said, gesturing toward the brown haze in the distance. "Cheechakos have no idea how to use fire in this country. They build fires without clearing the duff down to bare soil first, and don't make sure the fires are out. The fire smolders along under the surface until it reaches a tree or bush. Then, voila! A forest fire!

"We came to a burned stretch that lasted about ten miles. Trees had fallen across each other in big piles. We walked those logs for miles. The ground was still smoking. Under the surface the roots and moss were smoldering. We were constantly afraid we'd break through. Every time we came to water, we took off our boots to cool our feet!

"We helped each other over the worst places, and we made it. You can too, if you use common sense, and accept help when it's offered."

Yes, that was true. Sometimes, though, Melinda wondered if she overrode her common sense with fear of what might happen. Isn't that what landed her out here in the wilds of Alaska in the first place? Well, if Lillian could make it, so could she.

Lillian talked on. "Anyway, about Captain Abercrombie. I heard him say he's reporting to the government that the glacier is not a feasible way to reach the Interior. That's why he hopes instead to connect the Keystone Canyon route with the Klondike gold fields."

What if Quin had decided to go on to the Klondike? That could surely be part of the story he wanted to tell his readers. She'd heard the Klondike region lay more than 170 miles beyond Copper Center. She still didn't know if he'd reached the former settlement.

Lillian paused. Then she asked, "What about you, Melinda? I thought you'd be well on your way to Copper Center now."

Melinda told her friend about the Prosper party taking them in. "The men decided to try their luck in the hills not far from here, so Caroline and I are running a restaurant until they get back."

"Oh, I did something like that for a while," Lillian said. "The men traded flour for my apple dumplings, and they gave me other things too, like this." She showed her the small vial of gold dust that hung around her neck. "Someone even gave me a good heavy pair of German socks. They'll keep my feet warm on the glacier."

Melinda dreaded the trip back across the glacier. She told Lillian about getting lost in the storm and the close call trying to cross the crevasse. "But," she said, "if I find Quin, maybe we'll make the trip back together!"

Lillian returned to her camp with a promise for more visiting before she left. Later that same day, a short, copper-skinned man, Klutina River Joe, hiked into Peninsula camp with his young adult son. They spoke fairly good English, especially the younger man, David. They planned to cross the glacier to hire on as packers for gold-seekers still trying to reach the Copper River.

Each one wore an odd assortment of white man's clothes. David's heavy trousers were cinched around his waist with a piece of rope. He wore tall boots that looked too big for his feet, a flannel shirt under a too-tight, stained woolen suit coat, and a cotton cap atop his long black hair. The father wore plaid pants and a shirt of a different plaid, a top hat that had seen better days, and lace-up boots. Clothing traded from returning prospectors, Melinda supposed.

They carried a few belongings on their backs. She saw blankets, cooking pots, and skin pouches that probably held food. The loads were suspended from tump lines, bands of fabric they wore across their foreheads.

She'd seen Indians in Everett, but she'd never had a chance to get acquainted with any of them. Even though the country had belonged to the native peoples for hundreds of generations, the new residents looked down on them. They'd been forced into reservations on the most undesirable remnants of their vast original territories. She wondered if things were different here in Alaska.

While at the Everett waterfront, she had seen some Tulalip reservation women from across the bay climb out of their canoes with handiwork to sell. The women carried burdens suspended from tump lines, much like these two.

David removed his tump line to set his load on the ground.

She saw that the band, striped in brown, orange and yellow, appeared hand-knitted. Even though it was dirty and frayed, she was positive she recognized it. Yes. It *was* the scarf she had knitted last Christmas, the scarf she herself had placed around Quin's neck!

CHAPTER TWENTY-FOUR

SURPRISES

"David," she gasped, "Where did you get that tump line?"

The smile left the young man's face. His eyes narrowed. Melinda realized he must think she suspected him of stealing it.

"No, no ... it's okay. It's just that I made a scarf exactly like that for the man I'm looking for. His name is Quin Chenoweth."

Evan had noticed the look on David's face. "She made one for me, too," Evan told David.

He ducked into their small tent. She heard him rummaging through the belongings stored there. In a moment he reappeared, waving his own scarf, knitted in the same bright stripes.

Sympathy took the place of anger in the young man's eyes. "I found it in the river," he said. "Caught in tree roots."

Melinda gasped. *Did that mean Quin's boat had capsized? Was he dead?*

"I looked for the owner, but didn't find him." David said. "I will give it to you."

She tried to steady her breathing. "No, you must keep it. You've put it to very good use."

She offered the two men coffee. They sat cross-legged on the ground, drinking it, while she told them about Quin. Joe remembered a man he'd met at Copper Center. He pantomimed using a camera and writing on paper. Melinda relaxed. Who but Quin would be doing that? If he had reached Copper Center, that meant he'd survived the Klutina, whatever accident he might have met.

Melinda showed him the portrait in her locket. "Was this the man you talked to?"

Joe peered at him closely. "Maybe. Much hair on face now." He ran his hand over his own hairless chin.

"He said he might go to the Klondike. But then he asked about a guide to take him down the Copper River." Joe said he didn't know what Quin had decided to do, but he had introduced him to a friend who knew the big river well and could take him at least part of the way.

Lillian appeared from her camp to see what was going on.

The father and son were from the Ahtna tribe, they said. Some years previously they'd lived in a now-deserted village near the other end of Lake Klutina, where the river flowed out of the lake and on to the Copper. The villagers had mostly moved downriver to Copper Center after the government people came through and took the children, including David and his sister, away to Sheldon Jackson boarding school in distant Sitka.

"I was five years old when the missionaries changed my name to David," the younger man said. "The government thought if they took us away from our families and culture, we'd become like the white people. They whipped us if they caught us speaking our own language."

Melinda imagined how bewildered and unhappy those children must have been. The very idea of such arrogance angered her. "Did you forget your culture?"

"We were lucky," David said. He explained that at the time Klutina River Joe's children were taken away, the Indian schools claimed legal custody of the children in their care and refused to let parents visit them. Some parents went to court in 1885 and won the right for their children to return home. That victory didn't last long. But while it lasted, Klutina River Joe retrieved David and his big sister and hid them from the authorities until they were too old for school. The family now lived near Copper center.

When Lillian Moore heard that Joe and his son hoped to work as packers for gold seekers going to and fro over the glacier, she hired them on the spot.

That night, when Melinda and Caroline finished cleaning up after their supper customers, they sat down to rest beside the campfire. As the last color disappeared from the western sky, stars popped out one by one over Klutina Lake. Voices murmured around other campfires.

Lillian's skirt rustled as she made her way across the clearing and dropped down beside Melinda on her log.

Mosquitos whined around Melinda's ears. "Evan, would you find our hats, please?"

She put hers on and tucked the netting down inside her collar. Lillian also wore netting around her head.

"Well, Lillian." Caroline spoke. "What did your partners have to say about your hires?"

"They thought I hit pay dirt," she said. "They know the Indians are hard workers, and can carry more than we can. I can take my whole outfit in one trip now."

"I'll miss you," Melinda said. "Do you think we might meet again?"

"I hope so. The fellows are good company, but there's nothing like a woman to understand when someone needs to talk! You're fun to talk to, but you know when to be quiet, too."

"Well, thank you."

Lillian laughed. "That was a compliment!"

They were silent for a while. The stars dimmed in the northern sky while a greenish light rose from the horizon. The light spread, grew brighter, and began to ripple like a dancer's swaying skirts. Awestruck, Melinda watched the aurora borealis play above them.

After a while, the conversation turned to Lillian's adventures with the Abercrombie expedition. This was not the Captain's first time in Alaska, she said. As a young lieutenant in 1884, William Ralph Abercrombie had been sent to the Copper River's outlet, some distance south of Valdez. His assignment: ascend the river to investigate rumors of hostile natives in the upper Copper River territory. The U.S. government knew Americans would be settling in Alaska and wished to avoid conflicts with the original inhabitants.

"If he'd come in winter," Lillian told them, "travel on the frozen river would have been easy. But they'd arrived in late June. The expedition fought all summer trying to accomplish their assignment.

"Captain Abercrombie told us how they lined their boat up the river past impenetrable brush. They waded in that glacier water until they couldn't feel their feet. It rained and rained. Everything they owned got soaked. When they passed the Miles and the Childs Glaciers, they had to dodge icebergs rushing toward them. Then they came to rapids they couldn't get around or through. They named the rapids for Abercrombie.

"On the way downstream they got caught in whirlpools that spun them around and around and threatened to take them to the bottom of the river. Raging waves pinned them against huge boulders. Oh, it must have been awful!

"They eventually made it back through the maze of shifting channels and sandbars of the Copper River Delta to Eyak Lake and then they made a short portage to salt water. The Lieutenant took some men with him across the Sound to what is now Valdez and looked for a route he'd heard of that crossed the Valdez Glacier. That is the same trail we followed to get here."

Now, 16 years later, Abercrombie was back in Alaska looking for a better route into the Interior for laying out a road, Lillian said. Some of his men would descend the Copper on their return to Valdez.

"Maybe Quin will meet the explorers in Copper Center," Melinda mused out loud. "He might try to come back to Valdez with them by way of the Copper River, if he doesn't find an Indian guide."

Or, she thought, Quin might decide to travel on through the Interior of Alaska to the Klondike. She'd never catch up with him, either way. Should she take the risk of getting stuck in the Interior or on the Yukon with freeze-up close at hand? Neither could she risk taking Evan down that river where Abercrombie had met defeat.

What should she do now?

CHAPTER TWENTY-FIVE

BERRIES AND BEARS

Lillian Moore, her friends, and the two Ahtna packers started up the trail to the glacier the next morning. Every member of their party was heavily loaded. Lillian had copied the Indian method of burden bearing, suspending her pack from a bright fabric band across her forehead. It was secured with two sets of straps, one fastened at the waist, the other high on her chest.

The younger Ahtnan, David, touched his own tump line as he passed Melinda and mouthed "Good luck."

Melinda waved in acknowledgement and watched them go, wishing she had the carefree confidence that Lillian had. As they disappeared up the mountainside, she thought, too late, of another possible solution to her dilemma. She could have returned to Valdez with Lillian and waited there for Quin.

She sighed and returned to the cooking area. "What would you like me to do today?" she asked Caroline.

"I just put on a big kettle of bacon and beans. They'll be ready in time for supper." said the woman, indicating the simmering pot at the back of the stove. "Why don't you and Evan pick enough berries for a couple of cobblers? That's everyone's favorite."

"All right."

"Yesterday, I watched a squirrel harvesting mushrooms. Morels. They're delicious. I thought I'd try to find where they're growing. They'd be a great addition to our menu."

"I've seen squirrels hiding nuts and evergreen cones for the winter," Melinda said, curious. "But wouldn't mushrooms spoil right away?"

"They would, if they were stored fresh. But the little guy I saw carried them up a tree and lined them up along a branch to dry in the sunshine. Some he'd put there earlier were already dry. They'll keep all winter in a hollow tree."

"How smart!" Melinda thought of the two Indian guides. Their people had been here for who knows how many centuries. They looked healthy and strong. This land where some newcomers were starving held plenty of nutritious food, if they only knew what to look for. Just the other day, a recent arrival had seen a bear near the trail, digging for something. Maybe roots? The Indians dug roots to eat, as well.

"Benjamin left his shotgun," Caroline said. "I'd feel better if you took it with you, knowing that a bear has been seen not far away. Do you know how to shoot?"

"I could if I had to," Melinda answered. Though she'd not seen any bear sign when they'd collected berries earlier, she took the proffered gun and dropped some shells into her pocket.

"Evan," she called. "Ready to go?"

Evan told the dog to stay behind. "Bears don't like dogs, Mr. Prosper says. We don't want a bear to attack you, Bear!" He laughed at his own joke. The animal whimpered, but obeyed.

Together, she and Evan started up the mountain toward a high clearing where the brush glowed red and yellow. Autumn was near. She'd have to decide soon in which direction to travel. On through the wilderness, or back to Valdez. Meanwhile, the sun was warm and the berries, though close to the ground, were so plentiful they could scoop them off the plants by the handful. Propping the shotgun against a rock, she began to pick.

Now and then, she sat back on her heels and popped a few juicy blueberries into her mouth. She gazed down the valley where the river flowed out of Klutina Lake and through the forested interior. Smoke from wildfires blanketed the Copper River Valley with a brownish smudge. In the distance, several volcanic peaks in the Wrangell Range poked through the haze. From the biggest volcano (Mt. Wrangell?) a white plume, smoke or maybe steam, rose into the sky.

She looked around for Evan. She spotted him further up the hill. He'd found a patch of plump raspberries growing in the shade of a high outcrop of boulders. They'd be delicious mixed with the blueberries they'd already picked. He beckoned her to join him.

She started toward him, smiling at his big purple grin. Suddenly, only fifty yards beyond the boulders, something moved. A large, brown, furry something! She froze, and her heart seemed to stop. That mounded hump! Was it the back of a grizzly bear? The blood pounded in her ears.

Evan's grin faded as, watching her, a puzzled look spread over his face. Before he could speak, she put her finger to her lips and signaled. "Quick! Leave your bucket. Climb those rocks!" Hopefully, the outcrop was too steep for a clumsy-looking animal like the bear to climb.

Evan glanced over his shoulder. He saw nothing, but obeyed. Scrambling to the top of the rock heap, he raised his head above the highest boulder, then ducked.

She left her berries where they were, and crouching low, she grabbed the gun, crept to the rocks, and clambered up beside the boy, trying to make no noise. She peered over the boulder.

Evan's eyes were round. "That's a really big bear, Mindy," he whispered.

She stared at the brownish coat and humped shoulders, so different from the black bears she'd seen at Monte Cristo. "I think it's a grizzly, but not fully grown," she whispered back. "Bears don't see so well and I don't think it's smelled us yet. Maybe it will go away." She hoped the mother was not near by.

For a few minutes they watched the bear snuffling through the blueberry patch. It raked the berries off the low bushes and stuffed them into its mouth.

Evan stifled a giggle. "He reminds me of Jake or Lafe when they're hungry!"

The bear must have heard the giggle. It stopped, listened, then rose to stand on its hind legs. Its head swung from side to side. The leathery nose twitched, teasing their scent out of the air. Then, still on its hind legs, it took a cautious step in their direction.

She heard Evan's gasp. He recoiled against her.

She grasped his hand. "If it keeps coming," she whispered in his ear, "we'll both jump up and make ourselves look big and fierce. Yell as loud as you can!"

Curious about the strange scent it had detected, the bear waddled a few more steps toward them. *For all the world like a plump, shaggy man,* Melinda thought.

"Now," she whispered. Together, they leaped atop the highest boulder. They jumped up and down and shouted at the top of their lungs.

Evan clapped while he yelled. Melinda snatched off her hat and swung it in one hand, the gun in the other. "Get out of here. Shoo! Shoo!"

Startled, the grizzly tumbled backward in a comical somersault and scrambled away as fast as it could go. As it fled, it let out a terrified bawl.

Evan bent double, howling with laughter. She felt a little annoyed, but as long as he was making noise ....

Suddenly, a bellow echoed down the mountain. Melinda yanked Evan down behind the boulders. The mother bear, only a little bigger than her yearling cub, came galloping to the rescue. The two bears reached each other. The young one looked back over its shoulder while the mother gave it a good sniffing. Evidently deciding her baby was unharmed, she led the cub away from the unearthly racket that had so frightened it.

"All right, they are gone," Melinda said. "Let's take our berries home before Mama Bear comes back to investigate."

They grabbed their berry buckets and hurried down the mountain. Melinda shook so hard from the adrenaline that had flooded her body during the encounter that she feared she might spill her berries. She stopped to draw a deep breath. Evan stopped too, and looked up at her. His mouth twitched and he laughed again. "That was funny, Mindy!"

"I'm glad you thought so," she answered grumpily. Then, remembering the cub's scramble to get away from them, she too broke into laughter.

CHAPTER TWENTY-SIX

A LETTER, A DECISION

They found the worktable scattered with plump morel mushrooms, fissured like small gray-brown brains. Caroline had evidently found the source of the squirrel's harvest. But why had she left in the middle of cleaning them?

Melinda set their berries on the table and looked toward a commotion near the lake. She spied Caroline with a crowd surrounding a boat that had just come in. A man in a red flannel shirt and a leather hat lowered a ramp to the shore, then led a packhorse off the boat.

"That's Peter Jackson, the mail carrier," a passerby called. "Hey, Pete! Any mail for me?"

Melinda started toward the boat, which some of the campers were boarding. They carried someone down the ramp to shore. His leg was wrapped in bandages, as were his hands.

"Careful! Fred's been badly burned," she heard the man's mining partner say. He was middle-aged and hungry-looking, like so many on this venture. Melinda could hear the concern for his friend in his voice.

Caroline looked toward their camp. Seeing Melinda, she called, "Melinda, please heat some water. And bring those rags I washed yesterday."

Melinda stirred up the fire. She set a kettle of water on the stove, then took the rags down the hill to where other campers were helping the uninjured prospector, who'd introduced himself as Max, set up a tent. They unfolded a cot and lifted the hurt man on to it.

Fred groaned as Caroline bent to unwrap his foot and leg.

"Sorry. It's ugly," he gasped. "We were walking through a burned stretch. The ground looked cool enough, but I broke through into a pocket of hot embers before Max pulled me out."

His partner added, "Pete Jackson and his horse came along just in time."

As Caroline unwrapped the burned limb, Melinda's stomach turned. She stepped in front of Evan to keep him from seeing the ugly wounds. The mail carrier was sorting through a bundle of mail for letters directed to people at the camp as the men crowded around.

"Why don't you see if there's anything for us?" she suggested to him, though she didn't believe there could possibly be a letter.

"Melinda," Caroline said, "will you tear some of these rags into strips? Then, when the water is warm, bring it here. And some of that lye soap."

She was glad to get away from the smell of the man's wounds, but forced herself to stay when she came back with the soap and water. One of the bystanders brought a small flask of whiskey. "This will help the pain," he said. The injured man gulped gratefully, but still he screamed as Caroline gently washed the raw and blackened flesh. Afterward Melinda helped Caroline to wrap the leg and foot in clean bandages.

Then they re-bandaged the man's hands. "These will heal faster than the leg, since the burns aren't so deep." Caroline told both men when she finished. "That's all I can do. We'll just have to pray no infection gets started. If you can get back to Valdez, you'll find a doctor there."

"Thank you, Ma'am," Fred said weakly. He lay back and closed his eyes.

"We both thank you." Max's gaze took in Melinda as well as Caroline. "Neither of us expected to find a couple of angels waiting on shore."

The crowd around the mail carrier had mostly dispersed when he found the letter Evan waited for. Waving it in the air, Evan ran to their campsite. Joyfully, Melinda joined him and slit the packet open. A letter for each of them. She handed Evan's to him and tried to steady her trembling hands as she unfolded hers.

Copper Center, Alaska
August 7, 1898

Dearest Melinda,

The summer is passing quickly. Fireweed fluff is already floating on the breeze, ferrying the seeds for next summer's plants to new locations. Leaves are turning crimson and gold. This has been an adventure I'll never forget, and I'd have loved to share it with you, except for the times I got dunked in the icy Klutina River.

It comforts me to know you are happy and busy with your studies there in San Francisco. I'm sure you are keeping your promise to write to me, but I'm always on the move and so far, none of your letters have caught up with me.

The mail carrier is here but will not stay long, so I'll skip the details of my journeying since the last letter.

Copper Center is a busy little community of log cabins and tents. It has a roadhouse, a store, and a post office. Prospectors go out from here to explore and look for gold, and come back to resupply. They have some fascinating stories. I've been busy interviewing them and photographing them at work.

Copper Center is about 100 miles from Valdez. It's been quite a journey to get this far. I'll be leaving soon, but crossing the glacier once was enough for me. I could accompany some prospectors who are traveling to the

Klondike gold fields, then take a steamer down the Yukon River to St. Michael's on the Bering Sea. That would make an interesting addition to my series.

Or I can hire an Indian guide and take a shorter route, down the Copper River to Prince William Sound, and from there find a ship returning to Seattle.

I will try to keep you informed of my time of return. Then, when your classes are over, you can meet me in Seattle. God willing, our wedding will follow shortly.

I miss you, dear girl. I can't wait to kiss those little freckles on your nose!

She lowered the letter with a smile. Did she still have freckles on her nose? Did she even look like a girl anymore? The past couple of months had aged her, she was sure. But her heart felt comforted. Quin still loved her. He missed her as much as she missed him.

She had a choice to make.

Should she try to catch up with Quin or not? His letter didn't help her to know in which direction he would go. It was already past mid-August, a week and a half since he'd written this message. He'd survived at least two dunkings in the icy Klutina River. Perhaps the danger in her nightmare had already passed. If not, could she find him in time to warn him?

CHAPTER TWENTY-SEVEN

BACK TO THE GLACIER

Next morning, Melinda addressed the letter she'd written earlier to her mother. She'd told Rose Skinner about the glacier crossing and the new friends, and the little restaurant she and Caroline were running. Now she added a bit about receiving Quin's letter, and promised to write again as soon as she had more to report. "I miss you, Mother. I wish you could see Alaska, too, or even better, that you could join us after we are all back in Washington again."

Evan wrote his own note in the space at the bottom of the letter. She sealed it and took it to the mail carrier, who was ready to head for Valdez.

She thanked him for helping the injured man, and added, "Caroline says she's done all she can for him. Do you think a doctor in Valdez might be willing to come?"

"I doubt that there's much a doctor could do to help him here, even if one could come," he answered. "But the army has a small hospital there. I'll ask if they can send a rescue party to get him."

"That would be good. Thank you." She paused. "By any chance did my fiancé mention to you where he was going next?

The mail carrier swung the mail bag across his horse's back. "No, but the group he was with planned to continue north to the Klondike. They wanted to prospect near Dawson for the rest of the season, then spend the winter there. If your man goes with them, he'd try to go on to St. Michael before the Yukon freezes. But if it's an early freeze-up, he'll be stuck."

"How far is it from Dawson to St. Michael?"

"About 1700 miles."

Seventeen hundred miles! Plus the many miles to the Klondike. Trying to find Quin in all that distance would be a horribly risky gamble. She and Evan could also find themselves marooned by freeze-up, with no supplies or friends to help them survive. She imagined Quin's dismay if he should reach Seattle ahead of them and then found she was stuck for the winter somewhere in the wilderness of Alaska.

She hoped he'd chosen the Copper River route. Whichever way he'd gone, he had too much of a head start. She'd never catch up.

And whichever way he went, he could be in danger. She still felt the need to warn him. But she had to consider Evan's safety too. Should the two of them return over the glacier to Valdez now? Maybe it would be best to go back to Washington and wait for Quin there?

She'd just have to leave him in God's hands, as she should have done in the first place. After all, Quin would be the first to say he was safer there than any where else.

Melinda spent most of the day distracted. First she released her churning thoughts, putting them in God's hands. Then she'd take them back and worry her limited options like a puppy worrying an old shoe. She'd been so convinced that the nightmare was a portent she needed to act on. But so far she'd accomplished nothing.

She opened the oven to check on the cobbler's progress, and bumped her knuckles against the hot rack.

"Oh, drat!" She grabbed a dipper of cold water and poured it over her burns. She held her hand in the wash basin until the stinging lessened.

Caroline stopped work to inspect her companion's scorched fingers. "Melinda, you're not yourself today. Is something bothering you?"

"Sorry. I was just careless. But yes, I guess something is. I keep worrying about what I should do next." She repeated the last part of her conversation with the mailman.

"You are more than welcome to stay with us, whatever we do," Caroline said. "But do you want my best advice?"

"Mmm ... yes. I'm beginning to think I should have listened to advice long before this."

"I think you ought to get back over that glacier before the autumn storms begin and wait for your young man in Valdez. If it makes you feel better, you can send him a letter with the next person heading for Copper Center.

"Thank you." Melinda gave her friend a quick hug. "I don't want to give up, but I know you're right."

That evening, Evan came running from the lakeshore. "Mrs. Prosper, Mindy! Look! Jake and Lafe are coming. And Mr. Prosper and Mr. Gilvray."

Their boat coasted through the sunset reflections and nosed into the sand of the beach. Caroline welcomed her family back as other campers lent a hand unloading their gear.

Melinda joined them in time to hear Benjamin Prosper say, "No gold up the creeks we followed. Time we head for the Copper River!"

Here was her answer. Now she must part company with the Prospers and retrace the route across the Valdez Glacier. She'd send a letter with Caroline, who would find someone to deliver it to Quin.

Her friends were eager to get to Copper Center before winter. They decided to send Lafe and his brother back to Valdez for additional supplies. The others would pack everything into the boat tomorrow for the trip over Klutina Lake, then down the lower Klutina River. They'd build a cabin for their winter quarters at Copper Center.

Melinda and Evan would travel to Valdez with Jake and Lafe.

The next morning, the two bundled their tent, stashed the supplies they wouldn't need in the boat for the Prospers to use, and left their campsite as clean as possible.

"Thank you, all of you, for being so kind to us. I'll never forget you!"

Melinda hugged Caroline and promised to write her in care of the post office at Copper Center when they were settled back in Washington.

Caroline sniffled and wiped a tear. "Be sure to tell me all about your wedding!"

She spoke gruffly to her sons. "You big galoots take care of these two." She gave the young men a list of supplies to purchase in Valdez, hopefully enough to see the family through the winter, and hugged them. Her husband and Mr. Gilvray shook hands. Amid a chorus of goodbyes from family and neighbors, the four shouldered their packs and, with Bear at Evan's heels, turned their faces toward the mountains.

Melinda plodded up the trail, her thoughts in a whirl. Was she giving up her quest too easily? Even though Quin had no idea they were in Alaska, she felt as if she were abandoning him. But she had to think of Evan. What else could she do?

Lafe carried her small stove and tent. Jake's load included firewood to use on the glacier, plus a larger tent. Melinda had packed food for them all in Bear's load, plus the fish Evan had dried for dog food. She took just one kettle and a few plates and utensils. With bedrolls and clothing, their own packs were full.

Despite the heavy loads the Prosper brothers carried, Melinda, Evan, and Bear soon lost sight of them on the steep, twisting trail. They planned to stop and set up camp when they reached the foot of the glacier. Still, remembering the encounter with the bears, she wished they wouldn't get so far ahead. To her relief, she caught sight of Jake and Lafe at a curve in the trail above. They waved, and she realized the boys were keeping an eye on them.

The older Prospers and Conroy Gilvray had planned to leave Forest Camp as soon as they finished loading their boat. Maybe they were already on their way down the lake. When the mail carrier returned to Copper Center, they hoped their sons could accompany him with the additional supplies.

Melinda thought of the note Caroline carried for Quin. She'd told him where she was and why and that she was returning to Valdez where she'd wait for him. "It sounds foolish, I know," she wrote. "But I've had a dream that you could be in great danger. Please be especially careful around water." The Prospers would see that the note got to him, if anyone could.

She stumbled on the rocky trail and brought her attention back to what she was doing, thankful for the tent pole hiking sticks they carried to steady themselves.

At the steepest, narrowest places on the trail, they had to be especially careful. Sometimes their passage dislodged stones, sending them bounding over the precipice. A misstep could send a careless traveler into the rushing water.

At mid-afternoon, she and Evan stopped to drink from their canteens and to chew on some jerky. They watched the gray river swirling below, swollen with melt water.

"Did you know, Mindy, that the silt in the river makes a hissing noise against the rocks? If you're really quiet, you can hear it."

"No, I didn't know that."

"I heard it. I was lying on a big smooth rock at the edge of the water, wondering why I couldn't see the bottom. I dipped out some in my hand and looked at it. It was just full of tiny, sparkly specks. Mathias told me as the glacier moves, it grinds the rocks underneath into flour. It's those tiny bits of rock flour you can hear." He chuckled. "I don't think it would make very good bread."

She thought about the fine silt that settled out wherever the water moved slowly. "Mud pies, maybe?"

Rays of the lowering sun were spearing between the western mountain peaks when she and Evan finally reached their previous camping spot at the bluff near the foot of the glacier. The Prosper brothers had set up their own shelter. A pan of their mother's stew sat warming beside a small fire. They'd retrieved Melinda's sled from its protected place beneath the overhanging rocks.

While Jake took their walking-stick tent poles and set up her small tent near theirs, Melinda dropped to a seat on the sled and gratefully inhaled the warm scent of stew. Evan and Bear flopped on the ground beside her. "We're exhausted!" she told the brothers. "I thought going down the mountain was hard, but climbing up was harder."

Lafe agreed. "We're not at the top yet," he said. He gestured toward the snowy slope. "See how the glacier has melted back since we were last here? It's slushy too. We'll need to start out early tomorrow while the crust is frozen. We'll try to reach the top before the sun softens it."

They ate every last bit of the stew, then took the pan and dishes to the edge of the glacier and scrubbed them with snow. Melinda wrestled the sled into the tent and unrolled her sleeping bag on it. Evan spread his bed on his wolf skin.

"Let's pray for Uncle Quin," Evan said as they lay down.

"Thank you for remembering. Are you sorry we have to turn back?"

"Yes. I miss him, Mindy."

She reached for his hand. They prayed together for Quin's safety, and for their own journey. She fell asleep thinking of Quin and the way the corners of his eyes tilted when he smiled.

Long before she wanted to wake, she heard the brothers stumbling around the campsite.

Brrr! The tent felt frigid as the inside of an icebox even with Bear curled at their feet! A picture came to mind of thieving Wentzel spending the night on the glacier with only his filthy horse blanket to keep him warm. She wondered, had he survived?

Sitting up in the dark, she groped in her pack for the coat she hadn't worn since coming over the glacier. She opened the tent flap to let the big dog out, then donned an extra pair of warm socks and her boots and found her scarf, heavy mittens, and floppy-brimmed hat.

"Roll out, Evan. Time to get going."

"It's not even morning," he wailed.

"I know. But the snow is frozen now, so it will be easier to travel. Maybe we'll be able to stop and rest early today."

She found his warm clothing. "Put these on," she urged. "you'll soon get warm." With Evan's help, she rolled their bedding and took down the tent.

The brothers hadn't built a fire because they were eager to get underway. There'd be no coffee this morning. Jake chewed on some jerky as he came to see if he could help.

"We're almost ready." She handed Evan some jerky and dried fruit from one of Bear's packs to put in his pocket, and put some in hers. "For breakfast on the trail," she said.

The brothers added their camping gear to the sled and tied a canvas over the load. Evan harnessed Bear, and with all of them pushing and pulling, they wrestled the sled over bare rocks to the frozen surface of the glacier.

Melinda paused to look out over the valley of the Klutina. A faint glow lit the sky above the ridges to the northeast. To the west, a slice of moon dropped toward the peaks. Its light reflected from the snow, illuminating the steep slope above them. Dense, dark clouds spilling over the pass they must cross didn't look good to her.

But Bear strained at his harness, eager to go. Lafe grabbed a line to help him pull. Jake put his shoulder to the high back of the sled and pushed. Nothing for Melinda and Evan to do but pick up their packs and fall in.

Trudging up the glacier as the sun rose behind them, she wondered where the rest of the Prosper party were on their journey to Copper Center. The first part, boating down the lake, would be enjoyable. But after that came a long stretch of river, with miles of swift current and many rapids. That part wouldn't be easy.

Once more, she hoped that Quin had chosen the shorter route along the Copper River for his return, and that her warning would somehow reach him in time.

Chapter Twenty-Eight
Glacier Demon

As they neared the top of the pass, the sunshine disappeared. Melinda knew she'd been right to feel uneasy about the clouds piling above it. They'd deposited a fluffy blanket of new snow. Crystals swirled through the air and prickled their faces. In mid-August!

Evan danced around, sticking out his tongue to catch the flakes, as delighted as if this were a proper first snowfall of winter.

"We'd better not linger here," Lafe said. "No one's been over the trail yet. We don't want to lose it, especially with the snow falling so thick."

"Just follow Bear," Evan told him.

Evan was thinking of Bear's efforts to keep them on the trail when they'd become lost on the way to Twelve-Mile Camp, she knew. But the ruts left by the summer's traffic were deep, and not completely hidden by the snow. They should be all right. They started down the steep descent, Evan and Bear in the lead and almost hidden by the blowing snow. The others came behind to hold the sled back.

So intent were they on keeping the sled upright that no one said anything for awhile. Suddenly Bear pricked his ears. Evan turned. "Someone's coming."

Melinda heard footsteps and the jingle of a bridle. They stepped to the side of the trail and waited as the whitened forms of a couple of soldiers and a packhorse laboring to pull a toboggan-like sled appeared out of the falling snow.

"Halloo," one hailed them. "How much farther to the top?"

"You're nearly there," Lafe told them. "Weather's nice on the other side."

"That's good news. How much farther to Peninsula Camp?" Jake told them.

"Are you the soldiers the mail carrier promised to send for the man who got burned?" asked Melinda.

"Yes, Ma'am. We're to bring him to the military hospital," one answered. "Do you know how he's doing?"

"He was in a lot of pain when we left," she answered. "He really needs a doctor. We're glad to see you."

She wondered how they'd been able to come so quickly. Of course, the mail carrier on his horse would only need a long day to reach Valdez. If the soldiers started right away, they'd have made good time too, even if they weren't riding.

The soldiers climbed on toward the summit, while their own party made its way down the slanting wall of ice. Now it took all of them pulling back on the ropes to keep the sled from running away. By the time they reached the bottom of the long pitch, the snow had stopped falling.

Twelve-mile Camp lay mostly deserted. Their muscles cried out for rest, so they lit a fire in the small stove for tea. Caroline had sent along biscuit and bacon sandwiches. Melinda warmed them in a pan while waiting for the snow to melt and come to a boil.

They'd passed a few people hoisting sled loads of equipment to the summit by means of block and tackle, as they themselves had done earlier. Prospectors who planned to stay in the Interior for the winter, Melinda thought, or packers hired to carry supplies.

As they finished eating, another party entered camp. The two well-dressed young men leading heavily-laden pack animals appeared carefree and adventurous. Win and Louis Fletcher were brothers. They lacked the usual pickaxes and other gold-miner's equipment, and were accompanied by two people Melinda had hoped to see again, Klutina River Joe and his son David. They were both heavily-laden as well.

She greeted the two warmly, and introduced herself and her companions to the newcomers.

"We're out to see for ourselves what all the excitement is about," Win, the taller man, said. "We've been reading stories in Seattle's Daily Dispatch about the Copper River Gold Rush. Looks like Copper Center might hold some business opportunities for us."

"You couldn't have chosen better guides," Melinda said, nodding at Joe and David. "Who wrote the stories you read?"

"Fellow named Quintrell Chenoweth," answered the other. "He's a good writer. Doesn't exaggerate the situation, but still, we want to see for ourselves."

"That's my uncle!" Evan declared.

While Evan told them more about his uncle, Melinda asked Joe if Lillian Moore and her friends might still be at Valdez. He shook his head. "No. She told us, take her things to the wharf. She was afraid. She wanted to get away from Valdez as soon as possible. A ship was ready to leave, so she got on. I think her friends left, too."

Lillian, afraid? That didn't sound like the Lillian she knew.

"We're hoping my fiancé decided to come down the Copper River," she told Joe. "We plan to wait in Valdez for him."

Joe nodded. "Yes. Smart."

She hoped he was right. But what had happened to frighten Lillian? And why did Joe look so serious?

While Lafe and Jake, with Evan watching, helped the strangers set up tents and prepare to take smaller loads to the top of the pass, Melinda made more tea. Joe and David squatted by her little stove while she asked why Lillian was so eager to leave Valdez.

Joe gestured down the trail they'd just come over. He looked around as if fearful he'd be overheard. "We met a glacier demon," he said.

"No. Really?" Melinda was half amused, half incredulous.

Joe's face closed up. "I believe you, Joe," she hastily assured him. "But what is a glacier demon?"

"It looked like a man. But crazy, wild, very skinny. Talked crazy.

No coat or hat or gloves. Wore a dirty, ragged blanket like a cape. Snatched the food we put down for him like he was starving. When Miss Moore came close, he screamed and hid his face."

"He raved about a woman who spied on and betrayed him," said David. "I think he thought she was that woman."

With horror, Melinda realized that Wentzel the thief had gone mad. And he was still on the glacier.

"The men with Miss Moore grabbed the demon and tied him to one of the sleds," David said. "They said they'd take him to Valdez. But he screamed and fought until he broke the rope. He ran off toward a crevasse field."

"Your friend hardly said another word, all the way to Valdez," said Joe.

Poor Lillian. If she'd stopped talking, she must have been badly frightened.

This was awful. If they were to continue on down the glacier today, they'd have to spend the night somewhere between established camps. Maybe near where the "Glacier demon" roamed. What if Wentzel should come looking for food and supplies while they were sleeping?

Lafe Prosper had noticed Melinda's concern. He silently squatted beside her, listening to Joe and David's story.

"I know we're in a hurry to get the supplies for my family," he said to Melinda. "But we'd have to stop in another few hours anyway. I think we should stay here where there are more people. If the 'demon' *is* Wentzel, he's not going to want to come near a large group."

"I agree," Melinda said.

Lafe looked over at the two adventurers, who'd unloaded their pack horses and dumped some grain on the ice for them. They were ready to start ferrying their goods up the last steep rise to the pass. Joe and David hefted their packs once more.

"We'll be back tonight," David said.

"I'll go with them to help," Lafe said. "Jake, you want to stay and set up our camp?"

So while the five men set off toward the steep incline, Melinda, Evan, and Jake pitched their shelters and prepared for a night on the glacier.

That evening, a rising moon cast long shadows across the almost vertical trail as Melinda, Evan and Jake checked to see if Lafe and the others were in sight.

"There they are," Evan said, pointing. Sure enough, five small figures, still a long way above, made their way down the wall of ice.

Melinda gave a sigh of relief. "We might as well go to bed," she said. "We can get up early and fix a good breakfast before we start on our way."

Two hours later, she wakened out of a sound sleep to loud crashing, rumbling, and the terrifying feeling of the ice beneath them rising and falling. She sat up quickly and was tossed off the sled, sleeping bag and all.

"Mindy, is it the demon?" Evan cried.

Even in her fright, she wondered how much of the story he'd overheard. "No, I think it's an earthquake," she said. "Hold on to me."

The glacier jarred again and again, then shivered to rest. Next came the distant sounds of avalanches rumbling down onto the glacier from the mountainsides. Had Lafe and the others reached camp safely? Next to their shelter, Bear barked wildly. Another dog howled and horses whinnied. Melinda and Evan shoved feet into boots, grabbed their coats, and scrambled out of the tent.

"Stay with Bear," she told Evan. "I'm going to help with the horses."

While she and Jake attempted to sooth the panicked animals, she stole a glance up toward the pass. She saw no one.

"Here they are," Jake said. He left her with the horses and ran to meet his brother and the rest of the party, who had just arrived in camp.

Even in the dark, she could see that no one appeared to be injured.

Within minutes, the men appeared at their campsite. "What an adventure," Lafe exclaimed. "Are you and Evan okay?"

"Yes," Melinda said. "What about you?"

"It was crazy," he said. "The quake knocked us off our feet. Klutina River Joe yelled for us to hang on, but there was nothing to hold on to. I must have slid twenty feet before I bumped into a hummock of ice. I saw both Win and Louis go sliding past. I grabbed Louis by the coat tail, but Win had quite a ride before he came to a stop. Chunks of ice broke off and bounced all around us. Fortunately the big pieces missed us."

A few other campers came by to check on them, but soon all took shelter in their tents. An occasional aftershock rippled through the ice, waking everyone all over again. Terrifying, to realize that such shaking could rupture those hundreds of feet of ice beneath them and possibly open a crevice big enough to swallow the whole camp!

Such thoughts didn't bother Evan. Soon, Melinda heard his soft snore. In the middle of a prayer of thanksgiving for God's protection, she too fell asleep.

They hiked for another day and a half before reaching the bench where Melinda and Evan had spent their first night on the glacier. The group stood looking out over Prince William Sound and the settlement of Valdez. They marveled at the number of new buildings that had sprung up in the weeks they'd been gone. "It looks like a real town now," said Evan.

"Yes," said Lafe. "I hope we'll find the supplies we need."

"And a horse to carry them," added his brother.

"We won't need this sled any more," Melinda said. "Shall we leave it here for you to use on the way back? We don't need the stove or tent, either. If we don't find a room for rent, I'm sure we can stay with our friends, the Larsons."

"Sure," said Lafe. The brothers piled stove and extra items on the sled, covering it all with canvas to await their return. "Leaving our things unprotected like this would never work in Seattle," said Jake.

"Certainly not in San Francisco!" Melinda's thoughts flashed back to Wentzel, who'd stolen her money there. In a way, it was his fault she'd ended up here on this glacier in Alaska. The consequences of his act had been more severe for him. He might deserve what he'd got, but she grieved for him nevertheless. If he'd survived his time on the glacier, there was forgiveness. He only needed to ask God for it. But would his mind be clear enough to understand?

While the adults talked, Bear leaned against Evan, who hugged the big dog. She knew Evan hated the thought of giving Bear up. He'd keep his agreement with Bernie, but the boy loved that dog. She wished she could ease the parting that lay ahead.

They descended the last bench much faster than they'd taken to climb it with all their supplies. In no time at all they were walking into town.

For the past two days, Melinda had dreamed of a snug room, a bath, a chance to launder their ragged clothing and maybe even shop for something more presentable for the trip back to Seattle. Perhaps she would find Quin already here in Valdez. Ever hopeful, she said softly to herself, "It could happen!"

Among the people on the street, no one looked like Quin. But she saw one person she really wasn't eager to see, and of whom she'd barely thought over the past month. Ezekiel Cox.

Chapter Twenty-Nine

Valdez Again

"Hello, Mr. Cox."

Ezekiel Cox halted, mid-stride. His blank look told Melinda he didn't immediately recognize her. No wonder, she thought wryly, as unkempt as she undoubtedly looked. Then a smile of genuine welcome spread across his face. He swept his hat from his ginger-colored curls and bowed with a flourish.

"Miss McCrae. You're back, safe and sound. And the boy, as well."

"Yes."

His glance moved inquiringly over the Prosper brothers. "Your search was successful?"

"Did I find my fiancé, you mean? He's on his way." She hated to admit failure, but he'd ask more questions if she said nothing. "Quin was too far ahead for us to catch up with him, so when we heard he was returning by a different route, we turned back. We will wait for him here."

Was that a look of "I told you so" on the man's face? If so, she ignored it. "Please excuse my lack of manners, Mr. Cox. May I introduce our friends, Lafe and Jake Prosper?"

He shook hands with the brothers.

"Excuse our appearance, as well," she said. "We've been too busy adventuring to keep up with civilized amenities."

He smiled. "Adventuring looks good on you. Is there anything you need?"

"Is the Mercantile still in business?"

"Yes, and doing well."

"I think we'll find whatever we need there. It's good to see you again, Mr. Cox."

She nodded a goodbye and they continued toward town.

When they passed the Mercantile, Jake and Lafe went inside with their list of supplies. Melinda wanted to let Elizabeth Larson know they were back, so she and Evan bade the young men farewell. "I hope we'll see you again before you head back to the glacier. Thank you for everything," she said.

She hoped the Larsons could recommend a place to stay while they were in Valdez. They continued past Cox's Entertainment Emporium and a row of cabins toward the location of the Larson's tiny home.

There it was. Since they last saw it, it had been moved back from the boardwalk to allow for a generous front yard. The cabin now served as one room of a much larger home, not yet finished, but lived in, she could tell. The back yard was surrounded by a tall fence of rough boards. They could see into the yard from the boardwalk. They glimpsed the billy and nanny goats, fat and healthy-looking. The two babies, already half the size of their mother, head-butted each other outside their shed.

The children playing in front of the house stared at them. Then Nat and Nonnie recognized Evan and came running with shouts of welcome. The children took Evan and Bear to the back yard as Elizabeth Larson appeared in the doorway with the baby on her hip.

Delight wreathed her pleasant face. "Welcome back! Come in, come in, Melinda. I'll put the tea kettle on. I want to hear all about your journey. Did you find your young man? You'll stay with us, won't you? We're still not settled but as you can see, we're getting there!"

Melinda smiled at Elizabeth's excitement. "You'll have a beautiful home. You and the children look well! How is Mr. Larson doing with his mill?"

"Oh, he's so busy! Between keeping up with the demand for lumber and trying to build our own house, he's overwhelmed. But we're all doing well. We hear there'll be a school this fall. A teacher's already been hired. Isn't that great?"

Elizabeth set the baby down and pulled a chair out for Melinda. The little one toddled over and held his arms up to her. Melinda lifted him and settled him on her lap.

"Look at that! He's walking already." Melinda exclaimed.

His mother pulled the teakettle to a hotter spot on the stove and rummaged in the cupboard. "Yes. They grow up so fast," she said. "Oh dear. I baked cookies yesterday, but it looks like the children have helped themselves." She set the last few on a plate and made the tea.

Then the two women sat catching up with all that had happened since they last were together.

After a while, Melinda commented on meeting Ezekiel Cox. "He said once that he wants to be influential in building the town."

"I'm sure that's true. He seems to have his finger in every pie. But people respect him. He is a good businessman."

"What kind of business is his Entertainment Emporium?"

"I haven't been inside, but there's a big hall where he says someday he'll have concert artists and maybe an orchestra ... that kind of entertainment. Right now there is a sort of saloon. Liquor is discouraged in Valdez, so it's strictly managed. He has singers and musicians to entertain the customers."

"Hmm." Maybe the fancily dressed woman she'd seen with Ezekiel was one of the singers. Still, she felt still glad she'd not accepted a job in such an establishment.

"Tell me about your journey over the glacier." Elizabeth poured more tea.

So Melinda touched on the highlights of the trip and the many people who'd lent a hand when she needed help. She told about getting lost in the storm and being rescued by the Prosper brothers, and about helping run the restaurant on Klutina Lake.

She told about receiving Quin's letter and the difficult decision to give up her search, and her hope that Quin would come to Valdez.

"I see," said Elizabeth. "If Quin goes on to the Klondike, he will try to reach St. Michaels at the mouth of the Yukon before freeze-up. If he makes it there, he'd go straight to Seattle. If he comes down the Copper River, it's still a long, dangerous journey. I understand ships stop at Nuchek, near the mouth of the Copper. Do you think he might catch a ship there and not come to Valdez at all?"

"It's possible," Melinda sighed. "That's my dilemma. I did send a message after him that I'd wait at Valdez a week or so. If he gets my message, I'm sure he'll come here first."

"We'd love to have you stay with us while you wait," her friend answered.

So Melinda and Evan made their home with the Larsons for a week.

She bought traveling clothes for both of them at the Mercantile, and washed and mended Evan's outgrown things to leave for Nat. In the mornings, she sat with the older children around the kitchen table with small slates she'd purchased at the Mercantile and had them practice writing the alphabet and numbers. She told Nat and Nonnie they were getting a head start for when the new teacher arrived. As for herself, she loved the chance to teach.

They played arithmetic and word games. Sometimes she left Evan to lead the learning games and helped Elizabeth with her project of gluing heavy felt paper to the raw boards of the inside walls. The covering would help to insulate the rooms from winter's chill. When they could afford it, the Larsons would add real wallpaper on top of the felt paper.

One day when the children were playing a game of tag in the road that passed by the house, a man with a loaded donkey trudged toward them. Bear, who had been running alongside Evan, stopped short and pricked his ears. Then his tail wagged so vigorously his whole body contorted. The man bent and opened his arms. Bear raced to him, whimpering and wriggling with joy. It was "Bernie" Bernard, Bear's first human.

Melinda, who had been watching from the doorway, stepped out on the porch. She saw the look on Evan's face. This was the moment he'd been dreading, and her heart broke for him. He struggled to not show his dismay.

"You took great care of him, Evan," said the prospector. "He looks fat and sassy!"

"Thank you," Evan said. "He's a very special dog."

"Yes, he is, Mr. Bernard," Melinda said. "We could never have crossed those mountains without him." She told how Bear had helped pull the sled, how he'd kept them warm at night, and how he saved her life while crossing the crevasse. As she talked, she watched Evan give the dog a long hug, look into his eyes, and whisper to him. Then he slipped away into the back yard.

Bernie watched him go. "I should let the boy keep him."

"No," Melinda said. "We have a long journey ahead of us and we may not have a home for who knows how long? Besides, he's your dog. Anyone can see that."

"I'm living alone on my claim out of town," Bernie told her. "It will make all the difference to have my old friend with me through the long winter ahead."

"Of course," she answered. "Evan said his goodbye. Perhaps it would be easier if Bear just goes along with you now."

She watched them disappear around a curve in the road, Bear looking back as if wondering where the boy had gone. The other children continued their game. She went in search of Evan. She found him huddled next to the goat shed, cuddling one of the kids in his arms.

Her heart nearly choked her. "It's hard, isn't it, Evan? But you did the right thing. You were so brave!"

He set the little goat on the ground and came to her, tear-blinded.

She hugged him close and wept with him.

"I know you're sad about Bear," she told him. "You'll always love him. But someday, when we're home again and we're a real family, you can have a dog of your very own. Does that help?"

Evan lifted his wet face to hers. "Not very much."

She felt a tug on the strings of her borrowed apron, and twisted to see a baby goat chewing on them as they dangled just above its head. Evan swiped his eyes with his sleeve and gave a tremulous giggle.

The Larson's house sat on a rise, out of the reach of flooding when the glacier streams overflowed. From the top of the back yard, the comings and goings of waterfront traffic could be seen. The children knew Evan's uncle might be arriving soon, so whenever a boat came in, they'd run to let the adults know. Sometimes Melinda and the children made the walk to the waterfront a couple of times a day to watch the passengers disembark. But so far, Quin hadn't been among them, and they'd reached the end of the time she'd planned to wait.

Perhaps he had taken passage straight home from Nuchek. Maybe he'd gone to the Klondike instead. Maybe ... something had happened to him. She had to face that possibility. Perhaps there would be no marriage. She would have to find work to support herself and Evan. And Evan needed to get back for school.

It was time to head south.

CHAPTER THIRTY
COPPER RIVER

Quin Chenoweth turned the thumbscrew at the front of his #5 Cartridge Kodak camera. He brought the wild scene in front of him into sharper focus. Drawn up on the riverbank beneath him was the moose hide boat in which he and his Ahtna companions were navigating down the Aetna, or Copper, River.

Upstream, the river burst through a slit in the mountains whose walls of green schist rose to 400 feet. The rocky bluffs of Woods Canyon had constricted the massive river into a narrow channel. Quin's ears still buzzed from the roar of the water echoing from the cliffs. The strange vibrating sounds convinced his Indian guides that this place was the home of spirits. All of them were relieved when the river spit them out of the canyon into calmer water.

Throughout that wild ride, none of them had been sure they'd survive to see what lay beyond. Quin hadn't dared take his attention from the river, but fragments of thought flew to Melinda and his young nephew, Evan. What would happen to them if he should never get out of this dreadful place? But now, here he was, making camp for the night where the river spread itself out in braided channels among sandbars and quicksand. It filled the Bremner Valley to a width of at least five miles.

He thanked the Lord for their safe passage and pressed the shutter to capture his photograph. Leaving the film cartridge inside for now, he closed the camera's wooden body. The bellows contracted with a wheeze. Detaching the instrument from his tripod, he fitted it into its leather case, and looped it over his shoulder.

He didn't expect these photos to be used in his series on the Copper River gold rush. But he'd met prospectors looking for copper deposits.

Copper was in big demand for new industrial uses, and Quin believed that if copper was discovered in any quantity in these mountains, it would be of far more importance than the gold that very few people were finding. He would suggest a story or two on the subject to his editor, if he ever found his way back to civilization.

Civilization! To him, that meant Melinda. He thought of the golden flecks lighting her warm brown eyes, the curling auburn wisps that escaped the shining crown of hair the evening he walked her home from the Chautauqua. Her young scholars had done her proud that evening. She positively glowed in that beautiful dress the color of blue glacier ice. No wonder Anton Cole had fallen in love with her. But Quin was the one she'd promised to marry.

She must be nearly finished with her summer's studies by now. Soon she and Evan would be on their way north to Washington State. He intended to be there to meet her, Lord willing.

Quin took one more look around from the high point where he stood. The wind had picked up, sending the mosquito swarms to hide in the brush. His guides had erected the tents in the shelter of some scrubby willows. Out over the sandbars, clouds of silt lifted and blew downstream, cloaking the far end of the valley in a grayish haze. A lowering sun slanted across peaks already dusted with snow, setting the lower hills ablaze with splashes of yellow birch and willow, fiery buckbrush and red bearberries.

Tano, the older of the guides, stood on a slab of rock projecting into the river. He'd speared a couple of salmon and now he cleaned them, dumping the entrails into the river so as not to attract bears. His helper prepared a bed of coals over which to broil the fish. Their little group might be the only people in the world, so complete seemed their isolation.

Then Quin heard a shout from upriver. Another canoe rounded a bend and beached itself at their camp. Two more Ahtna men leaped out and pulled their craft out of the water. Quin's guides greeted the newcomers.

In a combination of sign language and limited English, the Ahtnas made known to Quin they brought him a message. One of them opened a bundle and handed Quin an envelope. He understood the message had come to Copper Center with a family of prospectors. "Woman says letter for writing man," the Indian told Quin. "You pay, she say."

The handwriting on the letter was Melinda's! Quin suddenly felt dazed, but he nodded. "Yes. I will pay."

While the newcomers set up their camp nearby, Quin's guides made tea and broiled the salmon, threading the halves on sharpened sticks and thrusting them into the sand next to the fire. Quin took the letter to his tent and sat down to read it. It *was* from Melinda, written from Klutina Lake. What in the world?

She told about the theft of her money in San Francisco, her precipitous return to Everett and the discovery that he'd gone to Alaska. She related a strange dream about him falling from a rocky cliff into the sea. She'd feared for his life and followed him to Alaska, hoping to warn him of danger, but when she heard that he'd either started down the Copper River or gone to the Klondike gold fields, she knew she'd never catch up with him. She hoped her letter would.

"Please, Quin," she pleaded. "Be careful. I'm sure the danger has something to do with water. I know that Alaska rivers, as well as the ocean, can be very treacherous. I am praying for your safety. I hope to see you soon in Valdez."

Quin read the letter again. And a third time. In his wildest dreams he couldn't have imagined something like this happening. He knew Melinda was independent, a one-of-a-kind woman. But this venture took more courage than most young women would be able to muster. He wondered where she'd left Evan. Maybe with the Swenson's. She loved his nephew like one born to her. Whatever she did, Evan would come first.

The sun had set by the time supper was ready. Quin sat listening to his companions joking together. At his expense? A couple of times he saw them glance his way and grin. Finally Tano asked, "Letter good news?"

Quin grinned too. "Very good news, I think. It was from my fiancee. The woman I am going to marry. She is in Valdez. But I thought she was far away, in the state of California."

One of the newcomers smiled slyly. "Oh. Woman do not know her place?"

Quin shrugged. Culture difference. He didn't try to explain.

Quin hoped he would find a check from his editor waiting when he got to Valdez. He had barely enough cash left to pay his passage home. So when he saw the two messengers eyeing his bear gun with admiration, he asked if they would take that for their payment. After all, Tano and his helper had rifles. They wouldn't lack for game, or for protection. And he'd have less to carry. He wasn't a good shot anyway.

In the morning, one of the Indians slung the gun across his shoulder and the two started back upriver in their skin boat. When they reached Woods Canyon, they'd have to carry the canoe over the trail atop the bluffs. No boat could make headway against those wild waters. Quin considered that the expensive gun was well-earned recompense.

Quin and his guides struck camp, tying the load down securely so if they ran into trouble, their equipment wouldn't float away. Tano pointed downstream, using his hands to indicate rough water. Quin wondered what the circular motions meant, but he nodded and stowed the precious camera where he hoped it would be safe.

The journey through the basin of braided channels was slow. They stayed near the main riverbank for the most part, except for sections where the current was actively undermining the roots of spruce trees. These sweepers leaned out over the water, their branches blocking the way. They eventually fell in, forming deadly traps for any boat or person that got swept into the tangle.

They passed a very large glacier on the right. Quin could see how it had obstructed the river, slowing the current so that sediments from upstream settled out to form numerous islands and sandbars. By afternoon, the river had wound its way around the obstruction and the current increased to a speed he estimated at close to seven miles per hour. Now the river butted up against what the Indians told him was Miles Glacier, on the left. This part of the glacier was covered with ridges of moraine carried down by the glacier. A dense growth of alders grew on the moraine, which protected the ice from the river's erosion.

High hills rose on their side of the river, forming a steep, brush-tangled wall. Here the Copper narrowed into the Abercrombie Rapids, so named by Abercrombie's party in their unsuccessful 1884 attempt to ascend the Copper River.

The Indians paddled with all their might toward the narrow, boulder strewn beach. Quin, in the rear, grabbed a paddle to help them. But the fierce current caught the boat and swept them toward converging waters which plunged over a reef and curled back upon themselves in a frothing mass.

Quin heard himself yell as the icy water crashed over them. They slid through, soaked but upright. Ahead, a series of whirlpools moved across the river, expanding, then contracting as they went. They could do nothing but try to dodge the whirlpools and make another attempt to gain the bank. Then he saw the grizzlies, a dozen or so, fat and glossy, snatching salmon out of the silty current. No one was willing to challenge the bears for use of their stretch of shoreline. Once past the bears, maybe they could wade and line the boat through the rest of the rapids.

Just ahead, two big whirlpools collided. The water rose into a heap at least eight feet high, then burst, leaving a churning surface through which the canoe was carried. Immediately they found themselves at the brink of another whirlpool. It caught the canoe and whirled them around the edge. Quin's stomach rose into his throat as the boat tilted. He looked down into a swirling green pit. The Indians screamed and so did he, but each dug his paddle in and pulled as hard as he could. Their efforts prevailed. Quin felt the whirlpool fling them against the shore. The Indians leaped into the water, grabbed ropes tied to the boat, and steadied it as Quin found a third rope and followed them over the side.

In the midst of the chaos, Melinda's plea for him to take care flashed into his mind. Was this her nightmare come to life?

They passed more rapids, a series of four in all. The men were bruised by slipping and falling against boulders. But, back in the moose hide boat, they finally came to a place of slack water. Across Miles Lake towered the face of Mile's Glacier. Chunks of turquoise ice, bigger than the tallest buildings Quin had ever seen, split off and crashed into the lake with a thunder that echoed upstream and down and sent waves over the expanse of water to rock the canoe.

Floating masses of ice blocked their way. When they saw a clearing on the river bank, Tano said they'd camp there for the night. Exhausted and shivering, they built a fire against a driftwood log. Wrapping themselves in blankets that had stayed fairly dry in the middle of their load, they wrung out their wet clothing and spread it to dry on bushes. Boots and socks steamed near the fire. Quin tended the fire and the boots while the guides set up tents. His hair and beard dripped and steamed too. If Melinda could only see him now!

He mixed some biscuit dough and cut sticks. Each man wrapped a glob of the dough around the end of his stick and roasted it over the coals as if it was a sausage. He wished they had sausages, but at least the biscuits were hot, and they had leftover broiled salmon to go with them.

Tomorrow they must pass Child's glacier, on their side of the river. Then would come miles and miles of channels leading through the sandy islands of the vast Copper River delta. He thought of Melinda's nightmare, glad of her warning. Death could have come at dozens of points during today's journey. He felt sure that only their heightened awareness, and God's protecting hand, had brought them through.

Originally, he'd planned to cross fifty-some miles of Prince William Sound to Hitchinbrook Island and the village of Nuchek, a long-time native settlement within boating distance of Valdez. Russians had built a stockade and trading post there a hundred years earlier, which had later been taken over by the Alaska Commercial Company. The trading center served all of south-central Alaska. From Nuchek he'd hoped to find passage on a ship to Seattle.

But Melinda's letter changed that. She said she'd be waiting in Valdez! He still couldn't wrap his mind around what that might mean. She loved him enough to leave the safety of her friends' home and launch out into the wilderness, alone. A niggling idea wormed its way into his thoughts: Did she think him not capable of looking out for himself? Surely not.

Even though a bad dream didn't seem a strong enough motive for such a venture as hers, obviously it had overridden her common sense, or what most people would consider common sense. Bewilderment, joy at the thought of seeing her, concern for the future now that she had failed to get her teaching certificate ... all these roiled in his mind until sheer exhaustion obliterated all thought. He knew nothing more until morning.

CHAPTER THIRTY-ONE

STORMY REUNION

Now that Quin knew Melinda waited in Valdez, he pushed himself and his guides to hurry. She'd written that letter nearly two weeks ago. She might give up and sail for Seattle before he got there.

Quin wished he'd done as his companions suggested and struck off overland toward Eyak Lake and hence to Prince William Sound. He'd thought it would be faster to follow the river through its delta to the mouth. But they'd been trying all day to find the right channels through the islets and sand bars that still spread many miles ahead of them. Now, the tide was going out. The river, already at its end-of-summer low, deposited them on a sand bar. All three men splashed over the side and pushed the boat after the retreating water.

After an afternoon of spending more time out of the boat than in it, they finally came to deep water. The silt-laden river colored Prince William Sound gray for miles. They camped on one of the uninhabited barrier islands beyond the delta. The next day, they paddled across the sound to Nuchek.

As luck would have it, a small steamer was making ready to leave at dawn for Valdez. Quin paid his guides for their work and secured a place aboard the ship. Lord willing, he'd see Melinda tomorrow.

Melinda rose early and dressed in the ready-made travel outfit she'd found at the Mercantile. She'd left most of her worse-for-wear clothing in Elizabeth's rag bag. Perhaps Elizabeth could turn some of the fabric and re-use it to make for clothes for the children.

She'd already packed their valises and sent the duffle bags to the ship last night. Now she took out her little black Bible and carried it to the window. It wasn't yet full daylight. Straining to read the tiny print. she turned to a favorite verse in Psalm 130. "I wait for the Lord, my whole being waits, and in his word I put my hope." She needed that reminder.

She slipped out to the back yard, climbed to its high point and peered down at the misty harbor. Their ship lay moored next to the dock. A clutter of smaller boats lay at anchor nearby. She'd spent the whole summer waiting for the Lord to help her find Quin. Should she wait a while longer?

Had any of those boats not been there last night? She didn't think so. Everything seemed quiet among them. If Quin was coming, he should have been here by now.

A sob worked its way up her throat. She choked it back. She just had to trust that he was alright. He could have been delayed by all sorts of circumstances. Maybe her letter hadn't reached him and he was already on his way back to Seattle. Maybe, maybe, maybe. Enough of that! Time to get busy. They had a ship to catch. The verse didn't say one should stop moving forward while they were waiting!

Elizabeth had breakfast nearly ready when she entered the house. Evan was slow to roll out of bed, slow to dress.

"I don't want to go yet, Mindy. What if Uncle Quin comes tomorrow and we're not here?"

"I think about that, too," she told him. "But I've already paid our fare. If he comes, he'll just take another ship and follow us."

Evan wasn't convinced. She felt as if she were pushing that sled up the glacier all over again to get him to the breakfast table, and after that, to the door, where they said their goodbyes to the Larson family.

"Are you sure we can't walk you down to the ship?" Elizabeth asked again.

"No, you're busy, and we're already late. We'll just make it if we go now. Thank you so much for being such good friends. I'll write and let you know what happens."

She hugged Elizabeth and the children, and hurried off down the street, Evan lagging behind.

"Evan, hurry up! Do you want to make us miss the boat?" She spoke sharply, then felt guilty. But she was too out of breath to apologize. Then Ezekiel Cox stepped out of the Emporium and stood waiting for them to reach him.

"Good morning, Miss McCrae, Evan. You're out early."

"Yes."

"May I help you with those bags?" Without waiting for an answer, he took one in each hand and fell in beside them. "I heard that you're leaving today. I ... Valdez ... will miss you."

"Thank you. I decided we'd wait for my fiancé in Washington, where we have friends."

"You have friends here."

Melinda knew that he was referring to himself, as well as the Larson family. "Yes, I know. And I'm grateful."

At the dock, they joined a line of people already boarding the converted sailing ship, *Josephine J.* Ezekiel set their valises down. She thanked him. He wished them luck, looking as if he wanted to say more, and watched her rummage for their tickets. She handed them to the purser.

Then Evan squealed, "Uncle Quin!"

She whirled and stared. Further along the waterfront, a small steamer's launch had just drawn up on the shore. But she saw no one she recognized among the disembarking passengers. Then a man dropped his bags and started toward them at a run. Was it really Quin? Dirty, bearded, but yes. It *was* Quin!

For a moment, her feet felt glued to the planks. Then she gave a glad cry and flew down the wharf and into his arms, Evan right behind her. She pulled away from the embrace first, her eyes fastened on his. The same warm, dark eyes that had smiled back at her from her locket every night of the eight months since they'd said goodbye. Had he changed? The rigors of his journeying certainly showed in his appearance, but the smile in his eyes was the same. The voice was the same as he breathed her name.

"Melinda! I haven't words ... Are you all right? I got your letter. Whatever possessed you ... ?"

Then for the first time he noticed Evan, who had a tight hold around his waist. "Evan! You're here, too?"

Evan stepped back and offered his hand, but before Quin could shake it, he came back for another hug. As Quin bent to embrace his nephew, his face reflected a mix of emotions. Bewilderment, relief, gladness, and something else. Disappointment? Anger?

Melinda, watching, also felt bewildered. What was wrong?

Quin's voice hardened as he straightened and looked at her. "Why did you bring my nephew here? I thought he would be safe with you."

Yes, it was anger. At her!

"He *was* safe with me!"

"That glacier, the rivers ... anything could have happened."

"But it didn't." Her cheeks flamed with answering anger. "Quin, I thought you trusted me."

"I left Evan with you, trusting you to look after him, didn't I?"

She looked him in disbelief.

"And you think I failed that trust? Quin, after all these weeks of trying to find you, and this is what you tell me?"

Quin looked miserable, but he blundered on. "Why were you trying to find me? Didn't you think I could take care of myself?"

Speechless, Melinda stared at him.

The purser called, "Are you boarding, Miss?"

She glanced toward the man. Everyone in line had boarded, and sailors waited to pull up the gangplank. Out of the corner of her eye, she glimpsed Ezekiel, still standing on the dock.

She turned from Quin, avoiding his unhappy, angry eyes.

"Let's go, Evan." She grabbed his hand and yanked him after her. As they passed, the purser reached for their valises and followed them up the gangplank.

"No, Mindy, no!" Evan tried to break away, but the sailors were already raising the walkway.

The gap widened between ship and dock. Melinda saw that Quin stood frozen where they'd left him. Ezekiel Cox looked shocked. Evan sobbed.

If ever a heart could literally break, that's what she felt hers doing now, though her face felt as cold and hard as stone.

Chapter Thirty-Two

DISAPPEARANCE

The Josephine J. plowed through the waters of Prince William Sound, slowly at first as the captain guided her past hidden reefs, then a little faster. As the passage widened before them, Valdez disappeared behind them.

As the town faded from sight, a sob broke from Melinda's throat. Before those standing nearby could notice, she hastily made her way to the cabin assigned to them. Evan followed, disconsolate.

How could she comfort him? Why, she'd just as much as kidnapped him, right under the nose of his rightful, legal guardian. She'd acted as his mother for so long, it never occurred to her to leave Evan behind. But now she thought of how it must look to Quin. And to the boy.

Oh, Lord, she cried silently. What just happened? Why was Quin so angry? What did I do that was so wrong?

She huddled on the edge of her cot, wrestling mightily to control the emotions that threatened to break out into an audible wail. Evan came to sit beside her. He leaned against her shoulder, mourning with her. At least he didn't appear to be angry with her, although he had a right to be.

After a while, she took a deep breath and put her arm around him. "We'll be alright, Evan," she said. "Let's go back on deck. A good, brisk walk around the ship will make us feel better. Maybe we can spot a whale or a seal!"

She checked the pitcher on the corner shelf. There was water, so she poured a little into the basin and splashed it on her face, drying it with a cloth hanging from a hook. She dampened a corner of the towel and wiped Evan's face too, coaxing a weak smile from him.

They soon discovered there were no other children aboard, so Evan frequently spent time watching the crew at their duties. Melinda could forget the present circumstances while talking with other travelers, though she paid little attention to the beautiful weather or the magnificent scenery.

Often, she sat alone in their cabin, a fog of grief and confusion enveloping her.

One incident did stand out. She and Evan had been watching from the ship's rail, as they threaded through some timber-crowned islands. They passed one whose black rock cliffs were patterned with streams gushing from the forest above.

Evan tugged at her sleeve. "Isn't this where we almost went aground before?"

He sounded worried.

"I think you're right. It doesn't look so scary now, does it?"

The sunshine brightened the rock face that had been so foreboding on their earlier trip; the heavy clouds that hid the forest and made the island seem much more massive in her imagination were gone. Seabirds still swooped from their high perches. Waves now scalloped a narrow beach, where earlier they'd crashed against the cliffs. What if she'd seen this version of the scene in her dream? She'd probably never have felt compelled to go to Alaska. What if she'd just waited to hear from Quin?

Stop it, Melinda. All the 'what ifs' in the world won't changed the 'now' of your life.

She knew Evan was grieving too, but what could she say to comfort him?

Finally, the Josephine J. entered the calm waters of Puget Sound. When the hills of Seattle came into view and they disembarked, she scanned the people on the dock. Strangers, all. No dear, familiar face waited to greet them. She'd left that face on the dock in Valdez, staring after their departing ship.

Now, aboard the train nearing Everett, she scarcely noticed the fiery vine maples shouting fall's approach to the deep blue sky.

"Oh, Lord, I acted too hastily, again. This time I've ruined the best gift you ever gave me. Why can't I learn to wait for you?"

A tear trickled down the side of her nose. She quickly swiped it away, but Evan had noticed. He gave her a quick worried glance before he returned to gazing morosely out the opposite window.

She squeezed his shoulder. "It's okay, Evan."

He turned back to her. "What are we going to do now?"

"We'll stay at Mrs. Collin's boarding house for a while. Maybe she will let me work for her while I look for a teaching job."

"Are you and Uncle Quin not going to get married?"

Probably not, she thought. "I don't know, but Evan, you mustn't worry. You will stay with me, unless of course, your uncle wants you to live with him. I don't know what his plans are, or what he wants to do."

"We should have stayed and talked to him. I would have told him I stowed away on the boat. It wasn't your fault I was there with you." The boy looked miserable. Her own heart was so heavy in her chest her stomach felt sick.

"He'll come looking for you. Remember the ship we saw following us into the harbor? Maybe he'll be on that ship."

"I don't want him to come for me unless he comes for both of us. You were supposed to be my mother."

All she could do was fold the child in her arms and let the tears fall.

With a screech of wheels the train jerked to a stop at the Everett station. Quickly she blotted her eyes and composed herself. "We're here, Evan. Where's your valise?

The conductor swung their bags to the platform, then helped them down. What should they do next? Find out if her former landlady had room for them, she guessed.

"Let's go see Mrs. Collins." Lugging their bags, she and Evan started toward the boarding house.

That night, Melinda sat cross-legged on the familiar bed in the boarding house. She turned the flame of the lamp up a little. Evan seemed to be sleeping soundly in the curtained alcove. She sorted the pile of letters in her lap, letters from Quin that her mother had forwarded from San Francisco.

Some were from her mother. Those she set aside for later. She opened Quin's earliest-dated missive and began to read his letters in order. Quin was such a good writer. No wonder he'd been chosen to write the Valdez Gold Rush series. She smiled as she read his descriptions of the Glacier ascent, and the beautiful campsite on Klutina Lake. She could put herself in the scenes he described because she'd been there too.

But it was the tender words meant only for her, the love and longing they conveyed, that made her choke back sobs. On the other side of the curtain, Evan stirred.

She slid the last letter back into its envelope and blew out the lamp.

Tired as she was, her brain wouldn't shut off. But by the time dawn crept into the sky she slept at last. She wakened to sunlight and the smell of coffee. She dressed quietly, wanting Evan to sleep as long as possible, and slipped down the stairs to join the landlady as the last of her boarders left the breakfast table.

"I overslept, Mrs. Collins. I wanted to be up early to help you."

"I managed just fine. You looked so tired last night. Did you sleep well?"

"I guess I slept very soundly once I got to sleep. I certainly didn't hear you at work down here!"

The landlady brought two steaming cups of coffee to the table, plus some biscuits that she'd kept hot in the warming oven above the stove. "I'll fix you and Evan some bacon and eggs when he comes down. But now, tell me all about your trip. Did you find that young man of yours?"

Melinda gulped and set down her coffee cup. She decided to start at the end, with the appearance of Quin just as they were ready to board the ship.

"I was so glad to see him. But when he saw Evan, he got angry and scolded me for bringing him to Alaska and taking him into the wilderness. That seemed so unfair, I got angry, too. I grabbed Evan's hand and pulled him up the gangplank after me just before the deckhands raised it. Quin stood there on the wharf, watching us leave. I felt so awful, but the trip going to Alaska was even worse, and it was so hard and so discouraging trying to find him in all that wild country ... and now he'll never want to speak to me again. And I'll never be a teacher!" The last words came out in a wail, and the tears gushed again.

Mrs. Collins' round, rosy face creased with a barely hidden smile. She reached to hug Melinda against her plump shoulder and patted her back. "There, there. That young man cares too much for you to be that easily put off. Once he knows the whole .story, he'll understand. You'll see."

Melinda straightened. "Do you really think so?"

"I'm sure of it. Now go wash your face and get Evan up. I'll start some breakfast for you both."

Upstairs, Melinda slipped into their room and poured water from the porcelain pitcher into the matching washbowl. She splashed water over her face, then patted it dry, inspecting herself in the mirror that hung above the washstand. She might look a bit frazzled, she thought, but nobody would ever suspect the adventures she'd just come through.

"Evan," she called softly. "Time to rise and shine. Breakfast's ready."

No answer.

"Evan?" She repeated, pulling back the curtain that hid the alcove.

The quilt had been smoothed up over the pillow. No shoes or stockings on the floor. No overflowing valise by the bed. No Evan.

She felt the blood drain from her head. She staggered over to sit on her own bed. She knew it. In her heart she knew it. Evan had run away.

CHAPTER THIRTY-THREE

SEARCH

"You're white as a ghost, child. What's wrong?" Mrs. Collins pulled the pan of sizzling bacon to the side of the stove and guided Melinda to a chair.

"Evan's gone!" Melinda realized she was trembling all over.

"Gone! Where?"

"I don't know. I thought he was sleeping. He must have slipped out after I finally fell asleep. I've got to find him."

"Maybe he's with one of the boarders. Remember how much they enjoyed him when you were here last fall?"

"Don't they all go to work?"

"Mr. Bennett is retired, though he sometimes picks up odd jobs at the waterfront. Maybe he took him fishing."

"Would you check to see if Mr. Bennett's home? This isn't like Evan, Mrs. Collinsl" Even as she said it, she remembered how Evan had slipped away from the Swensons to stow away on the Northward. She felt even more convinced that he had run away.

Mrs. Collins scrambled two eggs and put them on a plate with some bacon. She set them before Melinda with an admonition to eat. Melinda tried to obey, but her stomach rebelled.

The landlady left, then came back to the kitchen. "Mr. Bennett isn't here, but his fishing pole is on the back porch, so they didn't go fishing. I doubt he'd take the boy without letting someone know. Where else might Evan go?"

"He might try to return to Seattle to see if he can find Quin. He knows where the newspaper office is. Or, he might be looking for a way to earn money himself. He knows my funds are nearly gone." But Melinda didn't really believe the latter suggestion. Elbows on the table, she dropped her head into her hands. "He thinks the argument is his fault," she said. "Who knows what he might do?"

"If I were you, I'd check in first with the police so they can keep an eye out for him."

Embarrassing though it was, Melinda made the police station her first stop. The officer at the desk told her that most little runaways didn't go far and he'd probably come home soon. They wouldn't look for him until he'd been missing for 24 hours. His attitude made her furious. At her insistence, the policeman filled out a form with Evan's name and description.

Next she checked at the railroad depot. The train to Seattle had just pulled out, but no one had seen an unaccompanied child.

She started from store to store, asking shopkeepers if they'd seen a small boy with shaggy blond hair and sun-tanned face asking for a job. None of them had encountered such a boy. She then made her way to the Snohomish River waterfront that bordered the peninsula. She asked people working at the establishments there if they'd seen anyone of Evan's description. No one had, and her panic grew. He must have been more upset than she knew. The world could be a dangerous place for a child alone.

Late in the afternoon, exhausted, she found some cottonwoods near the river and dropped to a grassy spot where she could lean against a sturdy trunk and rest. Her stomach felt sick. She was thirsty, and as frightened as she'd ever been in her life. All day she'd been sending frantic, disjointed pleas for help heavenward. It seemed they were being ignored.

She lifted her eyes toward the clouds billowing above the distant mountains where Monte Cristo lay. "God, where are you? I need you."

Her heart heard the answer. "I'm right here."

A sensation of peace settled over her. Had she really heard a voice? Or was it just the rustle of the cottonwood leaves?

Whatever, her brain felt clearer and receptive. The fear drained away, like water gurgling from an overturned jug. "God, I'm so sorry. I presumed too much. I thought you were leading me to Alaska, but I didn't wait for your assurance. I'm waiting for you now. Please take care of our boy. Please help me find him."

She must have walked for miles. She'd missed lunch. Now it was well past time for dinner. Maybe it was the lack of food that caused her to feel sick. But how could she go back to the boarding house without finding Evan? A young apple tree hung over the street. It offered only a few apples, but she plucked one and polished it on her skirt. With the first juicy bite, her stomach felt better. She walked on.

The railroad depot came into view. She decided to stop there again and see if perhaps Evan had tried to board a later train to Seattle. The man behind the counter was different than the one she'd talked to in the morning, so she told the story over again.

"No, haven't seen him," the man said. "We'd not likely allow a child by himself to board the train, even if he had the fare, unless an adult put him aboard. Have you checked with the police?"

Melinda didn't explain that Evan was pretty good at getting himself where he wanted to go, fare or not. Nor that the police didn't look for runaways unless they'd been gone a full day and night. She thanked the man, and turned away, the fear rising again.

The depot's brass-trimmed door swung outward as she put out her hand to push it, and she nearly fell into the arms of a clean-shaven man with a small mustache and distracted dark eyes. He caught and stood her upright with a strangled exclamation of recognition.

The world around her whirled. Quin? Both stood motionless, blocking the open doorway. A very large lady harrumphed behind them.

Quin grabbed Melinda's hand and tugged her toward a bench outside the depot. Conflicting emotions raced across his face: trepidation, joy, longing. No anger.

Her relief was so overwhelming her knees gave way under her. Quin was here! She didn't have to face Evan's disappearance alone! And he seemed as glad to see her as she was to see him. They collapsed onto the bench, facing each other, their hearts in their eyes. Then, heedless of who might be watching, she fell into his arms again. This time for a long, wordless kiss.

At the curbside, a horse and carriage stopped. The driver hopped down to help the woman from the depot into the carriage. She'd been watching them with a bemused expression and seemed startled when the carriage driver spoke.

"Sorry," Quin said, half to the woman and half to Melinda. "I just couldn't help myself."

"I'm so glad you couldn't. Oh, Quin, I'm the one who's sorry. To think, after spending all summer looking for you, to leave you standing there on the dock ... even if I thought you were rude and unfair and unreasonable ...."

He held up his hand, laughing. "We can sort all that out later. Right now, I understand we have a problem."

"Yes, but first, tell me how you got here so quickly and how did you know where to find me?"

"Easy. The ship on which I came to Valdez left later that day, with me on it. I docked in Seattle yesterday and stopped to talk with my boss. He'd not seen you so I assumed you'd gone straight to Everett. Mrs. Collins confirmed that you were here. She also told me about Evan being missing, and where you planned to search for him.

"By the way, your friend Ezekiel Cox told me about our young stowaway. He said he was on the Northward when Evan was discovered. Nice fellow. He told me I was a lucky man!"

Melinda thought about this. Maybe she'd been wrong about Ezekiel.

"I owe you an apology, Melinda. Can you forgive me for doubting you?"

"Oh yes," she said. "If you'll forgive me for being so quick to take offense."

They sat silently for a few moments, each gazing into the other's eyes. A holy moment, she thought. Freedom. Forgiveness. Reconciliation. It reminded her of the moment when she'd first realized that God loved her, just as she was.

With a jolt, she came back to the problem at hand.

"Oh, Quin. I've looked all over this part of town and all along the riverside. I thought maybe Evan would try to find you in Seattle, but he didn't board the train. I just don't know where else to look."

"Maybe he wouldn't go south. Maybe he would go east."

"Monte Cristo? You think he'd try to go to Monte Cristo?"

"Maybe. But if I were him, I'd try to reach the Swensons in Silverton."

That made sense. She let out a relieved sigh. "The railroad bridge is still out near Robe, but he might catch a ride on a freight wagon, or even walk."

"There's a telegraph station here at the depot. Let's try to send a message to the Swenson's and ask them to watch for him. If that's where he's gone, they'll keep him until we get there."

What if Evan hadn't gone to Silverton? Then what? But Melinda didn't ask this aloud. She followed Quin into the depot and over to the telegraph booth. Obviously, while in Seattle he'd stopped for a shave and haircut. He wore a single-breasted suit and vest and a narrow-brimmed hat. He looked ... dapper? Handsome, anyway. She liked his new mustache, even if it had prickled her face. He'd taken off his hat as they stepped into the building, and she smiled to see his hair no longer flopped over one eye. That barber knew how to cut hair, she thought with approval.

"Do you have service to Silverton?" Quin asked the man at the telegraph machine. At his 'yes', he told him, "We want to send a telegraph to Mr. and Mrs. Ole Swenson. Let's see. It should say, 'Evan heading your way alone. Stop. Keep him there. Stop. We're coming. Stop.'"

He handed the telegrapher the amount he asked for, and checked on the next train leaving for Granite Falls. "Tomorrow morning," he was told.

Melinda thought of Evan, alone, probably hungry. If he really was heading for Silverton, he could ride the train as far as Robe. Then he might catch a ride with someone using the wagon road to Silverton, but knowing Evan, he wouldn't want to risk someone returning him to Everett. The alternative, the stretch of unused rails between Robe and Silverton, was a long walk for an eight-year-old. Who knew what dangers might lurk along the way?

Quin read her thoughts. "Don't worry, Melinda," he said, though she noted in his own face the concern he tried to hide. "Evan's resourceful. If he needs help, he'll find someone to turn to. Tomorrow we'll go to Silverton. For tonight, all we can do is leave him in God's hands."

His words reassured her. They walked together to the boarding house. Mrs. Collins sat with them while they ate, and Melinda told them both about her nightmare, Evan's surprise appearance on the Northward, the near shipwreck on the very island she'd seen in the dream, and the good people who'd helped them both in Valdez and on the glacier. She told them how the Prosper family had carried a letter for Quin to Copper Center.

Quin took up the story with his wild ride down the Copper River and how the messengers had caught up to him with the letter. "We probably passed the scene you described in your nightmare during the night, on the way to Valdez, but we went through other places just as dangerous," he said. "Your warning certainly made me more alert to the hazards."

"So you do understand why I had to follow you?"

"Well, I understand why you did it. I can't question your motives. But can you see how upset I felt to know you'd exposed yourself and the boy to such danger?"

"I guess so. But I tried to be careful, Quin. I did the best I could."

"It sounds like you did, Melinda," put in Mrs. Collins. "Quin's a lucky man to have someone like you on his side."

Quin laughed. "That's the second time recently I've been told I'm a lucky man." He looked fondly at Melinda. "But I'd say 'blessed' instead of 'lucky'."

"Maybe you've been blessed with a rather foolish fiancee," Melinda said. A picture of her near-disaster among the crevasses flashed through her mind.

She would have to tell Quin about that, later. "Perhaps after Evan turned up on the ship, I should have taken the next boat back when we got to Valdez. Do you know why he stowed away, Quin? He thought he was supposed to take care of me! An eight-year-old!"

A crestfallen look came over Quin's face. "I told him that, didn't I? It was the last thing I said to him!"

"Yes, and he's run away because he thinks he's responsible for our argument."

They went to their separate rooms to prepare for the morrow, but despite her exhaustion, Melinda's sleep was interrupted by dreams. Evan hiding in a chilly baggage car. Evan hauling himself across the Stillaguamish on the cable car. Evan lugging his valise up deserted tracks or maybe the wagon road while wild animals roamed the nearby woods.

Morning had brightened the room when a knock at the door below her window wakened her. A messenger left a telegram with her landlady, who brought it upstairs.

It was from Ole Swenson.

"Found him. Stop. Worse for wear but safe. Stop."

CHAPTER THIRTY-FOUR

TOGETHER

Melinda slid the telegram under Quin's door and tapped softly before returning to her own room. She hurriedly got ready for the day and packed what she'd need for a short stay at Silverton, wondering what Ole had meant by 'worse for wear'. She hoped Evan hadn't met with some accident.

The boarders had finished breakfast and left for the day. Mrs. Collins, a large basket over her arm, was just going out the back door. "Good news?" she asked, referring to the telegram she'd delivered.

"Yes." Melinda answered. "Ole found him, though it sounds like Evan had a hard time. We'll be on our way to reclaim him in an hour."

"What a relief!" She patted her basket. "I'll see what's available in the garden to send along to the Swenson's."

She indicated the bacon and pancakes she'd left in the warming oven for their breakfast, and closed the door behind her. Melinda found eggs in the pantry.

Quin came down the stairs with his bag and set it with Melinda's by the front door. He glanced around the kitchen, and seeing only Melinda, he took her in his arms and gave her a lingering kiss. "Mmmm," he said. "I could start every morning of the rest of my life like this."

"Me, too." She smiled, though she couldn't help feeling anxious about Evan. "Coffee's on the stove," she told him. "Why don't you pour it while I cook these eggs?"

He did so, and took a sip of his. "Where's Mrs. Collins?"

"Out in the garden," she said. "She's picking some vegetables for the Swensons. The season is so short up there in the mountains, they can't grow a lot of things."

She set breakfast on the table, wondering if the Larson family would plant a garden in Valdez next year. She remembered the cabbages and a few other cool-weather crops growing near the military buildings there.

Mrs. Collins came in with green beans, small potatoes, carrots and some almost-ripe tomatoes in her basket. She also had a cloth bag of apples. "Nell will think it's Christmas," Melinda told her.

"It's small thanks for taking care of our boy, the little imp," she replied. Melinda knew by the way she said it that she, too, was immensely relieved that Evan had reached safety.

She swallowed her last bite while Quin gathered the dishes. "Leave those for me," Mrs. Collins commanded. "You two don't want to miss that train!"

Melinda thanked her and ran back to her room for her jacket and hat. Then she and Quin hurried toward the depot.

She noticed the two box cars being hooked behind the baggage car as she waited on the platform. Supplies for the settlements along the route? Or maybe they were for picking up shingles from the mills along the way. Evan had probably stowed himself inside a car like that for the trip.

Other riders boarded the lone passenger car as Quin paid for their tickets and joined Melinda. The conductor handed up their baggage and the train chuffed away from the station. Tumbling into two of the last available seats, they turned to look at each other.

"Well," said Quin, glancing around the crowded car with a wry grin. "Alone at last!"

Melinda followed his glance. No one paid attention to them. Excited chatter rose from a family in the seat ahead and across the aisle. She and Quinn were not exactly alone, but ignored. Good enough!

But now that she was next to this man she'd been pursuing for so long, she suddenly felt awkward. She had more explaining to do. But where to start?

Quin solved the problem.

He took her hand. "The last letter you sent from San Francisco arrived here after you left," he said. "Mrs. Collins remembered it last night and gave it to me. I'm so sorry about that low-life stealing your money. I can see why you would want to join me in Washington." He paused. "I did write to tell you I was going to Alaska."

"I never got that letter," she said. "I would have found work and stayed with my mother until you got back."

"Well, what's done is done," he answered. "And now we're all together, or will be when we retrieve the younger Mr. Chenoweth."

The train rattled across the Snohomish River bridge and headed across farmlands toward the city named for the river.

"Tell me more about why you felt I needed to be rescued," Quin said.

"Not rescued, Quin," she protested. "Warned. 'Rescued' sounds like I thought you couldn't look after yourself!"

He raised an eyebrow. Her defensive hackles went up. "I told you about my nightmare. It haunted me. I felt compelled to warn you of danger. Especially after we passed the very cliffs I'd seen in the dream and the ship's propeller got tangled with debris and we nearly crashed against those same cliffs."

"It sounds like the warning might have been meant for you," Quin said, echoing the thoughts she'd had at the time.

"Except that in the nightmare, you were on the cliff and fell into the waves, and in real life, you weren't there. So I thought the danger must be still ahead."

"Did you know Evan was aboard by then?"

"Yes. Sailors found him the first morning out. During the storm, he was working in the galley to pay for his ticket. When the ship stalled, he came running out on the deck looking for me. Ezekiel Cox followed him and helped us both inside." She didn't mention how she had ended up crying in his arms. Quin thought he was a nice guy. Maybe she'd been mistaken about him.

Quin squeezed her hand and released it. "You're safe. I'm safe. And we both have stories we'll be telling for the rest of our lives! Let's talk about us, now."

"What about us?"

"Do you still want to marry me?"

"What if I said 'no'?"

Quin caught the mischievous glint in her eyes. "Then I'd kiss you, right here in public, until you said 'yes'!"

The train made a few brief stops along the way, but they never stopped talking. Melinda felt quite exhausted by the time the train slowed for the tunnels just before Robe. When Quin pulled her to him for a stolen kiss in the darkness of the "kissing tunnel," she rested her head on his shoulder. Happy. That's how she felt now, even with their uncertainty about the future.

The engine ground to a stop in a cloud of steam. The few passengers still aboard after Granite Falls got off at the hamlet of Robe, except for Quin and Melinda. They stayed aboard until the end of the run, at the store near where Bridge Number Two had washed out. Melinda told Quin about their ride across the river in the cable car and the journey to Silverton on Dan Sutherland's hand car 'railway'.

The conductor said Sutherland had not come that day to meet the train. But they could ride the freight wagon now loading supplies for people living in the valley. Quin helped the teamster transfer groceries and Sears Roebuck orders from a boxcar to the wagon. The wagon's high spring seat had room for the two of them beside the driver, so Quin helped Melinda up and sat beside her. The horses plodded along the same narrow dirt road she'd followed with Quin when they left flood-ravaged Monte Cristo.

Had Evan walked, or had he found a ride for the thirteen-some miles to Silverton, she wondered. With the sunshine warm on her shoulders, she felt drowsy, but the jolting of the wagon made sleep impossible. They stopped at communities called Turlo, Verlot, and Gold Basin. They ate the sandwiches Mrs. Collins had added to the basket. Where the road followed the river, they caught glimpses of nearby peaks. Finally they recognized the mountains surrounding Silverton. The driver pulled up at the railroad depot.

Melinda and Quin retrieved their baggage, crossed the Stillaguamish bridge, and followed the board sidewalk to the Swenson's boarding house.

Nell came running down the steps to meet them, followed closely by Ole, who cautioned her to be careful. Since Melinda had last seen her friend, her pregnancy had become obvious. Her alabaster skin and green eyes fairly glowed. Both of the Swansons enveloped them in hugs and happy exclamations. Evan must be fine or they'd not be so exuberant.

"The boys don't know you were coming," Nell told them. "I sent them upriver to Johnny's favorite fishing hole so we could talk a bit before Evan sees you."

"Is he all right?"

"Ja, just a few scratches and bruises," Ole said. "But he's one worried boy. He had plenty of time to think on his way here."

"Come in. I've got the coffee pot on," said Nell.

As they entered the living room, Quin handed her the basket of garden produce and the apples. "From Mrs. Collins, fresh picked this morning."

"Oh, thank you. What a dear lady! We planted green beans, but we've already had frost. They never got big enough to pick. We lost our tomatoes too." She smiled at her husband. "Ole's going to build us a greenhouse for next year."

The big Swede smiled back fondly, and nodded. "Nell loves to garden. A greenhouse will keep the frost out long enough for things to ripen."

Nell loved gardening? That was something Melinda didn't know about her friend. Marriage was certainly expanding horizons for both of the Swensons.

Once they were seated in the parlor, Nell took Mrs. Collins' gifts to the kitchen. She came back carrying a tray with three cups of coffee and a glass of water.

Ole interrupted his tale of finding Evan to leap up and take the tray from her. He set it down on a small table and handed each a cup. "Coffee upsets Nell's stomach now," he said, giving her the glass of water.

He sat down and continued his story.

"So, when I got your telegram, I took the wagon and started out to look for him. But where the wagon road crosses at Red Bridge, the railroad runs along the other side of the river. I didn't know which way he'd be coming."

Melinda thought of the trip on the hand car with Dan Sutherland. She remembered that section of track.

"I was sitting there in my wagon, wondering what to do. I thought I'd walk down the track a while to see if he was coming, and I saw him. But he didn't recognize me because I was too far away. He ran off into the brush to hide. In his hurry, he fell down the side of the berm, then got scratched in some thorn bushes. When I got closer I called and he knew it was me. I brought him here in my wagon, but he was too scared to talk until he saw Nell and Johnny." Ole had lost some of his Swedish accent, Melinda noticed.

"Then he talked and talked, although I could see he was exhausted," Nell said. "He said someone at Robe had found him in the boxcar and tried to catch him. He got away and hid, then made his way to the end of the line. He managed to get himself across the river on the cable car and started out walking."

"He said he saw a cougar, watching him from across the river," added Ole. "He thought it might try to cross the river."

Melinda felt the terror he must have experienced.

"Did he tell you why he ran away?" Quin asked them.

"He said you two were mad at each other and weren't going to get married. He thought it was all his fault."

"It had nothing to do with him, poor child," Melinda said. "Well, anyway, it wasn't his fault."

"So when are you going to get married?" Nell asked.

"The sooner the better." Quin grinned.

Melinda looked at him. "Not *too* soon, Quin. There are still the questions of supporting ourselves if I don't find a teaching job, and where we'll live. And my mother can't miss our wedding. She doesn't even know what's been happening. Well, I wrote to her before leaving Valdez, but who knows if she got the letter?"

"Sounds like you still have some decisions to make," Nell said. "As for Rose, why don't you send her a telegram?"

Evan followed Johnny through the back door, his blond head drooping, his face sober, contrasting with Johnny's bright smile as he laid their string of fish on his mother's work counter.

"Johnny, what a marvelous catch!" Nell exclaimed. Then to Evan she said, "You have company."

Evan looked up. A mix of emotions played across his face as he saw Melinda and his uncle: fear, relief, uncertainty. He froze, as if trying to decide which way to run. Relief won out and he ran to his uncle. He choked back a sob as he flung his arms around Quin's neck. Laughing through her tears, Melinda hugged them both.

"Oh, Evan, we're so glad you're safe! What ever were you thinking?"

During the happy reunion, none of them noticed Nell and her family slip out the back door.

CHAPTER THIRTY-FIVE

CATCHING UP

The boys helped Nell roll their trout in seasoned cornmeal. They lingered near the stove to watch it frying golden-brown and crusty while Melinda made a creamy sauce to pour over the new potatoes. No other visitors were staying at the Swenson's guest house this evening, so the six of them enjoyed a leisurely meal together.

Ole wanted to know how mining in Alaska differed from what he'd seen in Monte Cristo. "Well," said Quin, "I didn't see much actual mining taking place. I did see people using gold pans to wash out dust and small nuggets. Very different from the hard-rock mining at Monte. No tunnels, no explosives. The few successful miners I saw had found pay dirt close to the surface. They shoveled the dirt and gravel into a sluice box. That's a long slanted trough with riffles or slats across the bottom to catch the gold. Then they 'sluiced' water through the boxes to carry away the waste gravel and dirt."

"Did you pan for gold, Uncle Quin?"

"Sometimes. I wasn't very good at it. This is what it looks like." He pulled a small bottle from his pocket and showed it to the boys. They handed it around. Melinda shook the bottle a little, and fine gold mixed with black sand glinted in the light.

"Ja, I suppose what you find depends on geology."

"Right. Now, if all those gold-rushers had been looking for copper, they might have found the fortunes they were looking for. The Indians have always treasured the copper in those mountains."

"That's where the Copper River gets its name?" Nell queried.

Quin nodded.

"I'm curious," Nell said to Melinda. "Remember how real your nightmare about Quin being in danger seemed to you?"

"It's just as clear to me now as when I first told you about it," she said. "What I haven't told you yet is that we passed cliffs and waterfalls on the journey north that looked exactly like what I saw in my dream. It was stormy, with clouds hiding the top of the island. But we were the ones in danger. The waves carried a lot of garbage, possibly from a shipwreck. We didn't see a wreck. But our propeller got wound up in rope, and the engine stopped. By the time the sailors freed the propeller, we were nearly on the rocks. A lot of us must have been praying. They started the engine just in time."

"So Quin wasn't in danger?"

"I still felt he might be. That's why we crossed the Valdez Glacier. We didn't catch up with him, but I heard he might be starting down the Copper River. From what I'd been told about that journey, I knew it was no place to take Evan. So I sent a note after Quin, hoping he'd get it and take extra care."

"I did get it," Quin told them. "By then I knew for myself how dangerous the river is. I didn't understand Melinda's fear, but I knew if it was powerful enough to carry her through the country she'd already travelled, I'd better heed her warning."

"Do you think her concern was warranted?"

"Yes. I'll tell you more about the river later, but suffice it to say, that letter made me think about every move we made for the rest of the journey."

"And you got to Valdez just as she and Evan were leaving?"

"Yes. Not my finest hour, I must say. I didn't know Evan was with her, you see. And it seemed as though she'd been escorted to the ship by a good-looking man who obviously didn't want to see her go ...."

"There was nothing between us," Melinda said. "It wasn't my best hour either. I reacted too hastily. But our baggage was already aboard and the ship was pulling out."

"They acted like little kids." In the momentary silence they all heard Evan's whisper to Johnny.

Quin's and Melinda's faces reddened with embarrassment, but they laughed.

"Grownups do that sometimes, don't they?" Nell patted Evan's shoulder. "Why don't you boys play a game of checkers before bedtime? And Melinda, Quin ... it's a lovely evening for a walk."

At Nell's insistence, Melinda left her and Ole to put the kitchen to rights and followed Quin out the door. They crossed the bridge and turned east along the railroad grade.

The river burbled along below the tracks. A tree covered ridge loomed above the little town of Silverton and behind that, the rocky peaks where men still dug ore from the "45" Mine. Overhead, lines of a tram crossed the ridge and sloped toward the river. These lines carried large ore buckets, which were emptied into storage bunkers. There the ore sat waiting the return of the trains.

Would Silverton survive if the railroad was never rebuilt? What about Monte Cristo? As they meandered along, she asked Quin what he thought.

"People are resilient," Quin said. "Rockefeller and the other investors who put their money into Everett and the mines have withdrawn their support. They've made it clear they won't back a non-paying proposition. But perhaps other groups will step in. It's not only the miners who want the railroad back. Tourists have discovered Monte Cristo, and they're not pleased with access being cut off."

A trail led from the tracks down the bank to the river, where a big stranded log offered a sunny spot to sit and talk. Quin led the way to a narrow gravel beach. Melinda climbed onto the log and made her way out over the shallow current. Crystal clear water revealed gravel glistening in colors of caramel gold, green, black, white, deep red. Very different from the opaque gray waters of Alaska rivers, even though this water also started out as glacial and snow melt. She sat down, feet dangling above the water. Quin seated himself beside her.

"You know," she told him, "we never heard anything more from my stepfather after he left us in Monte Cristo to join the gold rush. I'd wondered if I might run across him in Alaska, but no one seemed to know him."

"I thought he wanted to go to the Klondike."

"Yes, but you'd think if he got there, he'd have sent word, if only to ask my mother to send money."

Quin took her hand. "I hate to say this, but you and your mom are both better off without him."

"It's sad. But yes, you're right." She paused a moment, watching some tiny fish dart below her feet. "And I'm so much better off since we found each other!"

Quin leaned close and bent to kiss the rosy lips turned up to his.

He pulled away, his breathing ragged. "You'd better sit a little farther away," he said. "You're more tempting than I might be able to resist!"

She giggled. "You're the one closest to the end of the log. You sit farther away!"

They compromised and stayed where they were.

"You know what I'm thinking?" he asked.

"What?"

"We should get married right here in Silverton. We could leave Evan with the Swensons for a few days and go camping at Monte Cristo for our honeymoon."

Melinda's thoughts swirled, and she said the first thing that came into her head. "Camping? Don't you think we've both had our fill of roughing it after a summer in the wilderness?"

He ran his finger along her jawline. "But we weren't together."

"Agreed. Camping with you sounds wonderful. But how can we get married now? I don't think there's a preacher in Silverton. And what about after we're married? We don't have a place to live."

"Last things first. Mrs. Collins will let us stay at the Everett boarding house until we find a place to rent."

"What about your job?"

"There are newspapers in Everett. Or maybe my boss will assign me as North Sound correspondent for the Dispatch."

"You've changed, Quin. Remember how you didn't want to risk getting married without a permanent job before I left for San Francisco?"

"I realize now what I've been missing out on." He grinned, and kissed her again.

Tree shadows lengthened across the river as the sun sank behind the mountains. "Let's see what we can work out with the Swensons," Quin said. "They'll know if there's a preacher nearby."

They walked back to the shore and he swung Melinda down from the log. They followed the railroad tracks back to Silverton and entered the house just as Nell lit the lamps in the parlor.

Evan and Johnny looked up from their checkers game. Evan studied their faces. Evidently he liked what he saw there. Even though Johnny took advantage of the distraction to capture several of his pieces in one jump, a small, contented smile played about his lips.

"Come sit in the parlor," Nell suggested to the adults. "Well?" she said, when all were seated.

"Well," said Quin. "Where's the nearest minister of the gospel?"

"Congratulations!" Ole beamed.

Nell jumped up and hugged them both. "We have a lady who holds Sunday school in her house for the children," she said. "But she's not a licensed minister."

"There's a preacher in Granite Falls who comes every couple of weeks to hold church services right here in our parlor," Ole told them.

"Do you think he'd come right away?"

"We can send a telegram in the morning. How soon is right away?"

Quin cocked an eyebrow at Melinda. "How long does it take to get ready for a wedding?"

"It took Nell and Ole a couple of days. But we won't need a party. I don't think we know anyone but the Swensons here. I can wear the blue silk dress you kept for me, Nell!"

"It's settled then," said Quin. "As soon as the preacher can get here."

Melinda thought wistfully of her mother in far-away California. How could Rose be left out of her only child's wedding? As soon as this was all over, she determined, she'd write her mother the best letter she'd ever in her life received. She'd tell her every detail.

Chapter Thirty-Six
WILDFLOWER WEDDING

The Reverend Garrett, pastor of a recently established church in Granite Falls, answered Ole's telegram mid-morning.

"He says 'Yes'. He'll come tomorrow," Ole said. "He'll stay over night and hold church the next morning."

Melinda, in the midst of pressing the blue silk dress her mother had originally made for Nell, set the flat iron back on the stove. She took a deep breath. Tomorrow! Her wedding was going to happen, tomorrow.

Nell clapped her hands. "Oh, Melinda. Isn't this fun!"

Melinda sent her a weak smile, then made a decision. She could fret about all there was still to do and what might be lacking for the wedding of her dreams, or she could be grateful to God that He was in charge. Since that was true, she'd just relax and enjoy events as they happened.

Quin came in from the back yard, where he'd been brushing the clothes he and Ole would wear. "Melinda, can you press these pants? I couldn't shake the wrinkles out."

"Yes. Just leave them here on the chair. Would you look to be sure Evan has a clean shirt and knickers?" She could hardly believe that soon the care of a husband's clothes would be part of her regular job description. How many more tasks would be part of her new job, she wondered? Quin would do his share, she was sure of that.

Quin came back to the kitchen with Evan's clothes to be pressed. "If you ladies will round up all the shoes, I'll get the boys to help me black them," he said.

See? she told herself.

"Let me get this cake into the oven first," Nell said. "And tell the boys 'no door slamming' till it's finished baking." To Melinda she said, "What do you think about decorating the cake with fresh flowers, if we can find any?"

"That sounds beautiful! Or autumn leaves, if we can't find flowers." Melinda sighed. They would even have a wedding cake!

That evening they had a quick supper of leftovers. Nell got the boys bathed and off to bed, and sent Quin and Melinda away for a few minutes together.

The two wandered down the river for a short distance, then perched side by side on a big rock overlooking a bend in the stream. Quin told Melinda he'd arranged for a couple of horses on which they'd ride to Monte Cristo, and a pack pony to carry what they'd need for camping.

"I overheard Evan telling Johnny this morning something about 'our honeymoon'," she said. "Do you suppose he thinks he's going too?"

"That's exactly what he thought," Quin laughed. "But I explained that a honeymoon is only for the bride and groom. I told him he'd get his new mama all to himself later."

She smiled. "Do you suppose he'll mind sharing if little brothers or sisters come along?"

He grinned back. "I think he'll be thrilled. How will you feel?"

"Thrilled. I think. But if that happens, I won't be able to teach."

"Let's leave that in the Lord's hands."

"Yes." She thought about the problems still to be solved. Quin's job. Hers. A place to live. Her mother, alone and far away. But they were in the Lord's hands. A good place to be.

The parlor windows sparkled. Ole had fashioned a pretty archway out of willow saplings to stand between the windows. Nell and Melinda twined it with vines and autumn leaves. The parlor furniture had been moved to one end of the room, facing the arch, and in front of that were benches with an aisle between. "Just in case we need them," said Nell. "The pastor will hold a service tomorrow morning before he leaves, so it will be all ready." She placed a garland of autumn leaves atop her piano. "How does that look?"

"Lovely. Thank you, Nell, for what you're doing!"

Nell gave her a hug. "Run upstairs now and get your bath," she said. "Then let me fix your hair."

When Melinda came back to the kitchen, Nell had spread raspberry preserves between the three layers of cake and was slathering it with creamy white frosting. "Look what the boys found," she said, indicating a bucket of lavender asters and clusters of little white flowers Melinda didn't recognize. "For your cake. And look what I made for your hair." She held out a circlet of white flowers woven together to make a tiara fit for any bride.

The pastor would be arriving mid-afternoon on the scheduled freight wagon. It was already lunch time, but first, Nell sat Melinda down, looping, tucking, and pinning her long auburn hair into a beautiful upsweep that showed off her slender neck. As a finishing touch, she took the curling iron that had been heating on the stove and wrapped a few strands around the iron to make soft tendrils framing Melinda's face.

"Your wife is a marvel," Melinda told Ole when the men and boys came in for lunch. "You've all been so kind. Thank you, Johnny and Evan, for the flowers. They're just what we needed!"

She sliced a loaf of bread while Nell put out peanut butter and jam.

"Everyone, make your own sandwich today," Nell said. "We've got a wedding to think about!"

Obviously, Nell had been already thinking about details that never occurred to Melinda. A neighbor lady dropped by to leave a tray of fancy little sandwiches covered with a tea towel. Someone else brought a platter of fruit. The man next door brought a huge pot of coffee and set it on the back of the stove to stay warm. Several women loaned pretty china cups and plates. Of course, all those people were invited to come back for the ceremony. That would happen shortly after the preacher arrived on the afternoon's freight wagon.

Earlier than expected, they heard a commotion outside on the boardwalk. It was the Reverend Garrett, accompanied by a number of townspeople. He would want to talk to Melinda and Quin before the wedding. She glanced through the open door, and her head began to spin. Not only was the dignified Reverend being escorted to the house, but ... could it be? Rose Skinner!

"Mama!" Melinda flew down the steps, laughing and crying, into her mother's arms.

Rose was crying happy tears as well. "Let me look at you! I've missed you so."

"Did you do this, Nell?"

"No. I swear, I knew nothing about it. Come in, Rose, Reverend Garrett." To the neighbors she said, "We'll ring the dinner gong when it's time for the ceremony."

Evan ran up with a glad cry, "Grandma Rose! You came for our wedding!"

Rose laughed. She handed Nell some white roses in a jar. "Mrs. Collins thought Melinda might need these," she told her.

The she caught Evan in her arms and swung him around. "My goodness, Evan, you've grown so much!" she said. "Not only am I here for the wedding. I'm back in Washington for good. I'll tell you all about it later." She turned to Nell and Melinda. "Now, how can I help?"

Nell and Rose covered the reception table with a damask cloth and arranged the food, with the cake in the center. Rose twined a wreath of wildflowers around the base of the cake and added a few to the top. She tied the roses into a bouquet with a white ribbon for Melinda to carry.

Meanwhile, Reverend Garrett talked with Quin and Melinda about the covenant they were about to enter and went over the ceremony with them.

"I have something to add," Quin said. He pulled a slip of paper out of his pocket. "It's my promise to Melinda. I'd like to read it before we say 'I do.'"

The pastor skimmed it. "Very nice," he said. "And what about music?"

"Nell will play the piano as we come in, and afterward." Melinda gave him the name of the song.

"Well, if that's it, you two had better get ready. I'll see you in the parlor in a few minutes."

Melinda found her mother in her bedroom, scrubbed and hair freshly combed. She'd changed from her traveling clothes and was ready to help Melinda dress.

"Mama, how in the world did you time this so perfectly?"

"I didn't. I'd decided to sell the house and move back to Washington. When I got to Everett yesterday, your landlady told me where you'd gone. So this morning, I caught the train, then rode for hours in that jolting wagon. My fellow passenger in the wagon was a pastor who was going to Silverton to marry you and Quin. He didn't know much more than that. You've got a lot of explaining to do, young lady!"

"Oh, I do." They both laughed.

"Later," said Rose. She had seen the blue silk dress hanging on the wardrobe door. "This is what you're wearing? I remember when I made it. Never did I suspect it would be your wedding dress!" She helped Melinda slip it over her head, careful not to disturb her hairdo, and fastened the little buttons up the back.

There was a rap at the door. Evan stood there, spick and span in clean shirt and knickers and freshly-blacked shoes. His blond hair was slicked down. He held out Nell's circlet of wildflowers and the roses. "Mrs. Swenson said not to forget these. You look pretty, Mindy."

Melinda dropped a kiss on his nose and told him he looked handsome.

While Rose pinned the flowers in her daughter's hair, Melinda told her mother about the ring of Monte Cristo gold that Quin had had made for her long before he asked her to marry him. Evan checked that the ring was in his pocket and Melinda made sure the golden locket which she'd worn since last January was still hanging around her neck.

She heard the dinner gong ring. Soon people began to enter the parlor.

From the piano came the notes of the two hundred-year-old hymn, "*Now Thank We All Our God.*" Evan scooted out to join his uncle and Ole in the parlor, and she picked up her bridal bouquet.

As Melinda and her mother came arm in arm down the stairs, people stood and turned toward them. They began to sing. Melinda's heart soared with the music.

"Now thank we all our God, with heart and hands and voices,
Who wondrous things has done, in Whom this world rejoices;
Who from our mothers' arms has blessed us on our way
With countless gifts of love, and still is ours today."

With her mother at her side, Melinda walked through the parlor to her waiting groom and her soon-to-be son.

As they approached Quin standing with Evan and Ole in front of the arch, Nell brought the song to a close and stood to join the bride as matron-of-honor. Pastor Garrett led the assembly in a prayer for the two being married. When he boomed out the question, "Who gives this woman to be married?" Rose spoke firmly.

"I do."

Melinda hugged her mother and handed her bouquet to Nell, then turned to Quin, who whispered, "You're beautiful."

Rose sat down beside Ole and Johnny.

The pastor continued with the ceremony. He paused before speaking the vows and said to the guests, "The groom has something he wants to say."

Quin took a step toward his bride and took her hands in his. His dark eyes looked deep into hers as he spoke his promise to her. "Melinda, I love you. I will only love you more as we live out the years God gives us to be together. I will never intentionally hurt you. I will support you in all your endeavors and protect you to the best of my ability. To you, I promise my faithfulness and loyalty."

Then he turned to Evan. "Evan, you have been like a son to me for three years. Today it is official. You will be our son, and we three will be a family."

Melinda thought her heart would burst with joy. She didn't know if she could speak or not, but she too had something to say. She turned to the pastor, and he nodded.

"Quin, Pastor Garett told us that 'plighting our troth' means promising our faithfulness and loyalty. I promise that to both you and Evan. I will respect you and honor you, Quintrell Chenoweth, and do my best to take care of both of you. From now on, we are a family."

Melinda and Quin repeated the vows after the pastor. Sniffles rose from the audience. Then the pastor asked Evan if he had anything to say. Evan and the pastor held a brief whispered conversation. Then the boy reached out a hand to his uncle and one to Melinda and spoke up loud and clear. "I, Evan Chenoweth, take you, Uncle Quin, and you, Mindy, to be my father and my mother from this day forward." He took the ring from his pocket and gave it to the pastor, who handed it to Quin. Quin slipped it on Melinda's finger. It still fit as perfectly as it had almost a year ago when he'd first asked her to marry him.

"I now pronounce you man and wife."

Evan tugged at the pastor's hand. "And son," he added. Everyone laughed. To Quin he said, "You may kiss the bride."

Quin did so while the neighbors clapped and cheered.

"May I present to you Mr. and Mrs. Quintrell Chenoweth."

Nell stepped back to the piano and the audience launched into the last verse of *Now Thank We All Our God*. Quin and their son escorted the bride down the aisle to the reception table at the back of the room. With grateful hearts, they joined the singing.

All praise and thanks to God the Father now be given,
the Son and Spirit blest, who reign in highest heaven
the one eternal God, whom heaven and earth adore;
for thus it was, is now, and shall be evermore.

       Amen

Chapter Thirty-Seven
More Monte Cristo Memories

Together, Melinda and Quin cut the first piece of wedding cake, and to applause, they served each other the first delicious bites. They stayed near the table to greet the guests while two of the Swenson's neighbors superintended the food and drink.

Nell softly played the piano as people offered congratulations. When she launched into a sprightly waltz, Quin whispered in Melinda's ear, "May I have this dance?"

Her beautiful silk skirt billowed and swayed as they circled the open space in front of the willow archway. Like dancing in a swirl of sunny blue sky, she thought.

Perfect, that's what her wedding had been. Later, after the guests had gone, Ole and Nell put the kitchen to rights. Melinda and Quin visited with Rose.

"Oh, Mother, isn't it all grand? I wanted so badly for you to be here. We even sent a telegram. But we didn't know the wedding would be so soon, or even if there'd be a wedding. How did you manage to arrive at just the right time?"

"I got the letter you wrote on the ship and sent when you reached Valdez," Rose told her. "But that was the last word I received from you. I knew something dreadful could have happened, but I decided even if I never saw you again, I didn't want to stay in San Francisco alone. So I sold the house, packed up my sewing machine, and here I am. I can buy a larger house in Everett with what I got for my house there, with room enough for all of us."

Melinda's thoughts whirled. Was this God's answer to their immediate need?

"That would be wonderful, Mother."

Quin looked a little dazed, but nodded agreement.

"Quin must find out where his job will take him. I'll need work, too. But we'd love to be with you, or near you."

"While you're off honeymooning, I'll go back to Everett then and see what's available in the way of housing," she said.

The Swenson's house was full that evening. A few other guests had asked for lodging, not knowing about the wedding. Pastor Garrett was staying for tomorrow's church service. Rose was given the room that had been Quin's, and Evan shared Johnny's bedroom.

Melinda waited in her room for Quin to arrive. In the darkening street, a few people sauntered by. Melinda, watching, turned at a knock on the door. She opened it to Quin, his bag in hand and jacket over his arm. "Hello, Mrs. Chenoweth," he grinned. "I've been ejected from my room. Will you take me in?"

She took his hand and drew him inside. He shut the door, pulled her into his arms and kissed her with a pent-up hunger that released her own passion.

After a while, she pulled away just long enough to close the curtains.

Melinda slept until the sun slanting in around the curtains woke her next morning. She opened her eyes to see Quin leaning on one elbow, watching her with a bemused expression.

"I'm a lucky man," he said.

"I think you told me that before," she murmured. She did not feel lucky. She felt ... blessed. She'd done nothing to deserve this happiness. And yet, here they were, sharing the same pillow, feeling the comfort of each other's bodies.

From downstairs wafted the smells of good things cooking. A soft knock at the door. Evan's voice. "Mrs. Swenson says, do you want breakfast in bed or do you want to come down?"

"We'll be right down," she called.

Hurriedly they dressed, took turns in the washroom, and joined their family and friends in the kitchen.

In the excitement of the celebration yesterday, Melinda had almost forgotten that Reverend Garrett was to hold a church service this morning. The wagon to Robe would delay its departure until afterward. Rose and the Reverend Garrett would leave midmorning.

"No, don't stay to see me off," Rose told Melinda. "You have a long ride ahead of you. I'll see you again soon."

Wordlessly, Melinda embraced her mother. They thanked the pastor for coming all that way. Quin slipped him an envelope with some money.

Then Ole brought the horses from a neighbor's barn. They loaded the pack animal with what they'd need. Melinda had told Quin that his cabin in Monte Cristo seemed in good condition, so they decided not to take a tent. He'd left his pots and dishes there, so all they took was food, blankets, and clothing. Quin also packed his Kodak.

"Are you sure you don't want me to come along?" Evan asked them. "I know how to light fires and catch fish. I could help."

"Thank you, Evan, but we'll be fine," smiled his new father.

Melinda hugged him. "I know you'd be a big help. I couldn't have made it in Alaska without you. But you deserve a vacation too. I want you and Johnny to have lots of fun. When we get back, we'll need you to work hard helping us make a home." She kissed the freckles on his cheek.

He snuggled against her. "All right," Then he added the word she knew he'd been longing to say almost since they met. "Mama."

Melinda slid from her horse to stand beside Quin, trying to stifle a small moan of discomfort.

"Yes," he said, stretching. "We're out of practice, aren't we?"

"Out of practice? I've never been 'in practice'." She laughed and patted her mount's neck. "That's the longest I've ever been on horseback in my life!"

"Well, here we are," Quin said, looking across the damaged railroad trestle. The deserted community straggled up the ridge between Glacier and Sunday Creeks. The Sauk River began below the ridge where the two creeks merged. It chortled through the lower townsite, past several flood-damaged buildings clinging to the bank.

Leading their horses, they walked the trestle toward the empty railroad depot, then crossed the bridge over Sunday Creek and followed Dumas Avenue up the ridge. Some sheds and outhouses had been splintered by the weight of winter snow; a few roofs sagged.

The Mercantile looked cared for, but the Regal Hotel, where Melinda had worked, was shuttered and locked. No familiar faces turned to greet them as they made their way along the planked street. They passed the lane to the schoolhouse. She wondered where her students were now.

Then they turned uphill. There was Quin's cabin, standing alone in the clearing where he'd made a snug home for Evan and himself. The window boxes held only debris from the surrounding evergreens, but the windows were unbroken. They tied each horse to its own tree, removed the saddles and the packhorse's load, and brushed the animals.

Then Quin unlocked the cabin. "Just as I left it," he said. He turned around, swung Melinda up, and carried her over the threshold. "I've always wanted to do this," he said before depositing her back on her feet.

She laughed, then wrinkled her nose. "What's that smell?"

"Probably just musty from being closed up so long. Let's air it out and see if the stove still works."

So while Melinda opened all the windows and swept and dusted, Quin cleaned the ashes out of the stove, opened the damper, and laid a small fire with some of the dry wood that still filled the woodbox.

"Help me take this mattress outside to air in the sunshine, Quin. It smells musty. Then if we can heat some water, I'll rinse the dishes and pots."

It took most of the rest of the afternoon, but when the cabin was clean, the mattress back on the bed and the blankets they'd brought in place, Melinda heated a can of stew for their supper. Nell had tucked a loaf of fresh bread in with their provisions, and even a couple of pieces of wedding cake for dessert.

"Delicious, Mrs. Chenoweth!" Quin patted his stomach and stretched. "But I already knew you're a good cook."

"I can't take credit for anything we ate tonight." She smiled. "Do you suppose we could leave the dishes for later? It will be dark soon, and I'd really like to go to the Pavilion tonight."

"Why not?" Quin grabbed the jacket he'd hung on a hook by the door and helped Melinda into hers.

The Pavilion still stood, a steep-roofed, open-air platform near the mountain wall where Sunday Falls patterned the rocks with frothy lace.

It was here, at the Chautauqua's box social, that Melinda had first worn Nell's blue silk dress. Here Quin had outwitted Anton Cole in bidding for her boxed dinner, and over there, on that flat rock overlooking the waterfall, they'd eaten it together. That had led to all kinds of trouble. But that was in the past. So was their long separation, and the foolish but never-to-be-forgotten adventure in Alaska. Now was now. And they were together.

The next day they packed a picnic lunch and set out to explore.

Ragged peaks speared into the blue sky ahead and to either side. They headed up Glacier Creek, past the huge and now-silent ore concentrator. They followed along the covered tram to the bunkers from which horses had hauled loads of ore to be crushed and sorted before being shipped to the Everett smelter.

Cables of the overhead trams glinted like spiderwebs in the mid-day sun. The still-attached ore buckets creaked in the breeze that carried the rushing of Glacier Creek's twin waterfalls to their ears.

As they neared the falls, Melinda bent to some low bushes and plucked a few plump blueberries. She popped one into her mouth and a couple into Quin's.

"You'd been picking blueberries up there in Glacier Basin, the first time I met you," he remembered.

"Yes, and after we argued about ... something ... I brought you blueberry muffins as a peace offering."

He grinned. "You thought I was too bossy."

"Well, you were!"

They both laughed.

"Is this a good place for our picnic?" he asked.

"Right over there." She gestured to a flat, rocky place where water from the split waterfall flowed on either side. They hopped across on projecting rocks, and sat down in the sunshine. While she watched Quin unpack their lunch, Melinda pondered the past few months.

San Francisco to Silverton, Monte Cristo to Seattle, up the coast of Northwest America by steamer. Valdez to the wilds of Alaska's Copper River country and back again.

So many mistakes. So many tryings again.

"Step by step, Melinda." The breeze, like a whisper from God himself, tickled her ear. "Walk with me. Don't run ahead."

"I'm trying, Lord," she whispered back.

And now Quin and she would also walk together. She looked at him, at home in the grandeur of this rugged country, and smiled.

The high peaks surrounding Monte Cristo hadn't changed. The gold was still there. Perhaps the little town could struggle back from the disasters that had assailed it. Or perhaps it would crumble back into the forest with scarcely a trace of the hopes that had once thrived here.

But God's Word, and His love, better than the gold of Monte Cristo, better than all the gold of Alaska, had never failed. It never would.

The End

About The Author

Joan Rawlins Husby grew up with four siblings in the valley of the South Fork Stillaguamish, near the site of Monte Cristo, the abandoned mining town in this book. Surrounded by reminders of the area's fascinating history, she came to love the places and the stories of the Pacific Northwest.

She taught in Washington State and then, after marrying, taught in Alaska. She loved the country and the people, and many of her writings are based on her Alaskan experiences. Her son and daughter grew up there. After her husband Bob Biggar passed away, she married Hank Husby and moved with him to the Stanwood, Washington, area. Together they have seven adult children.

Joan always dreamed of traveling to exotic places and writing stories set there. She found those places not that far from home. Her first 8 books were adventure-mysteries for middle schoolers, *The Adventure Quest Series* and *The Megan Parnell Mysteries*. She has contributed to a number of collections of short stories, articles, and poetry and has also written for newspapers and periodicals.

Her memoir, *A Logger's Daughter: Growing Up in Washington's Woods,* tells what life was like in the '40s and '50s.

Living Gold is the story of missionaries Dave and Vera Penz, who founded Kako Retreat Center for Alaskan Natives on the Yukon-Kuskokwim Delta, Alaska.

The Monte Cristo Memories Series thus far includes two historical fiction novels, *Heart's Gold* and this continuation, *Better Than Gold.*

You can visit her blog and website, RainSong Diaries: Stories of the Pacific Northwest, at rainsongpress.com, or contact her at Facebook.com/Joan Rawlins Husby. She would love to hear from you.

Bibliography

Abercrombie, Captain William Ralph, and other members of his military expeditions, *Explorations in Alaska*, 1884 and 1898. Copies of reports courtesy of United States National Archives.

Biggar, Joan Rawlins and Alaska Magazine Staff. *Trial and Error*. Alaska Magazine, August, 2000

Clark, Norman H. *Mill Town: A Social History of Everett, Washington, from Its Earliest Beginnings.* Seattle: University of Washington Press, 1970.

Lethcoe, Jim and Nancy. *Valdez Gold Rush Trails of 1898-99.* Prince William Sound Books, Valdez, Alaska. 1996

Moore, Lillian. Letter describing her July 1898 trip over the Valdez Glacier with Captain Abercrombie's expedition. Courtesy of the Valdez Museum.

Woodhouse, Philip R. *Monte Cristo.* Seattle: The Mountaineers, 1979

Woodhouse, Philip R., Daryl Jacobson, and Bill Petersen. *The Everett and Monte Cristo Railway.* Arlington, WA: Oso Publishing, 2000.

Map, courtesy of Anchorage Museum of History and Art, showing general area of route covered in the story. Adapted by Thomas Kauffman from a part of the *Geological Reconnaissance map in Glenn and Abercrombie, Explorations in Alaska, 1898.*

Outline map adapted by Thomas Kauffman.

History and Kid Stuff in the 1950s

Growing up in the Robe Valley, Washington, back in the 1940s and '50s, we neighborhood children were surrounded by reminders of history. Some of that history is found in this book and in *Heart's Gold*, a novel set in Washington State's gold-mining boomtown, Monte Cristo. To us kids, those reminders were just part of what made our community a fun place to live.

On warm summer days, wearing swimsuits under our clothing, we'd traipse through the woods to our swimming hole. We followed a narrow track that had once been part of the old wagon road that ran from Granite Falls through the valley. The road took us to Nichols Store. I remember stopping there at age four or five while my parents mailed a letter or bought milk.

The owner had abandoned the two-story, unpainted building when the present road bypassed it in the 1940s. We found ways to wriggle inside and explore the empty rooms. From the clearing in front rose a long, grass-covered ridge we knew had once been the railroad grade. The Everett and Monte Cristo Railway trains in the 1890s stopped at Nichols Store with tourists on their way to the mountain village. They carried loads of ore from the Monte Cristo and Silverton mines back to the smelter in Everett.

We crossed the grade where a short, timbered bridge spanned a creek full of little fish, then walked on through a park-like area beside the river. Someone had built a picnic shelter there, perhaps in the earlier days of tourist excursions. But no one came for picnics now, except us kids. The river ran past this grassy space and beyond lay the quiet eddy that was our swimming hole.

The remains of an old railroad-bridge buttress loomed above the hole. A deluge in 1897 had destroyed the original double-span Howe truss bridge that crossed the Stillaguamish River there. It also washed away the dreams of miners and mine owners at Monte.

If no parents were along, after our swim we dared each other to climb up the leaning uprights to the 12 x 12 inch timbers on top that had supported the tracks. Cushioned with moss, they made a soft place to dry off in the sunshine. We were careful though. We could feel the trestle wobble beneath us with every movement.

On the riverbank near the swimming hole was another temptation to adventurous kids—an old cable car, still attached to a fraying cable that hung above the river. The cable ran over rusty pulleys that were fastened to sturdy trees at each end. Floor boards were loose. Some were missing. We older ones could see the danger and only speculated about how much fun the ride must have been, once upon a time.

Recently I found a story in Philip R. Woodhouse's book, *Monte Cristo*, about what was likely this same cable car.

After the flood that destroyed the bridge and the railroad through Robe Canyon, people in Silverton and Monte Cristo held onto hope that repairs could enable mining to start up again.

Temporary repairs did start in the canyon, and while awaiting replacement of the bridge, a Silverton man established his own tongue-in-cheek railroad company—a single push car. Every day he coasted down the deserted tracks from Silverton to a cable tram installed near the site of the missing bridge. Mail and supplies for Silverton were piled on the tram and sent across the river. Then he loaded them on his man-powered push car and pumped his way back to Silverton.

The cable car must have been over fifty years old when a neighbor boy talked my little brother David into taking a ride. They hauled themselves across the tumbling river without losing fingers to the cable or falling through the rotting boards. It must have been a scary trip because once safely on the far side, David refused to get back on. The older boy left him behind and got word to our father about the situation.

Fortunately in late summer, the river was not too high. But it was swift, and the rocks were slippery. Dad waded across and carried a frightened David on his back to the other side. Then he destroyed the tram so that no other kids would be tempted.

We didn't know then how the old bridge abutment or the abandoned cable car tied into the story of Monte Cristo. But as young adults, we got to know the old ghost town up close and personal. It is still a favorite hiking destination for hundreds of outdoor enthusiasts. Robe Canyon and the Stillaguamish River where we played is a well-loved recreation center for many more.

*If you would like to read more stories like this, you can visit my blog and website at **rainsongpress.com**. While you're there, sign up for my newsletter, **Sun Breaks and Rain Songs**. I'd love to make your acquaintance!   Joan Rawlins Husby*

Made in the USA
Middletown, DE
09 April 2024

52621919R00165